Before THE WAR

Fay Weldon started out as one of the
most successful advertising copywriters
of her generation. Her credits as a writer
now include classic novels such as
The Life and Loves of a She-Devil and
The Cloning of Joanna May. In 2001
Fay was awarded a CBE for services
to literature. She has eight children
and stepchildren and lives on
a hilltop in Dorset.

FAY WELDON

Before THE WAR

HEAD of ZEUS

First published in the UK in 2016 by Head of Zeus Ltd

This paperback edition first published in the UK in 2016
by Head of Zeus Ltd

9 7 5 3 1 2 4 6 8

A catalogue record for this book is available from the British Library.

Paperback ISBN: 9781784082086
Ebook ISBN: 9781784082055

Typeset by e-type, Aintree

Printed and bound by CPI Group (UK) Ltd, Croydon, CR0 4YY

Head of Zeus Ltd
Clerkenwell House
45-47 Clerkenwell Green
London EC1R 0HT

WWW.HEADOFZEUS.COM

Before

THE

WAR

PART ONE

The Proposal

Nine O'clock In The Morning, November 23rd 1922. Dilberne Halt

Consider Vivien in the year 1922. She's waiting for the London train. It's a cold November morning, the station is windswept and rural, the sky is threatening snow, and the train is late. Vivien is single, large, ungainly, five foot eleven inches tall and twenty years old. She has no coat, just a tweed jacket and a long brown woollen scarf to keep her warm. She snatched the scarf from a peg just before she left home for the mile long walk to the station. The scarf is a dreary dusty old thing. Moths have been at it. It's been hanging on its peg by the back door amongst old coats, jackets, hats and caps for years. Not so long ago the scarf would have been noticed, laundered, darned, ironed, folded and put in its appropriate drawer within the hour. But time has passed and wars have happened and these days one just can't find the staff to pay attention to detail.

I'm not asking you, reader, to step back in time. I'm asking you to stay happily where you are in the twenty-first century, looking back. Vivien has seared herself into my mind, this single stooping figure – she tends to stoop, being conscious that she is taller than most women and quite a lot of men – as she waits alone for a train on a crucial day in her life in November 1922. So I offer Vivien and her fate to you, the reader. We like to dream the costume drama of Edwardian times, all fine clothes, glittering jewels and clean sexy profiles – but we are less drawn to the twenty years between the wars. Understandably. Limbless ex-servicemen beg for alms on hard-hearted city streets while hysterical flappers, flat-chested, dance and drink champagne in Mayfair night-clubs. Shell shock, the Fifth Horseman of the Apocalypse – what we now call post-traumatic stress syndrome – still stalks the land. Life expectancy for the poor is forty-five; for the rich, sixty-five.

Vivien is young and rich but no flapper. She is too large and ungainly to look good dancing, and one would certainly never guess she was rich from the frumpy way she dresses. Had she had a more exuberant personality her height would have seemed no great drawback; she could have sparkled and charmed and flung out her chest to the admiration of men and women both, but Vivvie was not like this. She suffered and let it be seen that she suffered. She stooped. For her special day in London she wears the long droopy brown scarf over a tweed jacket (taken also at random from the peg: it is actually her father's); her black skirt is ankle-length and she has rammed a grey felt cloche down over her ears. None of it does the poor girl any favours at all. Nor do her thick, flesh-coloured lisle stockings or her pointy black button-strap shoes (size 9). These clothes quite suit the flat-chested and lithe beauties of the time, a droopy weariness being all the rage, but Vivien is no beauty and has a noticeably large bust which she declines to bandage flat. She is, moreover, mildly Asperger's, though that is a word neither yet in use, nor a syndrome understood. She is often unaware of the impression she is making on other people – which is that she is decidedly odd and sometimes decidedly rude. When she does become aware of it, the understanding can be very painful. She does not mean to offend or upset.

Anyway...

The train is now eleven minutes late, which is not surprising since its driver feels obliged to stop for cows to saunter out of its way, workmen to leave the tracks, and for late-running passengers to reach its doors. Indeed, the 8.45 from Brighton, though it left on time, is not yet even in earshot. All is silent on the Dilberne Halt platform, no huffing and puffing in the distance, no mournful whistle as the steaming iron monster approaches, only the occasional cackle of crows in a dripping winter landscape. Perhaps it isn't coming at all? That sometimes happens. Vivien looks at her little gold watch – too small on her large wrist – but finds it has stopped. She shocks herself. She hates the unexpected. She, usually so careful, has forgotten to wind the thing up. She must be more nervous than she realised. And she so much doesn't want to be late; this is an important day for her.

Woman Proposes, Man Disposes

It is in pursuit of a husband that Vivvie is going to London this morning. She means to propose to Sherwyn Sexton, an attractive and many say charismatic young man, if NSIT (not safe in taxis), who is in her own father's employ as an editor at Ripple & Co. In this she is very unwise indeed; she will suffer and be humiliated, but humiliation is her lot in life, as it is for most plain girls, forget one with an awkward nature. Indeed, it's a marvel any ordinary girl gets married off at all in

1922, the inter-war years being such a buyers' market, so many eligible young men of all nations dead and gone in foreign fields, and so many women left with nothing to do but mourn them.

We may see Vivien as living and dying in the past, before the days of the battery watch, but Vivien believes herself to be living in the present – as one does – and memories of her own past seem more than enough to put up with. You, reader, living now, have the advantage over Vivvie of knowing what will happen next in world affairs – though I can see to some of you that might seem a disadvantage – a mere increase in years of what can only end up, as Tennyson would have it, as 'portions and parcels of the dreadful past'. All times probably seem equally troublesome to those who live through them. Be that as it may, Vivien has had the experience of growing up through four years of a war in which old men found young men expendable, and expended them by the million, thus very much limiting her chance of finding a suitable husband.

Vivvie may be a wealthy young woman in her own right, which certainly helps, but she is seen as very tall in the age she is in, and a man still likes a woman to look up to him, not down on him. He certainly does not want her to loom over him as they stand at the wedding rail. Vivvie is just too large for the normality of the times, when a girl's average measurement is around 31-24-32 and her height five foot two. At the age of twenty, when her mother Adela last measured her and sighed rather loudly, Vivvie found herself 38-34-40, nearly six foot tall and suitor-less. Her height remains a disadvantage when it comes to marriage, even though her mother is Adela Ripple, née Hedleigh, cousin to Arthur, Earl of Dilberne, and wealthy girls of good family usually marry early. But she doesn't smile when she should, utter pleasantries when she ought, has no idea how to flirt, prefers horses to men (in particular her stallion Greystokes) and possibly women to men, though she doesn't like women much either.

But Vivvie is ambitious, intelligent and not without talent. Tucked under her long strong arm as she stands waiting on the station is a portfolio of her illustrations for *A Short History of the Georgians: An Outline*, to be published by Ripple & Co, her father's publishing firm, in the following spring. They are not bad, if not strikingly good. She is Sir Jeremy's only child and her father is training her up as he would a son to join him in the family firm. He has given up regarding Vivvie as a daughter since she has few feminine graces. He worries far less about this latter than does her mother, his wife Adela.

Woman Proposes, Writer Disposes

But I will not distress you with Vivien for ever. It is not normal in books, films or on TV for much attention to be paid to unattractive women of any age: few films are made, few novels written: the news camera instinctively seeks out the prettiest, youngest women in the street. Why should I break the rules? Vivien is to die before long, leaving girl twins (non-identical) behind, and at least one of them is very beautiful, though the other may be seen as rather plain. Even plainer than her poor dead mama: the kind of girl of whom my own grandmother (born in 1888) would say 'such an unfortunate face. Poor thing!'

But that's for the future.

Anyway, here is Vivien: mother-of-twins-to-be. Seared into my mind at the time she is, standing in her shapeless clothes waiting for a late London train, with no idea at all of what I have in store for her. I will give her an easy death. It's the least I can do. She will drift away painlessly from loss of blood giving birth to twin daughters a day after their apparently safe delivery. Ergometrine was not isolated until 1935. Had Vivvie given birth any time thereafter, she could have been saved by a swift dose of the stuff, but so it goes, as Vonnegut was to say in his excellent novel *Slaughterhouse Five*. So it goes.

Anyway. I haven't yet quite determined whose fault Vivvie's death is going to be, but it is certainly someone's. I will let you know. It's good to have someone to blame, so it's not just happenstance. The purposelessness of real life can get depressing.

A Matter Of Class

For some people a late train is a blessing. 'Oh thank heaven the train's late,' says a voice behind Vivien. It's Mrs Ashton, the widow who keeps the village shop, off to London to buy stock for the winter – the hot water bottles, lozenges, tonics and so forth the village will need as winter settles in. Vivien is glad at least someone else has turned up. The train begins to take on material existence. It may be late but at least someone else has faith in its eventual arrival.

Mrs Ashton, unlike Vivvie, is taking no chances with the

weather. She's a wizened rabbit-like creature herself, with a tiny face and a sniffling nose, muffled up in a rabbit fur coat with a fox-fur scarf dangling from her neck as well – little glass eyes staring out of its head one end, little paws, clawing at thin air, the other. Vivvie, who always does what she can to assist small wild creatures, thinks the scarf is gruesome, but wisely keeps her opinion to herself. Such scarves are very fashionable; even her mother Adela owns one, along with a pale mink coat for best and a sable jacket for evenings.

At least Mrs Ashton will be travelling Second or Third Class, thinks Vivvie, so they won't have to travel together. Mrs Ashton is a perfectly pleasant person, apart from her desire to hang her body with dead small animals; but Vivien prefers to travel alone, if only today, to prepare for her coming conversation with Sherwyn Sexton. She herself will of course be travelling First Class.

'Aren't you cold?' Mrs Ashton asks Vivien as at last the train's whistle comes into earshot. It sounds singularly melancholy and forlorn, as if it knows it's just a steam flash in time's pan, that it's not long for this world, and will soon enough be replaced by an electronic wail. 'Shouldn't you have brought a proper coat?'
'I have a good scarf and the cold doesn't bother me anyway,' Vivvie replies as the train wheezes in with flurries of steam, black flecks of soot and motes for the eye, and Vivvie can move away from the one who too familiarly addresses her.

Vivvie comes from the Big House and Mrs Ashton comes from the village and was her mother's maid twenty years ago. It's not just that Vivvie has Asperger's syndrome – always a state more easily forgiven in men than in women, being expected, and one that makes social intercourse difficult – it's that the habit and custom of class distinctions tend to run in the blood of the nation. Vivvie knows that her natural place is in First Class, where the seats are upholstered leather, Mrs Ashton knows hers is in Second Class, where the seats are padded but one step up from Third Class where the seats are wooden slats and most people expect to stand anyway.

And though Vivvie's father Sir Jeremy Ripple, recently knighted by King George V 'for services to literature', is a keen supporter of the Labour Party, and increasingly admiring of the new Soviet Union of Russia, and has brought Vivvie up to believe all men and women are equal, Vivvie finds herself over-aware that Mrs Ashton was once the maid. In theory she, like the rest of her family, are on the side of the people, the proletariat – in practice she finds it difficult to talk to the workers on easy terms. Nor indeed does the cold bother her; though she shivers now, some echo from the future no doubt reaching her, just as it passes from her to me and makes me shiver too even as I write. Let's just leave it that Vivien prefers to travel alone in the eight months left to live that I have allotted her.

As they move together to board the train, Vivvie to the First Class carriage, Mrs Ashton to Second Class, Vivien hears or thinks she hears Mrs Ashton say: 'A lie if ever I heard one. Of course she's cold. She just can't find a coat to fit. Poor thing!'

Is it spoken or does Vivvie just hear what she expects to hear? Whatever it is, she is cut to the quick. She can never be like other people. There are tears in her eyes as she finds a seat in

First Class, all dark blue plush cushioning, amongst ladies like her, up to London for the day; but for lunch and shopping, not in a desperate attempt to change the pattern of their lives.

Anyway.

A Quarter To Eleven, November 23rd 1922. Ripple & Co Offices, 3 Fleet Street

Would You Marry This Man?

Now consider Sherwyn Sexton, at work in the editorial department of Ripple & Co in November 1922. He is a handsome young man of thirty-three, a Douglas Fairbanks look-alike, many say; that is to say lean, vigorous, muscular and clean-cut of feature, very much in the fashion of the day (but fair-haired and half an inch shorter than Douglas Fairbanks, who in spite of seeming so tall and swashbuckling on camera, was in real life a mere five foot seven). Sherwyn's lack of height greatly perturbs him. He sees his short stature as unfair. Fate gave him so much – looks, charm, wit, talent, a determined heterosexuality, a penis of remarkable strength, length and reliability – why had fate stopped when it came to this last stamp of natural authority – the ability to tower over other men? True, in his short stint at the front as a second lieutenant – 1916, six months – he was known to his command as Napoleon, which has reassured him a little. He may be short but he is recognised as a leader of men. His movements are quick and light. He is a fine dancer. He has bright blue eyes. He is excellent company when in a good mood and knows how to make women laugh. When he is not in a good mood he knows how to make them suffer for it. If you offend him he can sulk for days and days and how you might offend him is never made clear.

He is something of a dandy, in a bohemian kind of way. He wears a red cravat rather than a tie to signal his defiance of office convention. Like so many of his generation he has a small, well-trimmed pencil moustache and no beard – beards are for old men. A generation who saw active service in the trenches – in 1916 the average survival time at the front was a bare six weeks – have turned against beards. Beards interfere with gas masks. At least half way through the months that Sherwyn was at the front the War Office decided to distribute those effective if ugly things – before then a hopeless piece of fabric soaked in urine had to suffice for him. These things, however short-lived, can affect a man's outlook on life for ever. He is a man, not a lad.

Apart from the accident of lacking a few inches in height good fortune is usually on Sherwyn's side, though he rather doubts it at the moment, doomed as he seems to be to scrape a living – but perhaps he should gamble and drink less – in one of his employer's cold and draughty attic offices. Sherwyn is thirty-three and his ambition had been to reach thirty as a published and prosperous literary writer like his father before him. As it is, his life is running behind schedule. He lost a mother to a passing American lover and gained a stepmother whom he does not get on with, and has been thrown out of a comfortable home of his childhood and so has to fend for himself. He is obliged to spend time editing other people's books instead of getting on with his own. This has put his schedule back by at least three years. He doesn't for one minute doubt his genius – it is merely, cruelly, on hold.

Size Isn't Everything. What About His Prospects?

Sherwyn has at least just finished his first novel in the face of financial and personal problems which would have defeated a lesser man. The manuscript has been typed up by the girlfriend with whom he cohabits, but now sits waiting attention in a neat pile of other rivalrous works on the shelf behind Sir Jeremy Ripple's elegant Arts & Crafts rosewood desk. And there it has stayed unread for a full three weeks. Though Ripple & Co does not itself publish fiction, Sir Jeremy is a power in the profession (not yet described as an industry, and very much the preserve of amateur literary gentlemen) and his recommendation will go far. He has promised to recommend the novel – should he like it sufficiently – to Herbert Jenkins, an excellent publisher of popular novels.

But Sir Jeremy, to Sherwyn's rage and indignation, has not so far bothered to turn the pages, read and respond. Sherwyn does not suffer from literary self doubt – egoistical, vain little dwarf, as his enemies refer to him, those enemies being the husbands or lovers of girls he has seduced away. (In the rather louche literary and artistic circles Sherwyn likes to frequent, news of sexual prowess soon gets about.) It's just that a wait of a full three weeks for a mere recommendation seems out of order. A genius deserves better from the boss who is lucky enough to employ him. Too busy for three whole weeks? Poppycock! No. The boss, for all his affectation of proletarian sympathies, is at heart just another unscrupulous old man, the kind who let the Great War happen, filched what glory and profit from it he could, and now hopes to make money from a growing anti-war sentiment. Sherwyn doesn't trust him further than he could throw him. Which wouldn't be far: Sherwyn being short and Sir Jeremy being tall and well set up. But Sherwyn might ask his friend Mungo to do it. Mungo works in the office down the corridor, and is an Oxford rugger Blue.

Sherwyn's Better Self

Sherwyn has met Vivvie on occasion, mostly in connection with *The Short History of the Georgians, an Outline*. It was at Sir Jeremy's suggestion that Vivien, who according to her father has artistic talents (though Sherwyn doubts it – in his experience female artists are a good-looking lot: he lives with one; he should know), has suggested that his daughter do the illustrations and Sherwyn has politely briefed her as to what is required. He knows she will be dropping by during the course of the morning but to what end he has no idea, and will be horrified when he understands that the illustrations are a mere cover for her intention to propose marriage.

And on the Thursday morning when Vivvie walks into his office Sherwyn is already not in the best of moods.

Overworked and Underpaid

This is how Sherwyn sees himself: in this he is like most of Ripple & Co's staff – indeed staff everywhere. (Sufficient reward, thinks Sir Jeremy, to be employed by the nation's most prestigious and radical publisher: pay more, and staff might feel they were being bribed, not just employed.) Sherwyn, who feels he is entitled to lofty ceilings and general grandeur wherever he works, now finds himself housed in an attic room at the top of what was once a shop but is now an office building, with sloping garret walls crumbly with disintegrating plaster, low oak beams which catch the head and are powdery with what Sherwyn rather hopes is a deathwatch beetle infestation. At least, others might think, he has an office to himself with a door and a casement window, which is more than many an office worker has today. The window opens and he can feed the birds; he can look down to Fleet Street below – in his time a busy thoroughfare with both motor and horse drawn vehicles bumping up against each other, and the hoots and cries of angry travellers rising to the heavens.

News! News! News!

There is such a great excitement focused here – how can Sherwyn be immune to it? He is lucky. When he works late he hears the rumble of metal printing presses as they start up, shaking the whole street and stirring the blood.

On his way to work Sherwyn dodges the giant paper rolls as they're manhandled across pavements and lowered into the underground basements where the presses are housed; and thinks nothing of it. In the evenings he feels the whole street tremble as the great presses start up and takes it for granted. But he loves the smell of hot printing ink as it seeps up to his open window: exciting times, intoxicating! The nation is newly literate and hungry for news and gossip. Before TV, before even radio, there's only the printed word to tell you what's going on outside your own street.

Sherwyn feels it, and is happy to be part of it, if only obliquely. He is a novelist; he prefers to make things up rather than report reality. Besides, tomorrow the papers will wrap the fish and chips; they make sense of the tumult on the street outside for only a single day. Sherwyn hopes for immortality.

Rough, Raw Years

In the nineteen-twenties few understand their own motivations, their own compulsions. Freud is still sniffing cocaine, and feeding it to his unfortunate patients while he works it out. Self interest is at its height, compassion at its nadir. There is no benefits system, no assistance board, only the good will of a public who four years after the war finds pity has worn itself out. Fleet Street is one of the better places where derelict old soldiers can beg for alms – warm air belches up from the printing presses, kindly journalists occasionally bend an ear to their woes. But no-one really wants to be reminded of the war, a dreadful event which will never happen again. A blind patriotism led the nations into all that – well, we're past that now. Now we have reason, progress, science, the League of Nations. Why would anyone want war? As for the poor, they're always with us. Jesus said so. They must take their chances.

Anyway…

This morning a tall, ragged young man with haunted eyes, caved-in cheeks and one leg laid a begging hand on Sherwyn's arm. Sherwyn had told him he couldn't help him and that his own shoes let in water. The caved-in mouth snarled, showing the most disgusting broken teeth, and called out after Sherwyn's back, 'On your way, shortie. I hope you rot in hell.'

A short man can do anything – wage wars, write novels, bed a dozen girls, break a hundred hearts, be as clever and sophisticated as he likes about fine wines and cultural artefacts, political and social movements, past, present and future, predict the very disposition of the world to come – but if a tall man, starving and ill though he may be, refers to him as 'shortie', any bubble of self esteem is bound to be punctured. It is the one thing he can do nothing about.

Did that contribute to how Sherwyn reacted to Vivien's proposal? Yes, probably. His parts might be big but they were hidden: his height was obvious for all the world to see. Vivvie's faltering self esteem had been dented by Mrs Ashton's casual words: *She just can't find a coat to fit, poor thing.* So had Sherwyn's been by 'shortie'. If only some other people had kept quiet that morning, things might have turned out differently.

The Power Of Positive Thinking

Sherwyn gazes from his window at the wet slate roofs of the Royal Courts of Justice, smokes a Turkish cigarette and makes an effort to recover his equanimity. He is never, as it happens, to quite recover from 'On your way, shortie.' He is indeed to remember it on his deathbed sixty years later. Only then will it occur to him that if he had only given the beggar a couple of shillings at the time, a lifetime of remorse would not have followed. Such shameful memories as are bound to pile up in anyone's lifetime would have been so much the less. I would not go so far as to say Sherwyn was to die salvageable in the Maker's eyes, but at least at the time, in his nineties, after a lifetime of wrongdoing, he was a devoted follower of the Maharishi, and doing his best in the light of his own nature.

Even now, on that morning in 1922, as a young man, Sherwyn makes an effort of will and decides to give up cursing a cruel fate and concentrate on working out the new short story he has begun in his head.

Escape Into Fiction

Sherwyn's colleague and chum Mungo Bolt recently took him to lunch at The Ivy in Covent Garden where they'd watched fascinated as a very pretty girl pushed away her rare and expensive plate of whitebait – she just couldn't, she'd moaned to her embarrassed suitor, she couldn't – all those tiny black eyes staring at you! Sherwyn wonders now how a pretty girl taken to a restaurant in Morocco and faced with a choice of losing her virtue or eating a sheep's eye would respond. The art of fiction, he has heard his father declare, is to exaggerate reality and see where it leads you. A whitebait eye could become a sheep's eye, maybe a camel's eye? Perhaps you start from a title and work back?

There is the germ of something promising here, he knows. Would *Blackwood's* magazine perhaps take it? *Blackwood's* published Buchan and Kipling – Sherwyn would be in good company and they paid really good money. Sherwyn's shoes have begun to leak: there are worn layers practically through to the sock on both shoes but re-soling costs a one-and-thruppence he can ill afford. The sheer indignity of his current life is intolerable. *'On your way, shortie!'* How has he, a gentleman and a genius, come to this? Fit only to receive the insults of a hollow-eyed one-legged ex-soldier. And condemned to hell. But he already is in hell. Better not think about it. But perhaps *Blackwood's* might reject *The Eye of the Lamb*, and in so doing relegate him to the ranks of the lowbrow. Elinor Glyn could get away with sin on a tiger skin but that was commerce, not literature. The choice he is offering his heroine – sex or sensibility – might seem a bit blunt for a literary magazine. Perhaps the choice should be between money and a sheep's eye, not her virtue and a sheep's eye. The story would work as well? The borderline between being seen as a hack – plying for trade as did any hackney carriage – and a serious contender in the world of letters could be difficult to distinguish. A literary chap has to beware falling between the two stools.

Sherwyn had had a story published in the *Egoist* – undeniably highbrow – when he was twenty-six and working for the Ministry of Information. He'd been hailed in the *Times* as a budding young genius, been invited to the right parties, but injudiciously slept with one or two wrong wives. Since those unfortunate episodes he'd published nothing but badly paid, barely noticed essays and reviews in magazines no-one read. His father had flung him out: one of the wives belonged to his father's publisher. And now his shoes are leaking. And his future depends on a nod from Sir Bloody *Poseur* Jeremy. It is all an intolerable humiliation.

The Trials Of The Writer

The Uncertain Gentleman, his highbrow thriller – and such a thing is possible: isn't John Buchan respectable enough in literary circles? – has taken Sherwyn a whole three years to write because of his need to take paid employment to make ends meet. And Ripple & Co pay less than any comparable publisher – to have an editorial post in so prestigious a house was seen as compensation enough for paucity of salary. And Sir Jeremy, since his recent elevation to the knighthood, has turned, say all, into a moral sadist who will deliver a blow to any cheek turned to him, just as a moral masochist might turn his cheek to accept any blow. Sir Jeremy must find pleasure in tormenting Sherwyn, or why would he do it?

The Life Of The Publisher

The Ripple knighthood had been unexpected, and generally thought to be a mistake on the part of the Palace and something of a joke. In 1919 Jeremy Ripple published *Fortitude – The British Warrior*, an ironic history of military ineptitude through the ages written by a malcontent, but having been erroneously construed by a drunken reviewer in the *Times* as a tribute to patriotic fervour, went on to make a great deal of money throughout the world. The irony was not lost on Jeremy

Ripple but he was pleased enough to become a knight of the realm, and careful not to point out the error to anyone of influence. Within a few short months of his investiture the staff could no longer drift in and out of his office at will but must now first make an appointment with his secretary Phoebe, with whom he is rumoured, quite unfairly, to be having an affair.

It was in the eighteen-eighties that the whole institution of marriage had been predicted to break down when the first batch of young unmarried women had trooped into offices as typists: mature men in constant company with young female secretaries were likely to find them prettier and livelier than their wives and would be tempted. As indeed they often were.

Anyway.

The Publisher's Wife

Sherwyn sees in Phoebe temptation enough – she's a bright bouncy tactile bobbed blonde – but he does not want to believe the rumours. They seem unlikely. Sir Jeremy's wife Adela is a palely translucent fragile beauty who glides rather than bounces, looks down from a disdainful well-born height, and provides the money for the whole Ripple enterprise. Such women are hard to come by as wives and their alienation is not lightly risked. Besides, Sir Jeremy adores his wife, and has lately encouraged her to spend huge sums refurbishing Ripple & Co's foyer, reception area and his own comfortable and smoky offices (while quite ignoring the top floor – which leaks and crumbles, and where the real work is done) in the most up-to-date and fastidious Art Deco style. It even featured in *Home and Design*'s 'Offices of the Future'.

The Publisher's Offspring

Sherwyn, who runs across Vivien occasionally at this meeting or that, as she busies herself around the office choosing fonts and providing illustrations for various of her father's books, has always seen it as strange that Lady Adela Ripple's narrow fashionable loins could have given birth to a daughter of such excessive bulkiness. It would be grievous to any mother – so much hope goes into parenthood – to have given birth to such an untoward child, and an only child at that. Perhaps having had the one, they decided not to have another? That might make a short story: *The Shadow of the Nursery* or *The Peculiar Daughter* or simply *The Giantess*. He will consult with Mungo, who is good on titles. A good title is half the battle. Presumably, in the absence of a son, Sir Jeremy has been grooming Vivien to take over the family business. She is peculiar rather than stupid, Sherwyn acknowledges, and a pleasant enough person, if clumsy. She'd managed once to tip an inkwell over his valued Corona typewriter he'd bought from an army surplus sale with his last £50, the better to type *The Uncertain Gentleman*. His fingertips were stained blue for days.

The Writer At Work

But there is work to be done, and Sherwyn must get on with it and not let himself be distracted. He sits at his desk, rolls paper into his typewriter and types... *The Eye of the Lamb*. Seven vowels in five words: the more vowels compared to consonants in title, character's or author's name the better. He is not sure why he believes this but he does. *Taboo*, 3/2, *The Hairy Ape*, 6/5, *Abie's Irish Rose*, 6/7, all currently playing to enthusiastic audiences; Wharton's novel *The Age of Innocence*, 8/9, serve to make his point. His own name, Sherwyn Sexton, 4/9 – will just have to do. He will call the whitebait girl Claire 3/3, the hero – who? Delgano 3/4? That will pass muster, vaguely exotic yet not too foreign. The 'e' on the Corona is inked up as usual, so Sherwyn clears it with a hatpin kept especially for the purpose. Yes, Claire in the story will trade her squeamishness for her virtue: she will both eat, and satisfy her carnal appetites. Women have them – why is there so much pretence that they do not? – even, he supposes, girls like Vivien. Sherwyn has a spasm of pity for all the plain girls in the world, who so out-number the pretty ones. Once he has finished with *The Eye of the Lamb*, 7/5 – 'y's count as vowels – he will get on with *The Giantess*, 4/7. But then again, perhaps he won't.

Midday, November 23rd 1922. 3 Fleet Street

The Singlemindedness Of Vivien

It is even as he considers these things that Vivien turns up at the door. She's astute enough to know more or less how much attention Sherwyn will award her, if he notices her at all. Pretty women get noticed, those less so do not, as Vivvie is all too aware. This means only one woman in every ten gets any attention at all. It's the pretty ones that attract love and drive men to unreason and despair, and feature in literature and films; the others are just part of the furniture – unless, Vivvie thinks, they happen to have famous family names or be very rich. They exist to set men free for more 'important' and 'interesting' things, to keep fictional plots going as written by men.

Vivien is determined. She is damp though, from the London drizzle and fog – and wishes she had remembered to bring a coat. She flicks the scarf in a girlish fashion over her shoulder, but its fronds are actually quite wet and splatter raindrops over Sherwyn's desk. He barely looks up, doesn't recognise her, but brushes the drops away in irritation.

'Go away,' he says, going back to his machine. 'Don't you see I'm working.'

'You're very rude,' she says. 'But I suppose you haven't recognised me.'

Sherwyn looks at her properly and sees that this very plain, excessively sized young woman with a dull complexion in an ugly grey felt hat is Vivien, Sir Jeremy Ripple's daughter. It behoves him to be pleasant, but hardly flirtatious.

'Why Miss Ripple,' he said, 'I didn't realise it was you. I am so sorry.'

'There is no need to apologise. I am not sufficiently attractive to impinge upon your consciousness.'

He refrains from assuring her, as custom demands, that she is indeed attractive. She wouldn't believe him, and it wouldn't be true.

'May I – do something for you?' he asks, as she shows no sign of going, but continues to hover. He resents her. The order of his thought has been interrupted, violated. He has been inside the head of a pretty girl removing the heads of whitebait so as not to have to eat the tiny black eyes and he rather liked it in there. Now he must pay attention to the boss's daughter. Vivien nods and he has no choice but to offer her a chair so she can sit down. And this is how it goes.

Why? Why?

Vivvie unfolds her gawky self into a chair and Sherwyn perches on the corner of his desk. He finds the fashions of the day unappealing at the best of times – beanpole women with low waists and flattened chests, droopy attitudes, long beads, longer scarves: only the very good-looking can get away with it. But most at least make some sort of effort to please men. Vivien Ripple doesn't. She takes off her hat and shakes out her hair, and that at least is quite pretty. She has not had it bobbed and it ripples down her back in a reddish brown stream.

'Ripple by name and ripple by nature,' he says, courteously. 'Charming.'

'I'm thinking of getting it bobbed,' she says. 'People always admire my hair when they have to think of something complimentary to say. Better if they didn't say anything.'

He could see that on closer acquaintance she might be quite entertaining. She did say the unexpected and at least seemed to have a functioning brain, which was more than you could say for most of his female acquaintances. One never could tell, of course. So many girls were taught not to display intelligence in case it put men off, any female idiocy might well be mere affectation. The prettiest face might hide the wittiest brain.

Miss Ripple falls quiet again. She is more serviceable than pretty, he thinks. Her jaw juts as does her father's, but what proclaims a man as a master of lesser men makes a girl look sulky and stubborn, as though something went wrong at her birth. Well, her mother Adela's hips being narrow – perhaps there had been some breeding difficulty?

'Well?' Sherwyn tries to hurry Miss Ripple on and out. She seems reluctant to speak at all. His own position of rest – and he is aware of the paradox – is one of overwhelming impatience, a constant preparedness, alert for the next blow from the unexpected: words burst out of him all too easily. He stops his legs swinging. Miss Ripple might get a glimpse of the soles and despise him. But the state of his shoes is hardly his fault, but that of her father, of Sir Jeremy the hypocritical skinflint:

why should Sherwyn care what the daughter thinks of him? She for her part is dressed very oddly. There are actually moth holes in her scarf. Perhaps the father is as mean to his daughter as he is to his staff, which is why she dresses as she does? He feels a flicker of fellow feeling for her – they are both victims.

'I've had to "screw my courage up to sticking place" for this,' she says. 'I'd be glad of a little mercy.'

'You and Lady Macbeth?' he says. 'If you want me to murder Duncan you may have come to the wrong person.'

'You are not Duncan. Though you are to all accounts a virtuous and well-liked man.' Well, thinks Sherwyn, at least she knows her Shakespeare. Then she says:

'I am here to ask you to marry me.'

Just like that. Straight out. No preamble. Oh dear. Mad.

How very awkward. What is a man to do?

June 21st 1947. The Albany, Piccadilly

The Unwelcome Package

Sherwyn was to confide what happened next to Mungo, his colleague in the attic office next door. Mungo was also an aspiring writer – it was Sir Jeremy's policy to get young men of budding talent onto his staff, especially if they were good-looking – and twenty-five years on, in 1947, Mungo will include an approximation of the proposal scene in his own first and only novel *Vice Rewarded*. He will by that time be managing director of Bolt & Crest, his own advertising agency. A proof copy of *Vice Rewarded* will arrive unexpectedly at Sherwyn's bachelor apartment in the Albany, Mayfair – Sherwyn's between wives at the time, after finally divorcing Marjorie McShannon the Hollywood film actress. The maid has brought in breakfast from Fortnum & Mason down the road, but rationing is tight and she's only managed Camp coffee concentrate and scrambled eggs made from powdered egg and milk on dry toast with no butter. She's also brought in a package. It feels like trouble. Sherwyn had spent much of the war in Paris as an undercover SOE agent and that kind of thing makes a man wary, paranoid, even.

Sherwyn opens the package – only a book, with a covering letter from Samuel Epstone himself. He reads. Perhaps, Epstone asks, Sherwyn could provide a note of recommendation to go on the jacket of a new novel he was publishing, since Mungo, he gathered, was a friend of Sherwyn's back in the earlier days of Ripple & Co? In Mungo's *Vice Rewarded*, it seemed, Epstone saw another book as important as something like Camus' *L'Étranger*. Mungo Bolt, hiding his light under a bushel for so many years, is now revealed as an existentialist philosopher posing as an ad man: delving in this most thoughtful novel into the underlying nature of humanity: 'We can all recognise ourselves in these profound lines.'

What utter balls, thinks Sherwyn. Mungo has never had a profound thought in his life, all he's ever been fit for is advertising slogans like '*Buttoning's Such a Bother*' – and putting his prick where it doesn't belong. Not much of a prick, either, pretty pathetic: Sherwyn used to behold it in the showers when he was at the front, when was that, back in '16? Half the length and half the width of Sherwyn's own.

The clue of course was in the phrase 'we can all recognise ourselves blah, blah, blah'. It was a coded message. Epstone was warning him that *Vice Rewarded* was a *roman à clef*. He, Sherwyn, was in the book, might take offence, might possibly sue. He was being sounded out.

Sherwyn puts aside his disgusting breakfast – he will lunch at Rules, where at least you can get a good rabbit fricassee – and opens his former friend's, now enemy's, novel. It has a plain cream textured jacket in the French style, the paper is thick and the pages uncut: all the marks of a pretentious literary novel, one on which publishers were prepared to spend money.

Presumably Mungo had contributed to the cost. What was he playing at? Did he really have literary aspirations? He must know by now he was an awful writer. He had written one novel while working at Ripple's with Sherwyn, but no-one was prepared to publish it. While Sherwyn's career as a writer had blossomed, Mungo had cast himself on the wilder shores of advertising, where he flourished: '*For Added Strength and Security Say Yes to Crest Zips!*' or, more generically, '*Down with the Button, Up with the Zip*' was Mungo's level.

True, there had been that trouble over the twins, and Sherwyn had seduced Mungo's dull and skinny ex-wife to be revenged, '*but that was in another country, and besides...*' Mungo had never really liked her. But it probably hadn't helped. Mungo was the kind who nursed grudges. No-one keeps their mouth shut for ever, as Sherwyn had learned to his cost. Truth always emerged in the bitter throes of anger or divorce.

Something was up and it did not bode well.

Sherwyn let the book fall open where it would, to the pages where perhaps others had read before. And as he half expected, there he was for all to see and giggle over crucified upon the page, referred to as 'The Dwarf' along with poor Vivvie 'The Giantess', in a cruel account of that memorable proposal scene as long ago related to Mungo by Sherwyn himself. How misplaced that trust had been! Sherwyn read in horror. It was not done kindly: it was intended to humiliate and hurt. The Dwarf? Not only had a friendship been viciously betrayed but his wife's memory had been insulted and besmirched. True, it had been the briefest of marriages, shattered by her untimely death, but a wife is a wife.

Sherwyn had kept the proposal scene out of his own work (planning to preserve it for the great literary novel he looked forward to writing one day, when the popular Delgano seam finally gave out). It had been a memorable occasion, certainly. But it was so long ago! Had Mungo, the thieving, plagiarising swine, actually taken notes at the time? It was possible, even probable, and it seemed to Sherwyn as he read on, certainly so.

The Past Is Never Over

Vivvie's twin daughters, Mallory (the plain one) and Stella (the pretty one), were to pore over the passage when the same morning post delivered *Vice Rewarded* to No 17 Belgrave Square. It came out of the blue and had in fact been sent in error; a typist's slip as she sent off review copies to everyone on Samuel Epstone's list, either not noticing, or mischievously ignoring, the instruction 'not for Ripple family'. But the girls were not to know this and fell upon the novel with delight. Not only had the book been written by Mungo Bolt, the mysterious but jovial man who had called by their nursery when they were small, bearing gifts (rocking horses, dolls' houses, train sets – Mallory would engineer the most magnificent collisions), but it contained their only description of the woman they now knew to be their mother. Everyone seemed all too happy to forget Vivien – especially Adela. Any detailed description of her, 'Giantess' or not, was precious. At least it was confirmation that the Dwarf was indeed their father. In their young years they'd rather thought it must be Mungo who'd always brought such good presents over the years, better than Sherwyn's: exciting dolls' houses not boring rugs, glittery diamonds not tasteful pearls.

The Dwarf prided himself on maintaining an air of amused insouciance through all adversity, and when the Giantess made her outrageous proposal of marriage he did what he could to keep his face straight and preserve an air of equanimity. The Giantess was obviously unhinged or ill, or perhaps the victim of some sexual obsession that Freud would have something interesting to say about. The obvious thing to do was humour her. There might even be a way of turning this unexpected and uncomfortable situation to his advantage.

But unexpected events could all too easily lead to disaster. The Dwarf had already had his fill of them. His sister had been the victim of an incestuous assault by their uncle, his parents divorcing as a result; the arrival of a stepmother with a face like a horse had put an end to his hopes of inheritance. His dwarfish mind raced through alarming possibilities. Perhaps this was a Potiphar's wife scenario? If he rejected the boss's daughter she might cry rape and have him carried off to prison. Such things happened. Whatever her motives the utmost prudence was required. This over-tall, over-forward, singularly unattractive young person was in a position of power. Her story would be believed.

Yet she spoke composedly. She did not seem insane. Had something happened a fellow might have forgotten? He had got drunk at the last office party but surely not to the extent of losing his memory. The Giantess was not the kind one would casually flirt with. One would have to go on tiptoe to as much as kiss her. Office life had its temptations and its scandals – and a chap had had his fair share of amiable and passing office encounters – but nothing that could add up to an expectation of marriage.

33

Yet when the Giantess assured the Dwarf that she was making a business proposition rather than a declaration of love, and that she was without erotic intent, the Dwarf had felt vaguely disappointed. A man likes to be pursued. Though he had his pride and was hardly going to stand at the altar with someone who towered above him; that would be too ludicrous. But what was this about a business proposition?

'I am not a monster,' the Giantess was assuring him, 'though I think you see me as such; I am tall, but would not be out of the ordinary had I been born a boy.'

The Dwarf refrained from saying the problem was that she had not been. Priding himself as ever on his ability to charm he merely said, 'I am of course deeply flattered. But why me?'

'Because it is in your interests to agree. You are a writer. All writers need rich wives, at any rate my father tells me this is the case. He is a publisher. He should know. My wealth comes from my mother's side – on my 20th birthday I came into a not inconsiderable fortune: I inherited a small but prosperous mountain town in Bavaria.' He did not disbelieve her: it sounded so absurd it was probably true. 'I will pay off your debts: you are a gambler and a womaniser: I imagine you are on the verge of bankruptcy. You can scarcely afford the shoes on your own feet. The soles are on the verge of flapping loose. Marry me, and you will dress like a dandy and dine like a king for the rest of your life. You will have all the time in the world to write. My father will publish your books, and as his son-in-law do his best to make you rich and famous. It is

within his power. For my part I undertake not to stand between you and your pleasures. I am paying you to marry me not to sleep with me.'

The Dwarf began to view her proposition in a more favourable light.

'Prince Charming will never come along of his own accord,' said the Giantess. 'I realise he will have to be bought, and for me the sooner the better. I do not mean to live as a spinster lives, pitied by all. A married woman can be as tall, plain and ugly as she likes if she has the ring on her finger and had been chosen by a man – any man, be he oaf, cretin or criminal, he is still a man – and a man outclasses all women, no matter how pretty, witty or wise she is. And I am none of these.'

If only for decency's sake The Dwarf felt obliged to point out that she had other choices: these days she could live on her own as an independent woman, in whatever manner she wanted: he knew artists and architects who did that and even earned money enough to support themselves. He found himself relieved when she replied: 'But still she will be pitied and reviled for not following the life God decreed for women – to be subservient, serve men and propagate the race.'

The Dwarf, at bottom a man of infinite vanity and greed, weakened. The Giantess raised her black fringed eyes to his and they were suddenly beautiful, as was her voice, steady and soft now it had lost the slight whiny overtone of the peevish child and sang the siren song of wealth unlimited. He weakened more. He could see that a follow-ing wind of money might blow him to pleasant places. His talent could flourish in a world in which he was free of debt. He could write what he wanted, publish where he chose. And yet, and yet – marriage! Any form of commitment was dangerous. True, she offered him liberty to pursue his erotic inclinations, but once married she might change her mind, and turn into a shrew and a nag. If he waited just a little until he was famous in his own right he could have any woman he chose to fill his bed, and a (preferably titled) wife of his own choice, one of whom other men were jealous. Who would ever envy a short man who put up with a plain giantess for a wife?

But there was always divorce. A man could be so unkind to an unwanted wife she would be happy enough to put him away. The Dwarf weighed up the choices.

'Thank you for asking,' said The Dwarf. 'I would be happy to marry you.'

Storm And Stress

Sherwyn rang his lawyer, Bernie of Courtney and Baum, and said he meant to sue. Bernie advised against it. Hard to prove that being called a dwarf would make a reasonable person think any less of the person so described, though to be accused of having a dwarfish mind might possibly be defamatory? But what did a dwarfish mind consist of? The law was currently busy bringing to book men accused of hideous war crimes; Sherwyn would find little sympathy in the courts for so trivial a complaint. In five years' time, perhaps – now, no. More, Sherwyn would do himself no favours by objecting to a suggestion that he had married for money: the nearer a libel is to the truth the greater the damages. Sherwyn would do better not to draw attention to himself. As for the Giantess, it was impossible to libel someone after they were dead. Sherwyn broke off the call.

He would have then rung Jeremy Ripple, always good in a crisis and ever anxious to sue, but Sir Jeremy was dead and gone and no longer there for sympathy and advice. He had died a hero's death in May 1941, when bombs had hit the Law Courts, a fire had started in No 3 Fleet Street, and he'd rashly run back into the building in an attempt to rescue a whole first edition, piled up in the hallway and just in from the printers, of G.D.H. Cole's *A Chance for Everyone*. The *Times* obituary had run to a full half page, which in a time of war and a grave shortage of news-print, was quite remarkable. Sir Jeremy had been well thought of. '*A man of conscience, brave in the defence of the freedom of the fourth estate.*' Britain was fighting alongside the Soviet Union, and to be a fervent socialist was no longer a sin. The war was settling down in the eyes of many to a full scale battle between fascism and communism. It seemed that the *Times*, apologetic about its earlier pro-appeasement stance and early battles with Sir Jeremy, was doing its best to make amends.

Deprived of his customary allies, Sherwyn gave up his hope of rabbit fricassee, put on his bowler hat and leather gloves, took the No 19 bus and went to visit Rita in her Chelsea studio.

Eleven In The Evening, June 21st 1947. An Artist's Studio, Cheyne Walk, Chelsea

Sherwyn was at the time divorcing his third wife, and now wooing his fourth. His aesthete action hero Rafe Delgano, six foot two inches, was selling well in novel after novel. Two were in the pipeline to be filmed. The Moroccan restaurant Sherwyn first described in *The Eye of the Lamb* had become Rafe Delgano's gourmet safe house. The end of the war had not meant an end to food rationing – far from it; by 1947 the nation found itself hungrier than ever: even bread was rationed. Rafe's excursions into Middle Eastern cuisine as he dodged bullets, angry ex-wives and the caresses of various sultry temptresses found favour all over the world. Rafe Delgano cooked well, ate well, aimed and shot well, and made love well; he was Sherwyn Sexton's alter ego, only seven inches taller.

Sherwyn – disrobed, pale-skinned, lacking inches in height, but his member famously long and purposeful enough, and in general well muscled and proportioned – sank back into Rita's faded purple plush sofa. As artists' studios went Rita's was as good as any London could offer, Sherwyn thought, *bien situé* on the banks of the river, expensive, spacious and practical: wide, high windows letting in a good north light, smelling – as had all Rita's studios from the beginning and there had been at least five – of a heady mixture of oil paint, turpentine, Rita's

Evening in Paris scent, discarded silk knickers – or so Sherwyn liked to imagine – and the mildly exhilarating hot metal fumes from the Pither stoves that heated them. Like the sofa, memento of so many lovers, the stove travelled with her. And Cheyne Walk was a notoriously good address. All kinds of famous people had lived here, from Whistler's mother to Dante Gabriel Rossetti, Holman Hunt to Thomas Carlyle, and Sherwyn, famous writer, felt at home.

Rita, wearing nothing but a crimson silk kimono splashed with red roses, leafed through *Vice Rewarded*, occasionally laughing, occasionally snorting. Sherwyn watched her anxiously.

'It's not so bad,' she said at last. 'He's just an advertising man trying to write a novel, not a proper writer like you. He's jealous.'

'Why on earth should Mungo be jealous?' demanded Sherwyn. 'He's doing well enough in his own field. He makes as much as me, even more. Bound to. He tells lies. I tell the truth. Once he was my friend. Now he ridicules me. It's quite obviously an attack on me. Why else would he refer to me as the fucking "Dwarf"! I'm not tall, I can see that, but "The Dwarf"!'

'I can see it's awfully painful,' she said. 'But didn't you once go off with his wife?'

'I didn't go off with her,' he said crossly. 'I spent an hour or so with the wretched woman beneath the coats at some party. I was drunk, I can barely remember. She was very thin. I could feel her ribs, I remember that. And the elbows were sharp. It was at least twenty years ago, it was more her idea than mine. She was trying to make Mungo jealous, or so I imagined.'

'Well, she succeeded,' said Rita. 'And so far as I can tell you remember very well. Ribs and elbows.'

'And she swore she wouldn't tell. She was a department store heiress. American. What a nerve Mungo has, accusing me of marrying for money! He married his wife to get hold of a trivial zipper account for his agency.' Rita was beginning to laugh. 'Women always tell. Why do you think there are so many divorces? Perhaps she told him your cock was so much bigger than his. You men find it hard to overlook a thing like that.'

Sherwyn felt a little better. She was so right. Mungo's missile, his message would surely misfire. The short marriage of convenience to Vivvie was forgotten. The parentage of the twins was neither here nor there. But what a fool he'd been. Of course Mungo had taken notes. Indeed, he now remembered encouraging Mungo to do so: '*Be Boswell, Mungo, to my Dr Johnson. Write it all down for posterity.*'

And indeed, Mungo had, and posterity had caught up with them both. And there hadn't only been the matter of Olive Bolt, née Crest, Mungo's ex-wife, but the article he'd written in 1935 when Mungo had been awarded a CBE for services to advertising – to the effect that such a decoration was a sure sign of the decadence of the times. What was advertising but the glorification of the salesman, of snake oil merchants, confidence men all? Yes, Sherwyn could see that Mungo might have taken it personally and been annoyed. Mungo might not understand that anything went in love and war.

'No-one's going to recognise me, surely, as "The Dwarf"? It's intolerable.' He was still agitated.
'I shouldn't think so.' Rita was kind. 'Elvira hardly moves in modern literary circles. Her old books are for selling, not for reading.'

Which was true enough. Elvira was Sherwyn's intended fiancée, now that Marjorie the film star had retreated in a sulk and gone to Reno to see about a divorce. (Marry in haste, divorce in Reno. Everything can be arranged by those who have money.) Elvira might not be as young as she had been, but was still a favourite of the fashion pages, beautiful, decorous, intelligent – and much respected as a businesswoman. She bought and sold antiquities, Russian icons and rare books. Any man would see her as a prize, especially if they'd been married to Marjorie. But Elvira was proving difficult to woo. She was reluctant to put Sherwyn's ring upon her finger. She thought he was too easy in his affections.

Married, the Giantess explained, she could have her own establishment and with it her dignity. Unmarried, she was doomed to live with a mother who saw her as a freak of nature, a cross and a humiliation.

'At least Mungo got that right,' said Sherwyn. 'Poor old Vivvie. She was so desperate to get away from her Mama.'
'You're not the only one who's desperate,' Rita said, vulgarly. 'Look at you!'

It was true. Elvira was so slow falling into his arms, and the smell of Rita's studio was so familiar an enticement. Rita might be the age his mother was when she walked out on his father and left him to the mercies of the stepmother with the face like a horse, but the appeal was still strong. Rita did what she could for him, then put a sheet over him afterwards to cover his parts, still waving about but now without further purpose she reckoned, and make him decent, and went on cleaning her brushes. Her kimono fell open from time to time but now he took little notice. He was still too busy worrying away at the ins and outs of Mungo's betrayal.

'What astonishes me,' said Sherwyn, 'is that this preposterous tosh of Mungo's has actually found a publisher. He's hoping for a *roman à clef* scandal but he'll never get it. "The Dwarf", "The Giantess". So cruel. Something that happened twenty-five years ago, and not at all the way he remembers it. But who knows, who cares? All that rubbish about incest and my stepmother having a face like a horse!'

'A foul calumny, I know, I know,' said Rita. 'A betrayal not just of art but of friendship. Perhaps you should both strip naked and fight a duel. Then everyone could see from your balls who was the better man.'

'Why do you always laugh at me?' he complained. 'At least it's so badly written no-one's going to buy it, let alone believe it: "*Raising her black fringed eyes to his*"! Vivvie had rather short sandy eyelashes, poor thing, if I remember.'

'You're angry because you're saving it up for the memoirs you're never going to get round to writing.'

She went too far. She was not funny. She had grown hard and unsympathetic with the decades. Sherwyn had thought he could trust her but he could not; she was like Mungo, enemy posing as friend. He thought he might be angry: might walk out on her and go off to Rules for the fricassee: that would teach her. But then she came and sat composedly on the sofa next to him. He felt the touch of her thigh and forgave her.

Actually Sherwyn had indeed been saving the proposal scene for his own writing, though the occasion to use it had never arisen.

His bestselling novels and stories tended to feature epicurean, but tough, detectives whose hearts were in hock to unfeeling but beautiful wives who did not appreciate the heroes' cooking – and had no origin in Sherwyn's own life experience. Lately he had been on a winning streak with Rafe Delgano. But he wrote (which was customary at the time) as a neutral, anonymous observer of life, not as one who revealed any special or painful experience of it. To think clearly was surely more important for a writer than to feel deeply, which would be uncomfortable for both reader and writer: leave self revelation to the poet. Indignation, rage, social protest, appreciation of all things beautiful and even sensuous – such responses were acceptable, even necessary, but the chin must not tremble, the lip must not quiver; a cool impartiality must be maintained. Rafe Delgano hovered on the edge of acceptability, too commercially successful for Sherwyn's own literary good. As for his own memoirs, Rita was right, he would never get round to writing them. Perhaps he should feel more kindly towards Mungo, forgive him all that was past as the Lord's Prayer recommended.

Sherwyn recovered his composure.

'Poor old Mungo,' he said. 'He always was obsessed with bloody Freud. He has Vivien talking about stallions, parents and the primal scene. She would never have so much as mentioned such things.'

'I saw a photograph of her in her obituary,' said Rita. '*Tragic Death of Publishing Heiress*. If only she'd thrown back her shoulders and pushed out her bosom and smiled she could have joined the chorus line of the *Folies Bergère*. How a girl looks is so much a matter of how she presents herself. It's either take me or keep off me.'

'I tried to make her see reason,' said Sherwyn. 'I said she was far too young to be talking the way she did, that rich girls always found husbands in the end. And all she said was that she was proud, vain and ugly, and that was not an easy mix, and would I marry her. She was tired of being an object of mirth and derision, of having to put up with the leftovers of pretty girls.'

'You came home from the office drunk on the proposal night and told me all about it. I remember the phrase, "the leftovers of pretty girls". You had this cheque in your pocket you tried to hide from me. You owed me rent but you had no intention of giving me a penny. You'd already agreed to marry someone else but didn't even tell me. I don't know why I put up with you, then or now.'

'But you do,' he said, 'you do put up with me, you always have.'

'You were ashamed of me.'

'I certainly didn't tell Vivvie about your existence, though I daresay Mungo knew. All I wanted was to get her out of my office. She was just so large and looming. And frankly I was beginning to feel not just embarrassed but insulted. I was, I am, an English gentleman, a writer, a genius, not someone to be bought and sold in marriage like a slave. Vivvie was completely out of order. I thought perhaps Vivvie had somehow got me muddled up with Mungo. But she said no. Then she said that though she hoped I'd see fit to give her two sons for reasons of inheritance, I would of course be free to pursue my own interests, by which I assumed she meant someone like you.'

'How jolly generous of her,' said Rita. 'Posh, royal. An heir and a spare. But she couldn't have known about my existence.'

'It is possible,' admitted Sherwyn, 'though not likely. I was quite fond of Phoebe at the time, and you know how typists talk. I may have been indiscreet. Do you think that was why Sir Jeremy was always so disagreeable to me at the editorial meetings?'

When Sherwyn encountered Sir Jeremy on those Monday mornings long ago, he would find his employer oddly hostile. Sherwyn couldn't understand it. True, he would often arrive late, sleepy and unshaven when straight from Rita or Phoebe's bed. Sir Jeremy had taken to either ignoring or insulting him, calling him 'our lad from the orlop deck where the lowlife dwells', or 'our poor Old Pauline' – Sir Jeremy being an Old Etonian, as was Mungo, and Sherwyn merely an old boy of St Paul's, the lesser, if older, school. Mungo would be asked his opinion about, say, the length of the print run, the quality of the paper, the pricing of the finished volume – and his advice be then apparently accepted. Sherwyn's opinion would be publicly jeered at, if later privately followed.

'It is perfectly possible,' said Rita. 'I daresay as Phoebe's employer he thought he had prior rights.' Her fingers tightened, and the gentle scratches became less gentle.
'And I wanted to get on with my story. I was working on *The Eye of the Lamb*. You know they made it into a film?'
'Of course I know,' Rita said. 'They called it *Black Eyes* and you were stupid enough to marry the star. That's enough of your back. My wrist is tired and I've broken a nail.'
'I've made you jealous,' he said. 'That's good.'

Rita scratched harder still. Her mouth went down towards his member. It seemed undecided whether to rise or fall, as emotion

45

succeeded emotion, rising up with rage and vanity, falling with despair, regret and anxiety, but engorged by a generalised excitement of sudden and unusual event. Elvira's fastidious mouth was never likely to approach him in this way. The thought made him appreciate Rita the more; habit is strong, and the broken nail had actually drawn blood. For some reason neither of them cared to investigate, the blood stirred him on.

Afterwards he asked, 'And Rita, by the way, how are you so familiar with the tiny size of Mungo's cock?'

'Good heavens,' said Rita. 'Have you forgotten? When you were courting poor Vivvie you palmed me off on Mungo.'

'Oh,' said Sherwyn. 'Did I? Well, never apologise, never explain? In any case, in those days you were anyone's, more of an artist's moll than an artist.'

'True,' she said amicably enough. 'But I had become accustomed to yours, and his was such a little finger of a thing. The assertive and demanding is so much more appealing than the small and tentative.'

'You don't think mine has got smaller with the years?'

'I see no sign of it,' she said soothingly – and, thus encouraged, it leapt obligingly to life yet again. One way and another it was a pleasing afternoon, in spite of Mungo's outrageous offence.

Rita made him a cactus tea from the remnants of a powder which the married portrait painter Martin Dunsdale, one of the true loves of her life, had given her five years back and which made anyone who drank it agreeably foolish. Sherwyn sipped, and feeling braver and more relaxed, and a good deal less indignant, went back to *Vice Rewarded*, but Rita interrupted him.

'But you did marry Vivvie,' she said. 'You did. You failed me. You sold your soul and broke my heart. Say what you will about me, I never sold my soul.'

'No-one ever asked to buy it,' he said, more unkindly than she deserved.

A Long-Term Affair

Sherwyn had first met Rita in 1921, when she was nineteen, a voluptuous redheaded girl from Bermondsey living in a borrowed studio, no better than she should be, an artists' model, an artist's moll, presently to be known as a painter in her own right. Indeed, in 1976, when she was seventy-four, Rita actually had a three month retrospective of her own at the Tate Gallery, under the title *Love and the Artist*. Sherwyn, aged eighty-seven, didn't go, claiming the infirmities of age. Rita, feeling it was the least he could have done, was bitter.

(I, your writer did go along: large murky giantess figures without proper definition, lots of heavy purple and black, heavy gold frames not helping at all, not a patch on the work of some of those she had loved and who had loved her. I imagined it was Rita's notoriety as the mistress of so many luminous men of the art world which the curators supposed, rightly, would draw in the crowds. The work of the well known was reproduced in the catalogue, but only a handful of companion pieces by them could be afforded for the walls. I don't suppose the exhibition cost much to mount. But the reviews were good, and I was glad of it. Famous courtesans deserve some honour. The patience they must have had!)

Rita and Sherwyn had kept company most of their lives, in between his marriages and love affairs: witnesses to one another's life. We should all have such a relationship, someone to observe and comment. Rita didn't exactly love Sherwyn, that is to say he did not have the capacity to break her heart; but she cared for him, cosseted him and nurtured him, a strange verbal creature, a writer in a world of painters.

When Sherwyn and Rita pored over Mungo's *Bildungsroman* it was 1947 and Rita was forty-five. Her hair was no longer flamboyantly red but a kind of thinning, peppered chestnut. The flesh of her limbs was a little less resilient than once it had been, but she still looked good naked against the purple velvet. The fabric in its turn had faded and thinned with the years. It comforted Sherwyn to feel that Rita and he had faded together, melded together. The sofa had moved house and home with her wherever she went: a kind of magic token, he liked to believe, to keep him with her in spirit if not always in the flesh. And she would certainly tell him so – she was adept at flattery. Sherwyn would return to Rita time and time again to offer a progress report on his life: to lie entwined with her on her squishy purple chaise longue, share his disappointments and his triumphs, and rail with her against the ever increasing ranks of his enemies. They never married, nor had he asked her to. Rita was a bad habit. She was a costermonger's daughter, she had big raw, working hands and cigarette stained fingers. Vivvie had money, Marjorie had looks, Elvira had style: in the face of these three what could Rita offer, other than love and familiarity, and a role as witness to the life? Not enough.

They first encountered each other when Sherwyn was turned out of his family home by an angry father, and Rita was living in the studio where she had been set up by a professor at the Slade School of Fine Art. Some said it was Victor Hewtin, the landscape painter, others C.R.W. Nevinson, the war artist. Other lovers came and went. But all of them, so far as Sherwyn could tell, 'arty'. Keeping Rita was apparently seen as a joint effort.

Having nowhere else to go after a late party, Sherwyn had moved in to sleep on Rita's floor and pretty soon to share her bed, at least on a part-time basis. Victor Hewtin visited her whenever there was trouble with his wife but this did not happen often. The person who was or was not C.R.W. Nevinson visited more rarely. There was time for Sherwyn to conceal all evidence of his presence and move out for a day or two. He found these visits both annoying but oddly stimulating. As he noted at the time, painters, even more than writers, believed firmly that the creative impulse was dependent on the sexual availability of the Muse. And Rita represented that Muse, which she herself saw as a noble calling.

A Quarter Past Midday, Thursday November 23rd 1922. 3 Fleet Street

Other Things To Think About

Back in 1922, when he's a mere thirty-something, Sherwyn looks at his watch. He has no idea the future is watching him so closely. All he knows is that he needs to get Vivien out of his office as soon as he can. It's not just the embarrassment of the moment; the whitebait girl is scratching away at the edge of his unconscious and demanding attention. Her name is Patricia (4/4) or possibly Claire (3/3). Perhaps she means to be taken on a holiday by a woman friend but ends up alone in Morocco in the company of a sheik determined on ravishment and the sheep's eye is the price of her virtue? Perhaps Patricia/Claire isn't pretty at all, is not delicate and fastidious, but plain and somehow brutal – as is Miss Ripple, a pallid giantess hardly entitled to dietary fussiness – but still exotic in Moroccan terms, and desirable as the daughter of a powerful infidel diplomat called Delgano (3/4)? Oh dear, an extra consonant. It could be Delano (3/3) but that is one of President Franklin Delano Roosevelt's names (9/14). Delgano feels right.

Sherwyn finds it fascinating how it sometimes happens that the personal and the fictional world seem to clash and intertwine, jamming up against one another – how the gods of invention elbow reality out of the way, and render the writer at the mercy of what is laid in front of him. Sherwyn needs time to sort it out in his head. He must get Miss Ripple out of the sanctuary of his office, get rid of her as soon as is politely possible. He has to find time for Patricia/Claire and Delgano.

'Miss Ripple,' he says. 'Thank you for your proposal, though I must say it comes as a surprise.' How do men turn down women who demand marriage? It so seldom happens. There are few literary references. 'I need time to think, and I will respond within the week. But I am honoured and flattered that you should put such trust in me. I respect your confidences and can assure you I will keep them to myself.'
'Thank you,' she says. 'That is very prettily said.'

He tells Vivien he has a meeting with Mungo any minute now to settle the new timetable for *A Short History of the Georgians* and must hurry away. Will she leave the folder of illustrations with him? He admires her work and very much looks forward to seeing them. Mind you, the picture has changed somewhat since he last saw her. With the news that Joseph Stalin, a Georgian, had been appointed General Secretary of the Communist Party of the new Soviet Union, her father has expressed the belief that Georgia will cease to be just a place known only to the historians and intrepid travellers but will be celebrated by all who have faith in the future of mankind: Sir Jeremy anticipates that the book will sell well, and that, this being the case, more time and money must be spent on its production.

'Ah,' she says. 'Father is unusual in that he lives in such great hope of Utopia. I hope when I take over the business I can retain such trust. Don't think you are obliged to use my drawings just because he is your boss and I am his daughter. Myself, I would not think of employing me. There are others who cost less and do better.'

Pillow talk with such a one would require application, he could see. Sweet nothings would be rare. Intelligence, wit and honesty, in his view, are not necessarily desirable qualities in a wife: the girlish trill of vapid chatter might prove more restful.

She takes the hint and unfolds her long large self to leave. Good teeth, he notices, strong and even, though of gravestone shape and size. He prefers little sharp teeth, the kind that are almost translucent, like Rita's, like Phoebe's.

'I hope you will think seriously about my offer. It remains on the table. I think it would suit us both. You are the kind who finds fidelity intolerable and I am the kind who, frankly, finds male attention unbearable.'

Ah, that's the clue. She's an invert, a lesbian. Love between women is fashionable in some literary and titled circles. Free-thinking women drift from man to woman and back again, revelling in emotional storms, but some do seem to have an actual aversion to the opposite gender. She is probably one of these congenital unfortunates, and scared of the world's disapproval. To be married to such a one might do him no harm in literary circles.

And Vivvie leaves. He marvels. It seemed to be one of life's wonders – some writer said it – that nothing happens and nothing happens and all of a sudden everything happens. It is a sign from fate. He has no choice now but to hand in his notice. If he refuses her she may find a way of having her revenge. His career as a literary man about town has been hanging fire long enough. He must act, and now. Left to his own devices Sir Jeremy will never do Sherwyn any favours, let alone accept him for a son-in-law. Less than a year ago Sherwyn went to some trouble to write, at Sir Jeremy's behest, a series of articles for the house magazine *Futures* on the inevitable collapse of the Liberal Party. He doubted that these articles would ever appear in print and Sherwyn was right. What did happen was that Sir Jeremy kept them and used their substance in a lecture to the Fabian Society (watchwords: *Educate, Organise, Agitate!*) without so much as crediting the real author. And meanwhile *The Uncertain Gentleman* languishes on a shelf unread and ripe for anyone's stealing. Bitter, bitter. The novel is a thriller, true, inasmuch as a murder is committed, and by whom is the key. But what was the great Conrad if not a thriller writer? What else was *The Secret Agent*?

A novel with a strong plot can nevertheless be literature. Books can't be all reflection and contemplation. *The Riddle of the Sands* is much admired. Sherwyn thinks of poor doomed Erskine Childers, its author, even at the moment languishing in Dublin under sentence of death by an Irish military court. Childers' alleged sin? Carrying a pistol on his person – a Spanish-made 'Destroyer', a 32 calibre semi-automatic – the same one Sherwyn's Irish hero Patrick Vickery, goaded beyond endurance, uses in *The Uncertain Gentleman*. Childers' real sin? Writing a novel with a discernible plot. Perhaps the Irish connection – which Sir Jeremy always preferred to eschew on the principle that no good ever came out of Ireland – is unwise and will prejudice its reception. But too late now: the novel is written. Once those two fateful words 'The End' are written, there must, for the wise writer, be no going back.

Strange that Sherwyn's thoughts happened to turn to Childers that very day. On the very next President de Valera is to have the quixotic warrior-writer taken out and executed by firing squad, ignoring an appeal that was pending and never allowed to happen. But perhaps Thomas Hardy's 'Immanent Will', in his guise as Spinner of the Years, as the intricate set of gears that rule all our comings and goings, tends to engage a little more as anniversaries approach, move a notch on.

Sherwyn, ignorant of everything that is to come, and only vaguely aware of what is past (it being without the context of the future) takes a few minutes of his present to look at Vivien's portfolio of illustrations. He finds the fanciful pen-and-ink drawings of old Georgia competent enough – a peasant's hut, a pretty village, a child's face, various romanticised sanguinary battles. He himself has seen trench warfare in the flesh, an unattached foot here, a smashed in head there, and finds himself glad Vivien had been spared such visions. Already he seems to have protective feelings towards her.

Her illustrations will do. The production period won't have to be too much extended.

He does not think many will share Sir Jeremy's new enthusiasm for Georgia just because it's the up-and-coming Stalin's birthplace. He'll share a sandwich with his pal Mungo in the office next door and tell him about the extraordinary episode of Miss Ripple and her proposal.

Ten To Four, Thursday November 23rd 1922.
Dilberne Court Stables

Let's take another look at Vivien, since she is not to be with us for long. She takes the 2.20 Brighton train back to Dilberne Halt. She doesn't go straight home but drops by at the stables to compose herself and spend a little time with the being she describes as her best friend, her hunter Greystokes, a dappled grey, but his coat fading almost to pure white around the rump; a handsome creature, a good-tempered, gentle galloper and easy ambler, an ex-racer with a good pedigree but a bad record, since he is not given to exerting himself if he can help it. He has lost so many races he has been bought cut price by Sir Jeremy to be hired out for stud. Greystokes is a big horse of more than sixteen hands, and Vivien looks quite small as she leans against him for comfort and nuzzles into his warm neck.

Vivien is to marry Sherwyn, of course she is. At face value he is a rotter, a cad, a bounder, but Vivien is as clever as her writer in detecting Sherwyn's hidden virtues. He will live to be a perfectly amiable if rather vain old man with many tales of the past to tell; she, as we know, is soon to die giving birth to the twins, Mallory and Stella, who will inherit very different aspects of their mother's nature but not Sherwyn's, since he is not to be their father.

For a strange and unexpected thing had happened to Vivien a month earlier. She was half way through grooming Greystokes – her father kept the stables heated, as her nursery had never been – when an angel appeared in the doorway in the form of a well-muscled young man. That is to say he appeared to Vivien rather as an illustration of the Angel Gabriel she had once seen as a child, as he brought the good news to Mary, outlined against brilliant light and with a discernible halo, though that might have been an optical illusion, because of the way the sinking late October sun was shining through the curved slats of the stable door. A slit of clear sky must have opened up where black storm clouds had been gathering in the West.

An Innocent Girl

Bear in mind Vivien's extreme innocence, or ignorance as some might call it. General conversations did not drift to sexual matters as so many do today: bodies, except for an expanse of flesh around female shoulders in the evenings, were by and large kept shrouded. Revelation was left for the marriage night. Vivvie has never had the opportunity of seeing a naked man. (She has visited Vienna, but there sculpted genitals were hidden by fig leaves.) She did not examine herself 'down there', 'down there' being vaguely indecent. The nooks and crannies of the female body were best left ignored. Parts remain unnamed and without words the owner is left as though blind in the land of the sighted.

Vivvie had quickly averted her eyes when once she came across her parents entwined on the marital bed in some surprisingly noisy and impulsive act but did not care to dwell upon the detail. She had seen mares covered by Greystokes often enough but made little connection between animal and human behaviour; that of humans must surely be more dignified and affectionate than that of the beasts.

The young man with the halo wore stable overalls. He was remarkably handsome. He said something in a foreign language but whatever it was seemed polite and pleasant enough. She did not understand why but she unpinned her hair, which was her best feature. Now it rippled glossily over her shoulders and almost down to her waist. He was taller than she was and that made her feel both secure and helpless. She could even lean her head on a male shoulder. The Angel Gabriel for his part undid a couple of buttons round shoulders and waist and the overalls fell down and he was all skin, though she was so close to him and her skirt rucked up so that she could not see, only feel, the secret that had been kept from her.

One did not argue with a visitation from the Angel Gabriel; gratitude was expected. She was up against the stable wall; the unknown and unseen thing was inside her. She was aware of a kind of dark blanketing mist dividing her soul from her body and that it was best and certainly desirable to let the body have its way. Greystokes showed no surprise at all, which she took as his assent. And then the Angel Gabriel was buttoning up his overalls and he was gone, as lightly and pleasantly as he had come. She smoothed down her skirt, found her mitts – how had she come to lose those? – and went back to curry-combing Greystokes. The storm broke and there was a sudden shock of thunder and a flash of lightning lit up the stable but Greystokes calmed quickly. (Your writer feels it necessary to point out that if the breaking of Vivvie's hymen resulted in no trauma or bleeding, she is, remember, a keen horse rider, and any vigorous exercise can disrupt the fringe of tissue that is all a hymen is. She felt no pain, only marvel.)

Had that been the sexual act, the hidden thing? Vivvie supposed so. Did that mean she could have a baby? Probably not. Whatever it was, the event could hardly be classed as sin. It did not involve moral judgement. Besides she had been standing up and she had heard them say in the kitchens that you didn't get pregnant if you were standing up when you 'did it'. The Angel Gabriel has gone back to heaven or wherever such visitations go and left her cheerful and energised and with an understanding that sudden change is possible. She will beard Sherwyn in his den and propose to him.

Anyway, here is Vivvie, mission accomplished, nuzzling into Greystokes' glossy neck as the sinking sun shines through the slats of the stable door, and confiding the day's events to the dumb beast. She has to confide in someone, and if it's a horse who doesn't answer back or doubt her, and a horse who has witnessed what she remembers as a transfiguration so much the better.

A Woman Of Alpine Property

Vivvie had thought about it for a whole month before making her approach to Sherwyn. He seems a suitable candidate for marriage, a veteran, a man of action, not afraid of her father, able to charm her mother, someone who understood the importance of money – she had seen the soles of his shoes – and as such would protect her inheritance so long as it was to his advantage. She lacks the courage to confront her parents about the details of that inheritance, which she knows exists and is vast. Apparently she owns an Alpine village in Bavaria, church, inn, town hall and fifty houses (she receives ground rent and tithes from all of them) accumulated over fifty years. She seems to be a direct descendant through her mother's line of the Wittelsbach family, Counts Palatine of Schyren, and until the abolition of the German nobility in 1919 would thus have been entitled to call herself a Princess. For two whole generations Vivvie's long deceased grandmother Elise and her mother Adela had unjustly been barred from the inheritance for reasons of religion. Elise had turned Protestant back in the eighteen-eighties and angered her mother, Maria, a devout Catholic, greatly. This much Vivvie knows and supposes it to contribute to the palpable tension whenever she tries to bring up the subject of money. Since she turned twenty Vivvie's mother has been getting her to sign cheques for considerable sums. Vivvie does not like to press her father on the issue. He will just tell her to leave complicated matters to those who understand them.

Not Surprising, Look At Me

Her father's stud farm, Vivvie cannot help noticing, needs considerable upkeep. Greystokes is not kept all that busy – looks are not everything. He's big and strong, has got perfect conformation, great length to his neck, and big, powerful quarters; great, correct limbs; and plenty of bone, but his record in siring winners is declining. Vivvie has checked the stud book. Greystokes was enormously popular at first – out of Gainsborough the 1919 Derby winner out of famous Epsom Oaks Rosedrop – and covered a record two hundred and fifty mares in his first two years at stud, at around 150 guineas a shot. The year after it was down to eighty at a mere 100 guineas, this season it's down to sixty-five at 65. Costs exceed takings by a long chalk. The foals look good but don't make winners. But her father won't give in – he blames the mothers not the fathers for the failure of the progeny. Not surprising, thinks Vivvie, look at me. But given the right dam, he is convinced, sooner or later Greystokes will sire a spectacular winner and things will look up. In the meantime her father's incurable optimism makes the stud farm an expensive business. But she is not encouraged to raise doubts – financial matters are best left to men. She signs Coutts cheques, she notices, countersigned by Courtney and Baum, her mother's family lawyers.

So That's All Right Then

Anyway. Here is Vivvie, the enthusiasm inspired by the Angel Gabriel four weeks earlier having diminished a little, and what seemed so sensible in theory now seeming a little eccentric in reality, calming herself down by currying Greystokes and wondering if she has done the right thing. Greystokes' sturdy flanks are reassuring: they heave, they shudder, as she tugs with the comb. He understands her; he is on her side. More dark hairs remain in the comb than pale. Greystokes will be more white

61

than dappled by the time she is finished. Autumn is turning to winter. How beautiful will his progeny be.

Vivien, if asked, would have denied it, but she does share certain characteristics with her mother. Some things Vivien, as does Adela, just *knows*. To what degree she can foretell the future – how much her prophecy, when acted upon, really brings the future about, who's to tell? What Vivvie does know is that if Greystokes lifts his head in agreement she'll be right, if he lowers his head and whinnies she'll be wrong. He is all the oracle she needs, and he serves her well.

'Did I do the right thing, old friend?' she asks. 'Will I end up as Mrs Sexton?'

Greystokes lifts his handsome head and flurries and snuffles the air in apparent agreement, just as he did when the Angel Gabriel approached, all aglow with heavenly light.

So that's all right then.

Vivvie On A Horse

Vivien being so tall, large and bosomy, Greystokes is the only horse upon which she has ever looked good. Her quarrel with her father is that he restricts the amount of time she can ride Greystokes – on the somewhat unscientific grounds that too much exercise weakens and degrades sperm, be it of human or horse. Vivvie thinks maybe he is talking about himself – Sir Jeremy having been both a cricket and a rowing Blue when he was at Oxford and look at what resulted: herself, Vivien. She seems to have inherited her father's biceps as they were when he begat her, though twenty years on his muscles seem to have changed to flesh and fled to his belly, and he now looks as substantial and splendid as Edward VII in his prime.

Vivien knows she is over-fanciful: indeed, she reproaches herself for having an over-fevered imagination just as a contemporary girl would accuse herself of being paranoiac – the latter term being not yet in common usage. (Freud's work, *Certain Neurotic Mechanisms in Jealousy, Paranoia, and Homosexuality*, a successor to *Totem and Taboo*, was published in English that very year and made quite a splash.) Be all that as it may, she feels that if only she had more time with Greystokes his success rate as a sire would improve: he would breed winner after winner.

Once in a position to run her own establishment – which she surely would be when married to Sherwyn Sexton – she will take over the stud farm, turn it into a money-making proposition, and ride Greystokes as much and as long as she pleases. Sherwyn is not frightened of her father. With Sir Jeremy by his side everything will get sorted out. The world is full of hope and the promise of pleasure.

Her face as I regard her is gentle, relaxed and only mildly sorrowful. I see her as the slats of light come through the stable door and fall across her body. She unwinds her damp scarf and it drops where it falls, in hay and dust and stable muck. She doesn't notice or care. She takes off her hat and her hair falls rippling down, reddish gold, and glorious before the sun goes in when all things quickly turn to a kind of

63

newspaper grey. I see her as almost a ghost, but not quite, being fictional rather than real. Greystokes whinnies again. That is the scene as I remember it or invent it, I can no longer be sure which.

Five Past Four, Thursday November 23nd 1922.
The Editorial Office, Ripple & Co

Sherwyn had been Mungo Bolt's good friend – which was why he now takes the literary betrayal so hard. Both had been second lieutenants in the Artists' Rifles, invalided home for minor injuries at the same time, then both seconded to the National War Aims Committee where they worked agreeably together on advertising campaigns to persuade the public to do the right thing: *Follow the King! Eat Less Meat! Women Do Your Bit! Men of Britain Will You Stand for This?* and so on, which was not only fun but saved them from the trenches. After the war Mungo, like Sherwyn an aspiring writer with a North London literary background, followed Sherwyn into the world of publishing and eventually to Ripple & Co's editorial depart-ment. From here they look down in comfort on streets thronged with ex-soldiers, blind, halt, shell-shocked, hungry and cold, begging for employment. In the land fit for heroes the two of them at least have jobs: but then they are gentlemen with strings to pull. Nothing much changes.

Sherwyn and Mungo see themselves as young (as I too see them, a hundred or so years on, life expectancy being about double what it was in 1922, even including the sudden horrific dip in the four years of the Great War) but those born just a decade or so later see the pair as battle hardened and seasoned men of experience as they swan about the night-clubs of Piccadilly, picking off girls like grouse. They have been through the trenches and survived, and are envied as heroes. Girls swoon before them. Already younger men than they are beginning to lament that they have 'missed the war', and are preparing in their hearts for the next, which will be fought for more complicated reasons than love of country.

So much for the Great War, the war to end all wars; so much for patriotism, which begins to be seen as a great evil. A terrible cynicism rules the land.

Anyway. Sherwyn closes Miss Ripple's folder and goes into Mungo's office down the mean little attic corridor. A chap has to bend his neck to get along it. Nothing's fair; Mungo is lucky: his father Ambrose is managing director of Charlton and Hoare, a large and wealthy general publishers. Ambrose is from a generation which believes a gentleman should not be obliged to work for a living, and so gives his son a substantial allowance to add to his wages. Sherwyn is not so fortunate in his father, a writer, who thinks any man should be able to keep himself once out of Oxford. Sherwyn is finding paying his own way in the world increasingly difficult. Indeed, last time Sherwyn tried to book lunch at Rules he noticed a decided reluctance to take the booking. He was running up too high a bill for a customer whose shoes, should the maître d'hôtel look down, clearly let in water. Such a thing would never happen to Mungo. Nor need it ever happen to Sherwyn Sexton, he was already thinking, if he were husband to Mrs Sherwyn Sexton, née Ripple.

Sherwyn tells Mungo with dramatic detail how Miss Ripple has just proposed to him out of the blue and both men shudder at the thought. It makes a fine story. Both agree that while to woo and marry the boss's daughter would in most cases be both sensible and desirable, Miss Ripple could be a different matter. Prolonged intimacy with a giantess did not appeal, and what would the children look like? Sherwyn demurs at this and says the problem with begetting children at all is the element of chance involved: one simply does not know what will emerge from the maternal womb.

'Miss Ripple's father,' he says, 'is perfectly decent looking in Edward the Seventh style, and the mother's something of a beauty in a transparent kind of way, and to all accounts more intelligent than Sir Jeremy, who will let his heart rule his head. Miss Ripple's children might very well revert to type, and be perfectly presentable.' Mungo is taking notes, and Sherwyn, ever suspicious, asks why.

'I will be Boswell to your Johnson,' Mungo says. 'I shall preserve your *bons mot*s for posterity.' Sherwyn is satisfied. Mungo at least recognises who is top dog.

'However,' says Sherwyn, 'the next time I see Miss Ripple's father it will not be to ask for her hand in marriage but to hand in my notice. I cannot continue to work in a place where I am humiliated and scorned.'

'Oh come on, old pal,' says Mungo, who is a reasonable fellow. 'It's not as bad as all that.'

'My soul is shrivelling,' says Sherwyn, as if this was enough of an explanation.

Mungo murmurs that there is some work to do on *A Short History of the Georgians.* Sherwyn says he'd rather get on with his story about the girl and the sheep's eyes, but Mungo persists and points out that Sir Jeremy is convinced that the deep pool of right-thinking readers out there who've never heard of a place called Georgia will now be dying to find out. This very morning the great man put Mungo in charge of a new department to be called Publicity. The advertising budget is to rise by 150 per cent, from £23 to £57.10s. Mungo is to take out American-style ads in *The Ethical Socialist, The Schoolmaster* and *The Daily Chronicle.*

'How extremely vulgar,' says Sherwyn. 'And yet another slap in the face for me.' Mungo says not to worry, no extra money goes with the new title, just more work.

'But why are you to be in charge, not me?'

'Because you think publicity is vulgar,' says Mungo, who is getting slightly irritated. He is to go on to be managing director of Bolt & Crest, one of the great inter-war ad agencies. 'And I don't. Because he heard my vulgar little speech at the last monthly meeting, when I told the assembled company that love, hate, trust, fear, hope and greed were mankind's prime emotions. And the way to sell anything was to connect the product with two or more of these fundamental responses. It would work the same for books on politics as it did for the recruiting ads we used to do in the war – in the days when we were happy and young: *Daddy, what did you do in the war?'*

'But everyone knows that. Pavlov's dog stuff,' says Sherwyn, dismissive.

'It's not Pavlov, it's Freud's *Totem and Taboo*. And it sounded new and wonderful to Sir Jeremy,' says Mungo, 'which is all that matters. He envisages a new list which will change the world: *A Short History of the Georgians* is only the start. But it needs a new title: *Love, Fear and Hope in the Land of the Georgians* perhaps. I leave it to you. Just trawl primary emotions. Hate the capitalists, love the "communists" – that's the new word for bolsheviks. A fresh dawn breaking, new sun rising. *Workers Arise!*, all that. We must get the author's permission to change the title. *Georgia Awakes!* might do – it's shorter, and if there's time ask him for a new chapter on Stalin, the coming man, the new glorious son of the Caucasus.'

'Very flashy, the improved Ripple & Company,' says Sherwyn. 'The sooner I'm out of here the better. I am a king and country man myself: no kind of parlour pink. The Russians kill each other as others kill fleas.'

'They're the hope of the world according to our boss,' says Mungo, 'so perhaps you had better believe it too.'

He picked up Vivvie's portfolio and flicked through it.

'As for sacking yourself, think again. If I know the way your mind works, and I think I do, Miss Ripple is to be Mrs Sexton before long,' says Mungo, 'and how useful it would be to have your publisher as your father-in-law.'

'Absurd,' says Sherwyn. 'I write fiction. Ripple & Co publish non-fiction.'

'So it has crossed your mind,' says Mungo. 'I am glad to hear it. A pity that her drawings are so dull. Still, I daresay a dull wife is preferable to a skittish one.'

'You're out of your mind,' says Sherwyn. 'I am not the marrying kind.'

'If you're already making excuses for your future children,' says Mungo, 'and arguing that various obvious contrasts might work themselves out in the begetting, the deed is as good as done.'

Five In The Afternoon, November 23rd 1922.
3 Fleet Street

At five o'clock precisely Sherwyn went down to beard Sir Jeremy in his newly refurbished and opulent den. No 3 Fleet Street is a thin narrow building dating from the mid eighteenth century, once a master printer's residence, then a bookshop, then a disreputable publisher's; only now, passing into Adela's possession ten years back, becoming Ripple & Co. In its history, I may say, No 3 Fleet Street has periodically attracted the attention of authorities as a possible source of sedition and scandal, and agents of the police and government have knocked upon the door before. It stands where Queen Elizabeth's spymaster Sir Francis Walsingham once used a print shop to plant disinformation; it is where Adela's cousin Rosina wrote her work on the sex life of the aboriginals, and it is where now Sir Jeremy flirts with communism. Some buildings are just like that.

The first and second floors of the building have undergone a transformation. With the aid of a cheque from Coutts bank Jeremy's wife Adela has lately had the room redecorated in all that is latest in fashionable design. The place no longer looks like a working office, but more like a modern Art Deco drawing room. She has learned a lot, or perhaps indeed – who's to say – has inherited from her aunt Isobel a tendency to favour all that is latest and trendiest in contemporary design. Adela is cousin to Arthur, Lord Dilberne, who sold off most of the estate before decamping with his motor business to the US during the war, leaving not just No 3 but his ancestral home and its gardens in Adela's competent care and control, if not actual ownership.

Sherwyn finds the transformation from Edwardian respectability to Art Deco lightness and glitter extreme. The once latticed windows are now an expanse of plate glass, the old heavy mahogany furnishings thrown out, old wallpaper stripped, dusty old velvet curtains replaced by pale Venetian blinds, the old single central hanging light replaced by aluminium standard lamps – sinuous naked caryatids stretching high, bare-nippled breasts raised, embracing globes of diffused light.

A fortune has been spent on the first floors while the attic floor, where the workers toil away making money for the capitalist class, has been left to rot, as Sherwyn observes. Nevertheless, five o'clock being the time at which Sir Jeremy, a leading member of the Enlightened Publishers' Reform Committee, makes himself available for one-to-one approach by employees, Sherwyn is wise enough not to show any distaste as he enters the room. He knows the value of politesse. (He is scrupulously polite to his stepmother, the very plain woman who replaced his beautiful mother, still alive and breathing and living with her own mother in San Francisco.) Sherwyn is steady in his determination to quit his job, having cast aside Mungo's horrific prediction – Vivvie's proposal is pathetic, laughable and, worse, embarrassing.

A Happily-Married Man

Sherwyn finds his employer standing in front of an oval silver-framed cheval mirror and admiring his well-trimmed beard and moustache. Sir Jeremy is somewhat incongruous in his new Art Deco surroundings but oblivious as to how he seems to others, as are so many men of consequence and high self esteem. He is formally dressed in a heavy tweed suit complete with waistcoat over which his prosperous belly strains, sports a full beard, rather wild un-pomaded hair and a Homburg that he seldom removes even when indoors. He looks untidy, as if something was basically awry, as are his thought processes. His tie is not quite in the middle, he has an egg stain on his tie, he hasn't bothered to button his waistcoat properly, his shoes need a good polish. He looks, and is, in need of a valet, which the times do not allow him to employ. He is in his late fifties and has lived through Edwardian times, when it was rather bad form for a gentleman to look in mirrors, and would leave it to a manservant to improve his appearance before leaving the house. Since then there have simply not been enough servants around to do it. His wife, after more than twenty years of marriage and approaching her forties, automatically wipes him down and brushes him up whenever she sees him, while taking his appearance for granted. She is more concerned with her own. Which Sir Jeremy quite understands, adoring his wife as he does, confident in her respect for his vision and intelligence, as he respects hers, though her views are rather more spiritual and esoteric than his own, being concerned more with the Universal Oneness of all things than the dawn of the proletarian age.

73

Jeremy will adapt his office to the new world on her account, just not the way he dresses. He knows he is lucky to have married a woman both beautiful, intelligent, propertied and rich, considerably younger than himself. Their child Vivien was born when Adela was barely eighteen – and conceived out of wedlock, though no-one now would suspect such a thing. As others observe, his wife's smallest wish is his command. If legally much of the family wealth comes through the inheritance of their biddable daughter, the parents pay little attention to such detail. Moral right surely triumphs over the law and Courtney and Baum agree. The family lawyers are no longer young and are exhausted by a decade's worth of correspondence and enquiries into international laws of inheritance, and arguing the validity of the codicil of a will written in Bavaria in 1884 by a disagreeable elderly Princess, disowning her daughter, Elise Hedleigh, and her daughter's daughter, Adela Ripple née Hedleigh, but returning the Alpine estate to the granddaughter, Vivvie Ripple, on her twentieth birthday. Their funds, after all, come from managing the estate. If no-one argues, why should they? They are very old and one Ripple signature looks much like another.

Sherwyn first encountered Lady Adela on the occasion of the office party which celebrated Sir Jeremy's raising to the knighthood for services to literature. He had to gatecrash, too lowly an employee to be formally invited.

'A fair new look for a fair new society,' he overheard her Ladyship say to the somewhat sceptical group of publishers gathered for cocktails and canapés at the party. Evidently she, like her husband, believed that communism was to herald in a new Utopia. He did not fancy her: she was not his type, a porcelain, delicate, fastidious blonde – his own taste ran to the rounded, exotic and passionate – but he could see her desirability. That she was Vivvie's mother astounded him: how could such flimsy loins have given birth to so large and crude an energy? Vivvie had not been there at the party. He could see why. She would hardly have fitted in.

In The Afternoon, A Month Earlier.
Buckingham Palace

A Sorry Occasion

See, as I do, Vivvie trying to fit into the little gold chair she is expected to sit on as she watches her father's investiture. After today he will be not merely Mr Ripple, but Sir Jeremy Ripple. She is prepared to witness his elevation – Buckingham Palace, after all – but not to go to the party afterwards – though her mother tries to persuade her. The little gold chair collapses beneath her; fortunately before the ceremony is to begin – while the great and the good are still lining up, and the King has not yet taken up his sword – and she sits with a great thud upon the parquet floor in a welter of fabric, the Coco Chanel dress her mother insisted she wore and does not suit her at all, childishly girlish, with a striped white and blue grosgrain bodice, stiff but not stiff enough to keep the bulge of her breasts under control, topped with a ridiculous great white satin bow, on top of a very full floaty skirt which makes her look even more enormous than she is. Attendants rush to her side to help her up but have to sort out the skirt to get to her. People stare. Meanwhile her mother, dainty and composed, apologises for the fuss. Another larger more solid chair is brought. Now her knees are a hazard to anyone who tries to walk by.

The whole ceremony is stupid, her being here is even more stupid. She is out of place. She is always out of place. Why is she so doomed? And why, come to think of it, has she recently signed an enormous cheque for the Savile Row tailors who provided her father's new suit, and the one for the Coco Chanel silk georgette outfit her mother is wearing? Let alone the grosgrain monstrosity with the bow which her mother claimed made her look 'charming'. Vivien normally makes do with the Dilberne village dressmaker who is perfectly adequate. Aren't parents meant to provide for their children, not the other way round?

Doubts And Realisations

Doubt assails her just as the sword lifted by King George V falls upon her father's shoulder and he becomes Sir Jeremy. Does he deserve it? Why? How? The sudden uncomfortable and embarrassing thump upon her coccyx (though that's a knowledgeable term; 'behind' is what Vivvie would have called it; even 'bottom' seeming unladylike) seemed to have let loose a whole host of realisations and doubts. They come pouring in. There is so little in this world that you can depend upon. The Lloyd George government had made a great deal of money from the sale of titles, everyone knows.

Perhaps Daddy has bought his, perhaps she, Vivvie, is the one who paid for it? It's not as if she's ever consulted over anything; from the menus at the parties to the constant refurbishment of everything she takes pleasure in as it was to begin with. Come to think of it, she hates Syrie Maugham's passion for black and white and for mirrors everywhere – wherever you look you have to see yourself – at her father's publishing house, and now at Dilberne Court. The old bamboo furniture she loved has gone and the family portraits too: it's just more black and white and mirrors everywhere, not the nice speckled kind old fashioned ones but ones which throw back a hard, glossy and merciless reflection.

She hates the food Syrie Maugham serves for her mother's smart parties – bitter oysters Rockefeller and watery scrambled eggs – and most of all she hates the zebra rug (poor slaughtered beast) which now covers the lovely old oak floor of the morning room at Dilberne Court. And she is the one who has signed the cheques for most of it, so far as she can see, though there are more stubs in the cheque book than she can recall having written out… Perhaps her mother forges her signature? She complains often enough that it's simple and childlike. Which is true – though if she'd been allowed to go to school instead of having a series of inept governesses it might now have character enough. As it is, forgery would be easy. But that way madness lies.

Be Bold, Be Bold, But Not Too Bold

'Rise, Sir Jeremy,' says the King, and Vivvie's father arises. She feels a pang of pride for him, and of affection for her mother, sitting next to her in Coco Chanel black silk georgette and the dearest pink satin cloche hat, weeping a tear or so of happiness. But Vivvie can see change must come. She must take charge of her own destiny. No-one else will.

But what can she possibly say, and when, and how? Everyone gets angry and indignant if she brings up the subject of money, and tells her to leave it to those who understand financial matters. Her father once even said 'don't bother your pretty little head about it', which was fairly absurd since her head was neither pretty nor little. Her mother said 'we have family lawyers to look after all these things. They manage your Alpine estate'; but she had failed to give her the name of the lawyers and Vivvie hadn't liked to follow it up, which was silly of her, she knew. But they expected her to know things without actually telling her, and if she asked for detail saw it as evidence of her folly. She knew she wasn't half witted but they behaved as if she were. She's known for some time that when she reached twenty she would come into money but twenty had come and gone and she still had no more money in her purse than before, only now they put Coutts cheques in front of her which she was expected to sign. Early on she'd dared ask the crusty old lawyer who turned up from time to time, and in the presence of her parents, what the mysterious Alpine village consisted of, and been told it was a remote village sited on a lake amongst mountains, complete with an abandoned Benedictine abbey popular with visiting antiquarians, an old church, a town hall, a Gasthaus, a cluster of houses, some meadows and some cows and a goat herd and that was all. She should not make too much of it, but ground rents and tithes had built up while the will was under dispute, and she should consider herself wealthy.

'What a fuss about nothing,' Vivvie heard Adela say. 'It should all have come to me. No such thing in English law for disinheriting unto the third generation. No English judge would have allowed it.'

'Alas,' Mr Courtney had replied, 'he was foreign. As was your grandmother.'

Which, Vivvie thought, put Adela in her place. From the conversation which followed it seemed to Vivvie that the lawyers visited the village once a year but not Sir Jeremy ('*Too much to think about*') or Adela ('*Ugh, Austria. So primitive!*')

Vivvie had asked if the cows had bells and been told yes, to an impatient sigh from both parents – but then she'd read *Heidi of the Alps* and they hadn't. The village was called Barscherau, said Mr Courtney, and no, it was not a Swiss village but fortunately in Austria, where inflation had been brought under control, and not over the border in Germany where it was still rampant. Vivvie longed to go and see Barscherau. But who would she go with? Her parents would never let her go unchaperoned. Or perhaps they just needed her at hand to sign cheques?

Other girls of her age had husbands who looked after matters of finance and the law. What she needed was a husband brave enough to tackle her parents. But who? And how would she find one? Well, as one found anyone, she supposes. One asks around.

The band in the balcony strikes up with a medley from *The Pirates of Penzance*, rather feebly played, Vivvie thinks. Guests begin to file out. Vivvie's replacement chair causes an obstruction and has to be moved: she sees her poor mother wince. There seems no end to the humiliations. If she was married there might be fewer of them.

She decides not to go to the office party her mother is to give to celebrate Sir Jeremy's elevation. She will only be made to wear the dress with the big white bow – Coco Chanel, after all, her mother would insist. And she would have to admire the refurbishment and might blurt out the truth – that she hates it and misses the old musty, fusty, familiar offices her father used to take her to when she was little. Not that she was ever exactly little. No, she isn't going to attend. A humiliation too far. Anyway.

The Fate Of Nations

As it happens the investiture is held at three in the afternoon on October 22nd 1922 which also turns out to be a turning point in the fate of nations, as well as that of Vivvie. It's the day the coalition of Liberals and Conservatives finally fails; an event largely brought about by Balfour – a long time friend of Adela's, as it happens. Lloyd George is removed from office and Bonar Law, a modest Canadian businessman, becomes Prime Minister. Some days seem more conducive to change than others, and so perhaps it's no coincidence that this is the day Vivvie comes to the conclusion she does: she needs to marry, and to a man who understands money. A man whose boots let in water because he doesn't have the cash to pay the boot-mender understands money very well.

Five In The Afternoon, November 23rd 1922.
3 Fleet Street

The door stands open. Sherwyn finds Sir Jeremy admiring himself in the mirror, proof that Sir Jeremy does not stand on ceremony and treats his employees as partners. One could be buried alive, Sherwyn thinks, beneath the weight of so much hypocrisy. But everything, not just the hypocrisy of the rich and famous, now irritates Sherwyn. The lumbering daughter thinking she can buy him, Mungo with his private means saying flippant, self interested things. And Sherwyn has had to go without lunch – Rita having failed to make him sandwiches and his credit at Rules being unreliable. The state of his shoes; everything, the excessive luxury of the office, the vulgarity of the lighting caryatids – most of all the way his manuscript sits on Sir Jeremy's shelf because Sir Jeremy can't be bothered to read it.

Sherwyn is aware that he needs all the indignation he can muster to be able to resign in style. He is doing his best, while still seeing himself as a likeable fellow, and of an easy and amiable turn of mind. He is torn between a scowl and a sneer and goes for a curl of the lip, which comes easily enough, and always looks good beneath his moustache.

This is how the meeting was to go, not quite as Sherwyn was to report it that night to the lovely, lascivious Rita, with whom he temporarily shares the most bohemian of artistic lodgings, and to whom he currently owes three weeks' rent.

'Do sit down, my dear boy,' Sir Jeremy said over his shoulder but in jovial enough tones. Sherwyn sat. Sir Jeremy continued to admire himself. 'A glass of sherry?' Sherwyn nodded but Sir Jeremy chose to assume it was a shake of the head. Sherwyn, defeated before he began, gave up the sneer.

'No? Very wise. Drink not, fail not. Tomorrow I will be fifty-seven. For a man of my age I put up a good show, don't you think? Every day and in every way I am getting better and better. We need a list in the Behaviourist Sciences, don't you agree? I notice a growing interest. Pity George Stanley got hold of the Coué book. Should have come straight to us. Did terribly well and still is. *Self-Mastery through Conscious Autosuggestion.* Read it?'

'I haven't had the time, sir. I am quite busy. I work late.'

'Do I spot self pity on the orlop deck, Sexton? It won't do. Just read the book! Look at me. Good head of hair, slim waist, well set up and recognised by the King himself for services to litera-ture. Every day in every way I am getting better and better.'

'But how could such a thing be possible, sir?' asked Sherwyn.

'Don't mock me, boy,' said Sir Jeremy. 'I'm practising the art of autosuggestion. I recommend it. I grant you the slim waist is a bit of a challenge but one does one's best. I am glad you dropped by. Shut the door. I read your thriller. What was it? *The Uncertain Gentleman.* The title will have to change, for a start. But I liked it. Not exactly great literature, not exactly paving the way for the new socialist world order, not the new Coué, but for a piece of entertainment, not at all bad.'

Rage and resentment faded in Sherwyn's heart: a great gratitude took its place. He tried to prevent a smile: it did not do to show enthusiasm, let alone gratitude. He spoke casually and languidly.

'So you can see your way to recommending the work, sir?'

'More than that, old chap. I mean to publish it.'

'But we don't publish fiction.'

'We do now.'

'I see, sir.'

It transpired that Sir Jeremy was diversifying in the New Year into what he called 'intelligent commercial fiction'. He wanted *The Uncertain Gentleman* – provisional title, of course – to be the lead novel in his new list. He had taken his time getting back to Sherwyn until various boring details could be settled. He was sorry for the delay which had been of his co-directors' doing, not of his. The new list was to be announced with great fanfare in the spring. Sir Jeremy could see an encouraging future in fiction so long as it was designed to sell to the discerning and discriminating reader: pulp fiction was a thing of the past and not to be confused with what Ripple & Co, one of the great literary, intellectual and political publishers, was doing.

'I should certainly hope not, sir.'

'Quite at ease with the long words, aren't you, boy. Quite the Old Pauline. Do please translate "abecadarian" for me.'

'A beginner, sir. A dilettante. It describes my detective.'

'Um. Never overestimate the intelligence of the reader, boy. Modern publishing's first rule.'

'I'll remember that, sir.'

A publishing house, Sir Jeremy went on to say, must have its own character and nature, which must be recognisable and distinctive. Clever but not too clever. *The Uncertain Gentleman* seemed to fit the bill. These days a reader was as likely to trust a publishing house as a writer. Be as guided by a logo as title or author. He could see a future in jackets in a distinctive colour – pale blue, for example. Readers looking for intelligent but plot based fiction would look for the pale blue rather than the author's name. He'd discussed it with Mungo and Mungo thought it was a good idea.

'I might call the new list *Not for Numbskulls*. How does that strike you as a slogan, Sexton? You used to work with Mungo in public policy advertising.'

Sherwyn did not reply at once. His world was shifting and changing and resettling around him in a landscape that glittered with a thousand facets of fame and fortune, champagne and beautiful girls. A published writer! By Ripple & Co. Even though in a pale blue cover more significant than his name.

'Speak your thoughts without fear or favour, Pauline.'

The important thing, Sherwyn knew, was not to show gratitude. It was the emotion demanded by publishers as they sought to control writers; it made acceptance itself seem so great a prize that writers seldom asked for better terms. Publishers operated an unspoken cartel. Writers must not get above themselves. The initial opening gambit 'not exactly great literature' had been deliberate on Sir Jeremy's part, designed to ensure that Sherwyn did not get ideas above his station. 'Clever, but not too clever' likewise. And the notion of the colour of the cover being more important than the author's name was the same. Well, Sherwyn would respond coolly.

'*Not for Numbskulls*? Far too negative, sir, if I may say so. Ripple & Co must surely appeal directly to the positive aspirations in every reader. You might call it *Forward-looking Fiction* or something like that?'

Sir Jeremy raised his eyebrows in evident disparagement and doubt, but said nothing. Sherwyn decided that a lie was his best option.

'Actually I had thought of sending my manuscript to Duckworth's – they have a well-established fiction list – I showed the manuscript to you merely for an opinion in the hope of a recommendation. But there being a delay I sent a copy off anyway, and they've come back to me most favourably, though of course nothing's signed yet.'

'Um,' said Sir Jeremy. 'Thank you for confiding in me.' And then, 'I wouldn't think it wise for a writer of your capabilities to associate with Duckworth. They have such a fondness for seamy romances, bestselling or not; codswallop; cheap paper, cheap minds. All that madness of tender caresses. No, no, stay with Ripple, we are a serious house. Things are hard in the publishing business but we will make it worth your while.'

That was better. 'A writer of your capabilities. A serious house.' No-one had uttered the word genius but they might as well have. And Sir Jeremy had taken out his very expensive Waterman pen and his Coutts cheque book and was actually writing out a cheque, but for how much Sherwyn could not see. The stub and the date had already been filled in, but not yet the amount. Sir Jeremy put the cheque on the desk but kept it folded. Nor did he push it over towards Sherwyn. It lay there in front of them, a bargaining tool for an undisclosed amount.

'A word of warning, Sexton,' said Sir Jeremy. 'Steer clear of the markets. Keep your money under the marital mattress for the time being.' It must be a considerable amount if he was talking about investments. 'There's trouble brewing. Instability is inherent in the classism of the capitalist model. What's happening in Russia will be a financial upheaval, no doubt about it, but in a proper socialist economy stability will prevail. It must in the end. The Soviets deal in the reality of trade, of actual production, not figures on paper.'

'I'll bear it in mind, Sir Jeremy,' said Sherwyn.

'Of course,' said Sir Jeremy. 'I may be wrong about you and Duckworth's. It may be the very house for a man of your talents. I'll need to discuss it with my co-directors.'

His hand reached out as if to take back the cheque.

Sherwyn saw his new glittering landscape fading, the phantasmagoria dying: he was to be thrust back into his old world of disappointment, rejection, leaky shoes. Since there seemed nothing to be lost but everything to be gained he played his remaining card.

'As it happens, sir, I have news too. Talking of matrimonial mattresses, I am all too aware that mine is currently non-existent. But I am much encouraged by your reaction to my manuscript and think now is the moment to ask for your daughter's hand in marriage. Emboldened, indeed. I have come to know Vivien well in the last few months – and she, me. We have been working together on *A Short History of the Georgians*. To know is to admire, and to admire is to love. I admire her for her intelligence, her competence, her integrity.'

The fingers, which had seemed likely to snatch back the cheque, were stilled. Touch and go.

'That's very interesting, young man,' said Sir Jeremy, after a well-controlled blink or two. 'My daughter's hand in marriage. Very brave new world. Indeed, quite a turn-up for the books, as the bookmakers say. Hard to Adam and Eve it. You know we're shortly publishing a guide book to Cockney rhyming slang? No? Even East Enders now carry literary significance. In the new world we strive for, all men will be equal; Earl and bar-rowboy, Old Etonian and Pauline, humble worker and capitalist boss.'

'And here's the Joe's lamb to the slaughter wanting to get cash and carried to the office boy, I should bloody cocoa,' said Sherwyn, smiling his most charming smile, temporising, think-ing fast, arranging this new set of cards in his hand, working out in what order to play them. 'Which translated means the boss's daughter wants to marry the office boy. Why beat about the bush?'

'Really?' asked Sir Jeremy, increasing the pressure of his fingers on the folded cheque so it edged further towards him, and away from Sherwyn. 'You seem to do a lot of beating at our Monday morning meetings, should you deign to turn up. But perhaps you've been burning the midnights finishing your manuscript? One would hope so. But I'm only teasing you, dear boy. You're such a serious fellow in a world of fools. And Vivvie's actually willing, is she? So far she's frightened most suitors off. She finds it so difficult to smile, poor girl.'

'It was she who approached me,' said Sherwyn. There seemed little point in presenting the matter as other than it was. There are moments when it suits a born gambler – as Sherwyn was – to show his cards.

It is the right answer. Management's hand pushes the cheque a fraction further towards Sherwyn, but he resists the urge to snatch. He is not to be seen to be easily bought. Nor indeed, as a great writer, should he be swayed by anything as vulgar as money. The rich were truly bastards. He smiled on.

'Are you marrying the girl for her money?' asked Sir Jeremy and Sherwyn was taken aback, not for the first time in his life, or the last, at how swiftly delicate negotiations could degenerate into brutal confrontation. 'Because if you are you will find certain legal hindrances in your way.'

'I am sure it is not in my nature to marry for money,' Sherwyn said carefully, 'any more than it is Vivvie's to marry where there is likely to be none. And if I'm as good a writer as you say, earning enough for both of us should not be a difficulty. I would be happy to sign a prenuptial contract, of course. It would be the honourable thing to do.'

'And no more foolish talk about Duckworth's?'

'No,' says Sherwyn, simply. Lead title in a new fiction list at Ripple & Co was not to be sneered at. What he lost in literary credibility and pale blue covers would be made up for by healthy royalty cheques. But still Sir Jeremy did not push the cheque over.

'My daughter has inherited many things from me. Good teeth, a strong jaw and a height and scale which makes romance with ordinary men difficult. She also has, I do believe, inherited my gift for picking unlikely winners. If she has picked you that is good enough for me. And you're a competent enough writer and will look good on the back flap of the jacket. I have been talking to Mungo and he agrees with me that the way forward is to present the writer, like the publisher, as a marketable commodity, a personality. As to Vivvie, I will discuss the matter with Lady Adela. You actually love my daughter?'

'I do, sir,' said Sherwyn. What else could a chap say without being seen a thorough cad?

'Good,' said Sir Jeremy, taking back the cheque, crossing out what was written, altering figures and words, changing the amount on the stub, 'because I need to be able to tell my wife that.' Sir Jeremy slowly pushed the cheque over, mangled but legible, uncrossed. Five hundred guineas had been struck out and a thousand guineas substituted and initialled. £525 had become £1,050. A great deal of money. The thing to do was seem to be unimpressed.

Sherwyn studied the sum as if deciding whether to accept or not, nodded coolly, folded the piece of paper and put it in his breast pocket. It wasn't, after all, all that great a sum. You could buy a half way decent house for it, he supposed, and pay off a few debts, that was all. It is the sort of money a newly discovered writer could expect for a book but not the kind you would get for marrying an unwanted daughter, saving her from the shelf. Had she even told the truth about the Alpine village? He had assumed so – it didn't seem in her nature to lie – but supposing it was a fantasy? Supposing Sir Jeremy was sufficient of an old devil to be publishing his book as a bribe to marrying off his unwanted daughter? They might have conspired together. The trouble with being a writer of fiction was that the possibility of different plot flows was endless.

£525 for the novel, £525 for the wife? Or did they come as a £1,050 package? He had only himself to blame if they did. Asked if he loved Vivvie he had replied yes, and as he spoke it had not felt like a lie. Though that of course was the same for most lies: they work best if the liar believes them. He could hardly love the girl because he hardly knew her and she was certainly not attractive to him. But he did like her and the freshness, indeed the oddness, of her ways. She was at least not like other girls: she was no beanstalk simperer. A man could always buy built-up heels for a wedding, he would be allowed to go his own ways, there was money in his pocket and the world was his oyster.

But Sir Jeremy was still talking.

'See it as an advance on a dowry if you like,' said Sir Jeremy, 'but *The Uncertain Gentleman* – working title, of course – should at least pay its way. We'll talk about contracts in good time. I'm thinking of a royalty of twenty per cent on publisher price and thruppence on colonial and dominion sales. The book's already written so you have your advance. Just go and buy yourself a new suit and a decent pair of shoes from Lobb's, and come down to Dilberne for the weekend and meet the family. Get the address from Phoebe on your way out.'

Sir Jeremy had given up the sherry and now poured himself some whisky into a heavy frosted glass beaker with gold leaf trimmings – but failed to pour any for Sherwyn. 'But please don't let me delay you any longer, dear boy,' and he smiled his courteous Old Etonian smile of dismissal. 'I'm sure you must have many things to do and I certainly do.'

The Stars Look Down

Sherwyn went out into Fleet Street uncertain as to which of them had outwitted the other, but finding himself surprisingly languid, matter of fact. Well, one minute you're a poor man and next minute you're rich. It's the way things went and probably would for the rest of his life. His father had had his horoscope done when he was born – Libra in the ascendant, Jupiter, Venus and Neptune conjunct in the first house, somewhat opposed to Mercury in Aries in the seventh. Charming, witty, attractive, subject to strange events and violent swings of fortune. A thousand guineas in an uncrossed cheque. Doomed to prosperity and an unfortunate marriage; a vigorous Jupiter and a Saturn in Capricorn.

Coutts would be closed now but he could hand in the cheque over the counter at eight the next morning and collect the cash, though to be seen to be in a hurry would never do. But he has a cheque for an unimagined amount in his pocket and all things seem possible, fame and fortune at last within his grasp and Vivvie not such a bad old thing really. Just a pity she's so tall.

Six O'Clock In The Evening, Thursday 23rd November 1922. Dilberne Court

So. Vivvie has a suitor. Wonders will never cease. Jeremy thinks favourably of him. She is to meet him at the weekend.

Lady Adela Ripple finishes the call from her husband and puts the receiver back in its cradle with her tiny delicate hands, tipped with carefully manicured pale pink nails – scarlet and crimson are all very well for night but by day nails must be kept unobtrusive. A pity that Vivvie never bothers with her hands – raw, red, peasant things dangling from the end of intolerably long and large limbs. The girl is obviously a throwback – but to whom? Adela's father? A long line of personable aristocrats marrying beautiful women. Adela's mother? Did some giant of a mountains guide steal into a royal bedroom one night and lay a seed that was to flower generations later? No. More likely Jeremy's side. Army mostly, generals and brigadiers, horse breeders, someone along the way was bound to have gone native. Vivvie, married. Possible, peasant hands and all. But to what kind of person? What kind of breeding?

A Turn-Up For The Books

Jeremy's telephone conversation with her had been brief. He'd described Sherwyn as an interesting if impecunious young man who was a good novelist, would go far, and apparently wanted to marry Vivvie. He hadn't been to Eton but at least to St Paul's, which would do at a pinch. He could come down for the weekend so she might meet him and approve of him, or otherwise. She must bear in mind that Vivvie was certainly not likely to do better. All in all, so far as he was concerned, it was a consummation devoutly to be wished. He was working late; he would stay over at the Garrick, one of his clubs.

Vivvie and Sherwyn Sexton! Now which of Jeremy's young tyros was Sherwyn Sexton? Of course, the good-looking if short one with the bright blue eyes who'd gatecrashed the party to celebrate Jeremy's knighthood. It had been a splendid party even though Vivvie had done her best to spoil it – '*A Knight of the Realm? Daddy? Isn't that rather hypocritical for a social radicalist? I thought he was meant to loathe everything to do with the realm*' – and had even refused to turn up, which was probably just as well as she'd just have towered over everyone and insisted on wearing something dreadful; but it had rather upset her father. When Adela had tried to tempt her with the promise of lobster soup and oyster patties, Vivvie had said the money would be better spent re-thatching the stables, and the whole event was absurd. Vivvie was good at disapproval. And Sherwyn Sexton was prepared to put up with her? It was true that some men seemed to flourish under its weight. The handsomest *bons viveurs* often turned out to marry the plainest prunes of wives, bug-eyed Betties who tagged along at dinner parties as sort of walking consciences and were the kind who asked their husbands to fetch their fans or their handbags for them, and the husbands did. Perhaps Vivvie and Mr Sexton would be this kind of couple? The wife had to be good so the husband could be bad?

This Sherwyn Sexton had certainly showed a flirtatious spirit. He'd been rather drunk and so, she remembered, was she, though perhaps rather more with exhilaration than alcohol. She'd have thought she herself was more to his taste than Vivvie.

Extraordinary, thinks Adela. Vivvie and Sherwyn Sexton! Manly enough, with the kind of mobile, responsive face she herself found attractive but one so seldom met these days. She'd even rather shocked herself at the time, thinking if only she were not married to Sir Jeremy and didn't have an all too grown daughter and was twenty years younger – but that way folly lay. Don't think of it.

It had been such a triumphant party – though she'd drunk too much champagne; a really special day, the day she became Lady Adela Ripple; not as good as Adela, Lady Ripple, of course, as she would have become had she married a peer, but certainly more befitting her status than plain Mrs Ripple, née Adela Hedleigh. She'd been wearing a floaty pale pink Hilda Steward dress and was looking her best. She'd had Harrods cater the evening with the most delicious oyster soup and lobster patties. It was at the end of the evening that this drunk young man, this editor, this Sherwyn Sexton had taken her hand and held it a moment longer than a junior employee of her husband should, while fixing her with his blue eyes and saying something perfectly foolish and soppy: '*Oh the Lady Adela. Oh the delicacy of the damsel! The lightness of her being! I swoon, I swoon!*', which was not what people usually said, but for some reason made her feel light-headed and entranced. But then his friend had snatched him away before he could make yet more of a fool of himself, and just as well.

Sherwyn Sexton, interested in Vivvie. Why? Well, obviously for her money. Why else would anyone woo her? In itself it was not so bad a sin. Why did most girls marry most men? The marriages turned out well enough. Since girls felt no shame in marrying for money, why, in a changing world, should not men?

On Mother Love

Of course Adela loves Vivvie: Vivvie is her child, and one loves one's child but it is because of Vivvie that Adela must put up with the one child she has, and cannot try again for better luck with others. Vivvie was a big baby, and did permanent damage to Adela as she burst from the womb – such a young, frail, angelic mother, such a vigorous bouncing child – and Jeremy behaving as if the lying-in room was a windowed foaling box and cheering her on through dreadful agonies telling her to be a man, girl, bear up and don't let it get you down. None of her friends have had to put up with a man present at the birth. It is unheard of. Adela really does not like horses, nor has she since the birth. Adela nearly died. But she had a vision, when *in extremis*, of her parents beckoning her to paradise and knew it was a trap and stayed alive, to the doctors' astonishment. She had given up hope of Vivvie actually ever marrying.

Vivvie did one season, sat round looking sulky, refused to do another and has showed no interest in young men, only horses, ever since. Yes, decidedly Jeremy's side.

Money Vivvie may have – far more of it, technically, than Adela herself – but she does not have grace, and will sit around at home graceless, or such is Adela's nightmare, until she sees her mother out.

Then all of a sudden, a phone call from Jeremy and everything changes; the world lights up.

It occurs to Adela, with a great lifting of the heart, that married to someone like Sherwyn Sexton her only daughter might at last become a source of envy, not of pity. To have a daughter married to a successful and good-looking young man meant she, Adela, had not failed in her maternal duty. And since he was short and Vivvie was tall it might even itself out if it came to anything and they had children, and she could become a grandmother of perfectly acceptable children.

A Zebra-Skin Rug

Even as Adela recovers from her husband's news Vivien bursts into the morning room in muddy boots, and strides across the black and white zebra-skin rug that takes up much of the parquet floor. It must have been an enormous beast. Now its poor dead legs reach to the white sofa on the left and to the mirrored walnut cabinet on the right, its head – though at least without its original Van Ingen taxidermy head – to the mirrored club fender, and its tail to the new plate glass picture windows with their view of the drab winter garden. Lady Adela's best friend Syrie Maugham's taste is here too, as it is in the Ripple offices, but perhaps seeming a little out of place in so rural an environment, so old a country house. (The redecorating zeal of Adela's aunt Isobel seems to have been inherited, more's the pity. *Surtout pas trop de zèle?*)

Vivvie's boots leave strands of straw behind and tread mud into the striped white of the zebra skin. Adela does her best not to notice but her sensibilities are hurt.

Vivvie goes straight to the drinks cabinet and pours herself a large whisky, ignoring her mother. She is behaving rudely, reverting to teenager behaviour; albeit teenager is not a term to come into use for another forty years, when fifteen-to-twenty-year-olds with money to spare were recognised by advertisers as an identifiable consumer group.

'Such wonderful news, darling,' says Adela. 'You and Sherwyn Sexton. But what a delightful surprise, my dear!'
'Father phoned you?'
'He did. Apparently Sherwyn – I suppose we must call him Sherwyn – asked permission for your hand in marriage. What a delightful lad – so old fashioned!'
'That was quick,' says Vivvie. 'He didn't waste much time. And Father said yes?'
'He asked him to Sunday lunch.'
'Oh dear,' says Vivvie. 'That's a pity. Overcooked beef, soggy roast potatoes, flat Yorkshire pudding and disgusting trifle. Sherwyn is accustomed to Rules and The Ivy. I don't want him changing his mind. I suppose we don't have time to fire Cook?'
'No,' says Adela, flatly. And then, because in spite of all, she loves her daughter, 'Vivvie, I suppose you know what you're doing?'

'I wouldn't have proposed to him if I didn't,' says Vivvie, who has this unfortunate compulsion to tell the truth, if only because she can't be bothered to look for a polite lie. 'I just didn't know if it would work. But he must have gone straight down and asked Father. I needn't have worried. But Greystokes said I'd done the right thing, Greystokes always knows.'

'I do wish you'd stop this Greystokes nonsense,' says Adela, goaded. 'Greystokes is a horse. And I wish you'd wipe your boots before coming in from the stables. It's been raining.'

So much for the touching scene she has envisaged, but to which perhaps, she realises, only the mothers of beautiful daughters are entitled.

'Let Lily brush it up,' says her daughter. 'It's what she's paid for.'

Intolerably Grand

Vivvie can be intolerably grand. Adela marvels: a royal blood line seems to control so many of her daughter's sentiments, albeit housed in the body of a rough Alpine guide. Lily's the maid of all work, one of a staff of three. Lily, the cook, and an outside man: all of them live out, not in, which is something. The unspoken fear amongst the Upstairs classes was that Downstairs would creep up in the middle of the night and kill them in their beds. It did happen from time to time. But we're in 1922 now, and though the servant problem is worse than ever, at least it's easier to get menials to live out than live in, so it's safer. At the best of times Adela has never quite had the knack of keeping hers in control. Servants have always been a bother. When it comes to it she'd actually rather make a bed herself than have to instruct other people in how it's properly done. It's a matter of principle. She is, after all, like Jeremy, a socialist: she respects the proletariat. Besides, once servants were silent and shrinking (if murderous) when master and mistress passed by. Now they demand conversation, care and concern. They poke and pry and are as likely to despise you as to love you, and can be worryingly quick to take offence. If Lily is asked to clean up unnecessary mud she will probably do so. But she is bound to scowl; and look cross; best now to placate, not aggravate.

'Sherwyn Sexton is certainly a very good-looking young man,' Adela says cautiously. 'I met him briefly at your father's investiture party. The one you refused to go to, because you didn't like your dress. The Coco Chanel one with the bow. The bow was removable, didn't you realise? And so charming. And now suddenly an engagement! A wedding! Indeed, a wonderful surprise. I had no idea you and he were so close! How did it all happen? Do tell!'

Vivvie, almost deliberately, Adela thinks, shakes her boot so that more mud and straw fall onto the floor and then tips down her whisky in a great gulp, chokes a little and then says with a calm ferocity:
'We're not at all close, Mother. Do stop gushing.'

On Having A Difficult Daughter

It is not just her daughter's looks – or her lack of them – that so bother Adela, but how she can have given birth to someone who is so swift with the truth but so bad at light conversation. Or indeed a person of so much aggressive – how could she put it? – solid physicality? Yes, that's it. Solidity of body and mind, look at Vivvie now – she has been down at the stables again. Her great grimy hands seize the thick glass of the decanter and pour with no trouble at all, while she, Adela, a snowflake of a person, almost translucent – like an angel, admirers declare – can hardly get her tiny fluttering hands to lift such a thing, nor would it occur to her to pour such a drink for herself. Well, sherry, perhaps, whisky no.

She tries to absorb what her daughter has just said and plays for time.

'And doesn't one need more water in one's whisky than that, darling?'

'Spoils it,' says Vivien shortly, as she tips yet more golden liquid down her massive throat.

Vivvie doesn't sip, she tips. She is trying to annoy. But why? She should be really happy. Even if she did the proposing – an indignity to be driven to such lengths, Adela can see – but the response was positive. Engaged to be married, and after so many disappointments! Now a flake of mud falls off the hem of Vivvie's skirt onto the brilliant white of the shockingly expensive rug. It springs to Adela's lips to say '*I might be losing a daughter but at least I would gain a rug*', but she bites back the words. Her daughter is easily hurt and views parental witticisms with mistrust.

Adela loves Vivvie though she has difficulty showing it, as do most mothers of the time. The maternal role was to instruct, chide and feed. The paternal role was to educate: hugging and kissing was frowned on, as were any declarations of love.

Maternal embraces were what turned sons into pansies, daughters into trollops. The duty of the parent is to refrain from praise, no matter how naturally it sprang to one's lips, since it was what made boys self-satisfied and girls vain: better to search for reasons to find fault, so that the child strives harder. Never tell a girl she's pretty or it will go to her head and she'll end up on the streets. Never tell a boy he's clever or he'll stop trying and end up in the gutter. It is a world away from how we live now.

Anyway...

The Story Continues

'Vivvie, I wish you every happiness, you know that,' Adela says. 'Your father and I will be losing a very precious daughter. Just be sure you are doing the right thing. Such a good-looking young man. Most manly, though perhaps rather short.'

'Only in comparison to me, Mama,' says Vivvie. 'I expect to other people he seems to be within acceptable limits.'

'And well spoken. St Paul's, I believe. He must be really very clever.'

'I could hardly aspire to Eton, Mama. One must be realistic.'

One never knew when Vivvie was being sarcastic, that was the trouble. Adela decides, wrongly, that she is not.

'My dear girl! 'says Adela. 'You're not as bad as all that. You're a lovely girl and quite a brain box yourself. You should get on well. Like calls to like. Not everyone has the money for Eton, these days. But the main thing is for you to be happy.'

'Happy?' repeats Vivvie. 'Happy? What has happiness to do with anything?'

Adela supposes her daughter knows the facts of life, and what marriage entails, though it's possible that she doesn't. Vivien seems to lack the basic curiosity that other girls have. She lives in the country and will have seen the antics of livestock often enough, but it is still possible for a girl not to make the necessary connection between animal and human life. It's just not the kind of knowledge a refined mother can impart to a daughter without unease and embarrassment. Now is hardly the time to bring the subject up. She could envisage her own naked body next to Sherwyn Sexton's well enough, but Vivien and Sherwyn together made a comic scene.

'I just so hope you know what you're doing, darling.'
'I have no illusions, if that's what you mean. Sherwyn is putting up with my looks and nature in favour of my bank balance, and you and Father are anxious to get me out of the house, for fear of my having to live with you for the rest of your lives. Of course you want a wedding! Don't concern yourself. Courtney and Baum will no doubt look after my financial interests, or rather you will, as usual. Don't concern yourself. I will not interfere with our existing arrangements, other than perhaps take over Father's stud farm. At least Sherwyn is not like Father: he knows nothing about horses; and is concerned only with himself, his writing, and his sensual consolations. I hope to leave him alone as I hope he will leave me.'
It was a full half minute before Adela replies. Vivvie downs some more whisky.

Then Adela says: 'But darling, life can't be all practicalities and money. Surely there has to be a little love?'

Adela speaks with sincerity and from the heart. She crosses the room and touches her daughter's large red hand with her own little fingers; she is not quite sure why she does it, other than is this not the flesh of her flesh? Her own creation, however strange, burst from her loins, just as she herself once burst, a sensuous, passionate stranger, into her mother's chaste and abstemious life?

And as she does it the poor girl's face puckers and Vivvie explodes into tears and actually howls, and the hundred silver tipped prisms in the four concentric rings which compose the chandelier jangle and clink. When Adela cries she is an angel weeping for the sins of the world, which are far removed. When Vivvie cries she grows bloated and pink, and makes chandeliers rattle. Adela snatches her fingers away. She trusted where she had no business to trust.

'What love did you ever show me? All you ever wanted is to get rid of the embarrassment of me. Father couldn't wait, could he? Did he offer Sherwyn money to get me off your hands? Is that how it happened? And you with your "darlings" and "dears" and "do tells". More love in a day than I've had in twenty years.'

'Vivvie, you are very cruel and unreasonable. What I'd like is for you to go and fetch a dustpan and brush and clear up the mud your boots have left behind. Lily has enough to do as it is.' At which, after another gulp and a hoot or two at least, Vivien regains her composure and says:

'I am not your answer to your servant problem, Mama.'

And Adela, floored, thinks: 'Well, if this Sherwyn Sexton is prepared to take Vivvie on, he has my blessings,' and hopes that if children result the girls will take after their father. It doesn't matter so much about boys.

'And by the way,' says Vivvie, as she stalks in indignation to the door, and the ceiling chandelier shakes and rattles some more, 'if I am expected to pay for thatching the stable roof, I think the least Father can do is allow me to ride Greystokes whenever and however I want. And your friend Syrie Maugham is an idiot and ruins everything she touches. Ripple & Co now looks like some vulgar advertising agency, and as for this bloody morning room it's a joke. Before you spend any more of my money I'd like you to consult me. And I hate this rug.' And she stomps away to her bedroom.

Things Not Working Properly

This, thinks Adela, puts a new and rather alarming slant on everything. It is dark outside and the temperature is falling. There are scattered drops of rain on the inside of the plate glass window which can only mean it hasn't been fitted properly. Nothing ever works properly in the morning room. But then it's where in 1905 they laid to rest the body of her uncle Robert, Earl of Dilberne after his shooting accident – one could hardly expect the room to be cheerful. It's all very well in the summer to have the mirrored walls which Syrie Maugham so adores, but in the winter all they do is magnify a sense of desolation, surrounding one with the sight of dank lawns and decaying vegetation, not the fecundity of summer and the generosity of nature.

Memories of past litigation assail Adela, the anxious tedium of it all, the obtuseness of countless lawyers, decades of waiting while she and Jeremy fought through the international courts for their child's inheritance – the child herself seeming quite indifferent to their success or otherwise, only now at this late stage deciding to throw her weight (considerable) about and deciding to interfere in matters she knows nothing about: the art of interior design, for example. And heaven knew what kind of wild card this Sherwyn Sexton is going to turn out to be. What can Jeremy be thinking of? Doesn't he realise just how vulnerable Vivvie is? How delicate the situation?

Supposing this young man with his embarrassing '*I swoon, I swoon!*' – the words had been absurd but she remembers the touch of his hand and it was not unpleasant – decides Vivvie's money is better spent on her husband than on his parents-in-law? But with any luck Jeremy has left sufficient options open so that there is time to re-think the marriage, put Sherwyn off these absurd nuptials. One or other of the parties involved must be talked out of it. Well, Adela is good at that kind of thing.
She hopes money has not changed hands already, that they have not unwittingly dropped into breach of promise territory – though that is normally a defence for brides, not grooms. She hopes she has not upset Vivvie too much.

Adela fetches the dustpan and brush herself, dons rubber gloves (size: small) and sees to the straw and mud on the carpet herself. Lily has gone home.

Around Seven O'Clock, November 23rd 1922.
Cumberland Market, N.W.

It is in good spirits that Sherwyn approaches Rita's tall, thin, grimy little house on the South side of Cumberland Market. The wide, shadowy market place has seen many changes. Before the war it was where the hay carts which kept the horses of London fuelled would gather and unload, and here that the building stone which was needed to keep the city growing would be landed from the Regent's Canal. Now that the motor car increasingly usurps the horse, the fuss and bustle has moved on elsewhere, and Rita's second floor flat looks out on an almost empty square. But nothing is without benefit. As the saddlers, the stone masons, the porters move out the artists move in, rentals being cheap and available. Rooms might be narrow and staircases steep, but windows are large and let in good daylight, and the Slade School of Fine Art is just down the road in Gower Street. Forget that the air is often thick with coal smuts from the railway lines behind Euston Station and bronchitis is endemic. Let the working classes cough and spit and hawk and grow old before their time, the young bohemians will flourish and suck the area dry for atmosphere and cheapness and then move on to healthier climes.

At the moment the area suits Sherwyn very well. It's as well for a young writer preparing for great things to be living in sin in

Cumberland Market. Respectability was for before the war, this is now, now, now. Experience is everything. He is a little drunk. He stopped by at a bar he knows and shared a quick glass or two of absinthe with an acquaintance who seemed happy enough to pay.

'Rita, Rita,' he could say in exultation, 'we are rich! I have sold my novel! I am to be married to Miss Vivien Ripple the well-known giantess!' and they will share a good bottle of wine and he will leap on top of Rita on the purple velvet chaise longue she has just bought for two shillings in Kentish Town Market.

Commonsense Rules

No, on second thoughts perhaps that isn't all that sensible. Rita will be all in favour of him marrying for money – is she herself not kept as a rich man's mistress? Sherwyn must move out when he comes by – so that is no concern; if he says his novel is to be published she will be delighted; but when it comes to money he must be careful. If he says he is rich Rita will demand the rent he owes – how quickly sums do mount up. He mustn't forget he is seriously in debt. He owes his father some £265 (or £450 according to his stepmother, the horse-faced Enid); some £50 to various dining and bookmaking establishments.

And now he must outfit himself, not just for life as an up-and-coming young writer, but immediately for a weekend at Dilberne Court. He hates to be rushed when it comes to clothes. Serious and careful consideration must be paid to the impression they make; and he had so little of what is the correct wear for a handsome young suitor wooing a large, plain woman. No, he must not think like that. Flowers, of course. His mother had always bought hers at Moyses Stevens, but they were so expensive and at this time of year there would be nothing to find in his father's garden except a few laurel leaves. It would simply not be wise to tell Rita about the cheque.

What Has He Done?

For what is left after debts have been paid – horribly little – will have to support him for the couple of years it will take to write the next novel. Such is the writer's life. And at what cost has the money been earned? Engaged to marry Vivien Ripple! He can hardly imagine how in the course of a single day he has arrived at a situation which will take him weeks, months, to wriggle out of. Somehow or other the engagement must be broken off. With any luck Vivvie will do it of her own accord, if he shows himself to be impossible enough. Then he will be free as well as rich. A man with money in his pocket can take his pick of desirable girls. He will keep quiet about the cheque. Rita will not necessarily understand how much of a joke the whole thing is. She might even weep and make a fuss. You can never tell with girls – they sometimes seem to lack all reason.

No, better to keep quiet and content himself with the good bottle of wine he borrowed from the bar and leaping upon her on the purple chaise longue, to which he is greatly looking forward. Perhaps the whitebait girl has some of Rita's characteristics? Rita is not averse to all sorts of practices of the kind 'nice' girls would not even imagine, let alone think of doing.

She has turned out to be a real brick, and he is grateful for it, but she too might have to go. To be living with an artists' model is fitting for an aspiring young literary man about town, though for a successful writer perhaps not. Her father keeps a fruit stall in Bermondsey. These things count, no matter how much of a bohemian a man might be. Oddly, an Old Etonian can get away with anything, a Pauline, not so.

But Oh, Rita!

But it will be hard to let her go, she is so pretty and striking; almost Moroccan in appearance; dark-complexioned; small lithe limbs; big breasts and little ankles; enormous, blue reproachful eyes – and then this mass of wild dark red hair. When they go about together in the street he attracts looks of envious curiosity from other men. She earns her own living as a model for the figure- and head-painting classes at the Slade, where she's become so much of a favourite they've even let her enrol as a pupil. She spends her free time daubing away in her studio, and her nights – well, that didn't bear too much thinking about but at least for the moment she spends them with him. He started sleeping on her floor after a party but little by little has risen to become a fixture in her bed.

True, he once had to make himself scarce when the married lover turned up and demanded his dues. But when the lover turned out to be a famous landscape painter and a professor at the Slade, and not just some wealthy businessman, Sherwyn found his pangs of jealousy quite assuaged. He felt at least he was in good company. Rita denies that the lover pays her rent, claims she loves him passionately and that no money changes hands. Of course her lover pays her rent: why she demands that he, Sherwyn, pays towards it seems unreasonable. It is all very reminiscent of Alexandre Dumas' *La Dame aux Camélias*, not to mention *La Bohème*. It is the very stuff of drama. Fate, Sherwyn realises, is on his side, as so often happens in the making of a great writer. It will never let him be short of subject matter. A writer does well to be open to as wide a range of emotional experience as possible. As it is, he is able to record his own inevitable spasms of jealousy, while being set free every now and then to engage in other couplings of his own. The nights Rita spent with the professor are the nights Sherwyn spent with Phoebe. They were not very rewarding nights. She had no conversation and wept most of the time.

It might indeed be possible, Sherwyn supposes, to be contentedly married to Vivien Ripple while keeping Rita as a mistress. That would spare him the scandal and fuss of a divorce. He could be both emotionally and sexually satisfied, and still concentrate on writing. Wealth was certainly infinitely desirable. The cheque in the pocket was the key to creativity. Money meant the end to anxiety and freedom to the soul. And it could always be like this. He would not even insist on fidelity on Rita's part: she moved in interesting circles: as life went by perhaps others yet more famous and more fortunate than the landscape painter might join in her life and look good in his biography. One must always think of the biography. And of course Vivvie would have no option other than fidelity.

Sherwyn, thus tempted, climbs the steep grimy staircase to Rita's studio. He finds her standing barefoot in front of her easel, a coat over what seems to be her nightie, trying to use the light that comes from the gas-lamp in the street below to guide brush to canvas. She is annoyingly impractical, but so very beautiful.

Intermission

As it happens I know Adela, Vivvie's mother, well. I lived with her as her writer for five of her teenage years, over three novels of mine which took place between 1900 and 1905. I left her when she was seventeen rising eighteen at the end of *Long Live the King*. Book Two of the *Love and Inheritance Trilogy*. A very different kind of book from this. I reunited her with her affectionate aunt Isobel and thought I had finished with her. But no. Here she is, twenty or so years later. Odd that I never realised until now that she had the roots of evil in her: that she turned out not to be a good person at all. I am writing Vivvie's story, not hers. I saw Vivvie on the station platform at Dilberne Halt waving at me out of the past and stayed with her, and only then realised, of course, she was Adela's daughter, though as unlike her as chalk from cheese.

So here is dear Adela, back in this book. I had thoughtlessly given her too harsh and traumatic a childhood for her to lead a harmless life. Because people are victims does not mean they are necessarily nice: on the contrary, they tend to learn the same tricks as their oppressors.

Being the grand-daughter of a Princess and the niece of an Earl did not save little Adela from a disturbed, hungry and dysfunctional upbringing by parents who, while of the blood, were religious fanatics and convinced that to feed the body was to starve the soul. Feeling hopelessly guilty about the sexual act which had brought their daughter into the world in the first place all they wanted for her was to live an asexual life and to become a bride of Christ, Anglican not Catholic. But when Adela was sixteen her parents died in a fire in the rectory where her father was rector. Adela was saved. It was a tragic and terrible event, but it at least saved her from a future in a convent.

But now I wonder if something nasty entered her teenage soul during her brief stay at the Bishop's Palace in Wells after the rectory fire, from which she was rescued in the middle of the night, shivering and naked. Covered only by a blanket, she watched as the shrivelled and burnt corpses of her mother and father were carried past her on a stretcher, still sexually entwined. No-one had the forethought to hide her eyes. Perhaps whatever it was stayed and festered, having used the wound left by her parents' death as a point of entry. She'd had such a hard time from them that she scarcely grieved for them at all, and grief normally puts up a protective barrier against evil forces. The Bishop's Palace, where she received refuge, grand and beautiful place that it is, was no protection. On the contrary, where there are angels there are devils as well. It was from the Palace that the orphaned Adela fell into the clutches of spiritualist fraudsters, who put her on the stage as a medium and clairvoyant. And heaven knows what happened to her psyche there. Messing with 'the other side' can be dangerous.

And then of course Adela's cousin Rosina, with the help of the Theosophists, took her to Monte Verità in Switzerland and there she joined the community of hope and light – and where there is light there are shadows as well.

Adela believes herself to be a good person. She thinks that all her actions are justified, that anyone would do as she does in the circumstances in which she finds herself. But the more I write about her the more I have discovered just how awful she has become.

Mothers get the blame for everything as a matter of course, I know – too cruel, too kind; too cold, too enveloping; too discouraging, too full of unrealistic praise; too controlling, too careless; made me fat, made me thin; made me have an abortion, stopped me having an abortion; forced me to be an Olympic star, actress, opera singer whatever, stopped me being an Olympic star, actress, opera singer, whatever. Any stick will do with which to beat a mother. The truth being that most of us mothers do our best within the limits of our own nature. But I must say I think Adela was pretty awful when it came to poor Vivvie, even though once she spent so much time as my heroine. She just couldn't bear being mother to a plain daughter and let Vivvie know it. Adela's mother, of course, was a plain woman who couldn't bear having a pretty daughter.

Adela, in 1922, is still a large-eyed, beautiful, fragile little thing, with the tiny body, large head, hands and feet of a surviving anorexic, or anyone who for some reason didn't get enough food in childhood. As a young girl she had the vulnerable transparency and innocence which large tough men found appealing. It was on Monte Verità, whither he had come in search of a suitable author to write a book on the life of Madame Blavatsky, that Jeremy Ripple, the cricket and rowing Blue and gentleman publisher, clapped eyes upon the ethereal, well-born and well-spoken Adela. He fell instantly, hopelessly and permanently in love with her. He proposed marriage within the month and was accepted. A roll of thunder around the mountain tops was heard as he put a ruby wedding ring upon her finger. The ring as it happened was Adela's own, a present from Queen Alexandra herself, but it was the only ring available on the remote and unworldly Mountain of Truth where artists and thinkers gathered from all over the world to spread the message of truth and light, hear the music of the spheres and join in Universal Oneness, and where wedding rings were scarce.

Anyway.

How was Jeremy Ripple to know that his child bride – she was just eighteen – was eventually to come into possession of Dilberne Court and with the birth of Vivvie the premises at No 3 Fleet Street, which was one day to house Ripple & Co, Publishers. Though some did assume, unkindly and in error, that it was not so much love at first sight as a fairly obvious act of self-interest. Adela was an Earl's niece and Jeremy, from an army family and an Old Etonian, knew all too well the value of family connections in all parts of British society. But Adela believes in love, and how could she, or indeed Jeremy, or any of the Asconites gathered there on that momentous wedding day dismiss the clap of thunder which shook the mountains at the exact moment the tiny ruby ring was placed on the tiny finger? The Gods themselves were present, and a very harmonious marriage it turned out to be. It produced Vivvie, and out of Vivvie and the Angel Gabriel, Mallory and Stella. As it happens there was at the time a young White Russian Czarist refugee called Igor Kubanov, later to enter the fashionable world as a famous equestrian champion, working at the Ripple stud farm as a stable hand – a handsome fellow, and his blond hair could look quite angelic with the sun behind it.

As some people seem born to be, Adela remains event-prone – that is, major events swirl around her while leaving her untouched, undamaged. One meets such people in novels – it is Adela's intervention that saves the Prince of Wales himself to live another day – but also, I have found, on occasion, in real life. These are the individuals who walk unscathed from the rail accident, who stand next to the grassy knoll when Kennedy dies, who watch from the ship when Krakatoa erupts – the ones who seem fated to be witnesses, not the victims, of great events. Far worse to be accident-prone, the ones whom fate has it in for. Disasters and cancers strike them and theirs, law suits are lost, vital files misplaced – in the end a truck veers off the road and mows them down, a tile just falls off the roof when they pass by and knocks the life out of them. It's enough, if not quite, to make a writer believe in the machinations of a divine power. Some people are just born lucky, others just unlucky.

The other thing which impressed Adela in her girlhood was not just the beautiful spiritual sentiments of the Monte Verità inhabitants, but the flabby skin and scrawny limbs of those who most espoused them. (Jeremy by comparison was a smooth, sturdy tree trunk of a man in his prime, a man of virility and consequence.) There was great relief to be found in simply getting away from the black bristles which sprouted between the toes of elderly sandalled artists as they sunbathed naked, or from their armpits as they raised their arms in worship of the rising sun. It was in those Monte Verità months, no doubt, that squeamishness, if nothing worse, entered into her soul.

119

I know Adela to be capable of great acts of kindness and it is possible to see her decision to steal Vivvie's babies as an attempt to save the family from disgrace – but what disgrace? the children were legally Sherwyn's – his being the name on the marriage certificate – and a little care would ensure that no-one would suspect otherwise: it would be possible to claim that Adela wanted to redeem herself by being as good a mother to her grand-daughters as she had been a bad one to her daughter. But I think she was such a selfish bitch she thought that having small children at her knee would make her look young and envied by her friends and most of all she would punish Vivvie for having been born and so deprived her of having the children she deserved. And that is why when it became apparent on her wedding day that the girl was pregnant, it came to Adela that to bring up the Angel Gabriel's baby as her own was such a good idea. And it was a fairly commonplace occurrence at the time. The disgraced daughter lay low until the baby was born. Her mother or married older sister would step forward with the newborn, crying 'Look what I made!' Everybody knew, nobody told.

Adela sees herself as a good person, as do so many in this wicked world. And being a good person, how can anything she does be wrong? If she maintains that she is the mother of her daughter's misconceived twins – how can she possibly believe Vivvie's tale of the Angel Gabriel – how can any of us, come to that? – the family is at least saved the disgrace of their illegitimacy and ensuing social embarrassment. If she had known – as a modern scan would have instantly told her – that Vivvie was carrying twins, then Adela might have changed her mind – twins, as one might say today, being decidedly something else, even for a wealthy woman who can afford nursemaids. And she had enough to deal with without the extra burden and being in love with Sherwyn took up a lot of emotional time and energy resisting the temptation to go to bed with him. She was, after all, a married woman and had what was left of the vast and prosperous Dilberne estate to look after and keep up to date. The estate is now much reduced in size. When in 1916 the war budget demanded tax of five shillings in the pound, Arthur, Lord Dilberne, always an impetuous man, simply sold up and took himself, his family and his auto business to Chicago, handing over the ancestral home, Dilberne Court, a very pretty Jacobean manor house, a few hundred acres of tenanted farm-land, including a well-managed stud farm, to Adela's care. His mother Isobel claimed that Adela was the only one of the family with a head for business and so it proved.

There may now be only a staff of three to help Adela run the place, but all the same the upkeep of a manor house and grounds is not cheap. It was fortunate that money from Vivvie's estate was able to contribute, one way and another, to the refur-bishment and running of the property. Adela felt herself entitled, if only morally, to such of it as she could get her hands on. It is not nice, indeed it is unfair, to be disinherited, cursed even in utero, on the grounds of a mother's infidelity to the Catholic cause in 1883. Many felt at the time that the Bill of 1882 which allowed married women to own property in their own right was a great mistake; women, as everyone knew, did whimsical things.

The funds that came in from Ripple & Co were never certain. Sometimes the company was in profit, sometimes not, depending on how Sir Jeremy's hunches worked out. Adela was able to persuade Jeremy that if only his offices were refurbished in tune with modern times a new and upcoming generation of writers would flock to the firm and ensure that it prospered. The cost of the investiture party had been extreme – Syrie had upped her prices disgracefully – but there was surely something to celebrate, and many other London publishers had followed suit. Out with the old, in with the new! Keep up to date in style and a new literature for a new age would surely emerge, fit for the age of the League of Nations and universal peace.

In any case so long as Vivvie, justly inheriting, is wealthy in her own right, Adela, unjustly disinherited, feels morally entitled to at least some of her daughter's money to help with the upkeep of Dilberne Court, and it is indeed Vivvie who ends up paying for the splendid refurbishment of both the Court and her father's offices. Vivvie, such is the effect of what these days we would call her 'low self esteem', finds herself unable to challenge parental authority. She longs to please those she has so displeased by her existence: it is the least she can do for the mother who bore her, so disappointing a child for such a fastidious and beautiful mama.

And indeed it is no easy a thing for a pretty mother to give birth to a dull, ugly daughter. The mother will be deprived of so much: put the child in pretty frilly clothes and she looks absurd, dress her as a fairy princess for the party and friends just laugh. She must learn to put up with pitying looks – which is what Adela has most feared all her life. But the blow – for blow it is – goes even deeper. How has this happened? Adela vaguely fears that she has given birth to some ugly inner aspect of herself – her shadow side, as Carl Jung would have it, 'consisting not just of little weaknesses and foibles, but of a positively demonic dynamism'.

Adela, we must remember, spent time at Ascona, and though glad to escape, puts much faith in Jung, even occasionally reading passages of *The Theory of Psychoanalysis* to Vivvie as she grows up. Her daughter is not all marks of weakness, marks of woe: Vivvie is intelligent enough, but was never sent away to school to have the rough edges of human interaction rubbed smooth. When she was small she ate mostly at the kitchen table with the maid. Now she had grown to twice Adela's size she did her best to maintain a sulky silence at the dinner table.

Vivvie, who loves and admires her tiny mother intolerably, takes much comfort from the fact that at least Adela doesn't have to suffer the pangs of envy so many other mothers feel as their own beauty fades and that of their daughter grows, and of rage as the daughter takes the affection from the father that was once his wife's by right. And some comfort in that at least her mother has risen up the social ladder now that her husband has been dubbed a Knight of the Realm by a grateful monarch and at last has a title, 'Lady Adela'. She no longer feels so bereft at being so well born on her father's side and yet a mere Mrs, and actually a Princess on her mother's side had not so many European titles been abolished over the years by revolution and the fall of empires.

I think you know Sherwyn, Vivvie, Sir Jeremy and Adela well enough by now and I will move swiftly on, racing through the decades to slow up in 1947 by which time Vivvie is well-dead, brown-bread, and Mallory and Stella, twins, shadow sides of one another, beauty and beast, are twenty-three.

PART TWO

Scenes From Married Life, 1923–39

A May Afternoon In 1923. Dilberne Court

Adela was helping the seamstress with a fitting for Vivvie's wedding dress. Syrie had tried her hand at dress designing and the bridal gown was to cost £100, *prix d'ami*. The bridal gown was in elegant draped white satin so slippery it was hard to manage, but Syrie thought it would make a splash in the dim candlelit recesses of the church.

The seamstress, who as it happened was a sister of Mrs Ashton, the village store keeper whom we last saw with Vivien on the platform of Dilberne Halt, was busy putting a new set of pins along the front of the hem.

'I don't understand it,' Elsie was saying. 'I thought I'd got it right a month ago. But now the hem in the front is a good two inches higher than at the back.' Vivvie huffed and puffed and wriggled and shifted from one leg to another which didn't help.

'Then unpick, re-pin and re-do,' said Adela. 'Vivvie, do at least try and stand still.'

'Sherwyn stood in the mud at Verdun,' said Vivvie, 'and moving from one foot to the other was the only thing that stopped him falling down and drowning.'

'For heaven's sake, Vivvie, we are not on the battlefield. You are having a fitting for a wedding dress.'

Vivvie and Sherwyn had had a peaceful enough courtship. It involved no kisses or sweet sentiments, and neither talked about anything dear to them. The ring went on her finger on Christmas Day. The wedding was to be in May. Sherwyn visited weekly as seemed proper, and made it his business to charm Adela.

'Naughty boy! What a flirt you are,' Adela would say, and Vivvie would wince.

Adela put on scarlet lipstick when Sherwyn came round and wore her most flattering clothes. Vivvie abjured cosmetics – they seemed to her a form of cheating. When Sherwyn was alone with Vivvie he contented himself with telling tales of heroism in battle, mostly involving himself and mostly invention. If dates, times and places became so implausible even she objected, he would say, 'But I write fiction. I have to keep in practice.' And she would raise her bushy eyebrows and even egg him on. They got on well enough together.

There was to be a quiet ceremony in Dilberne Church on May 23rd. Neither Sherwyn nor Vivvie wanted a big wedding. Mungo suggested that readers preferred their male authors unmarried and as Ripple & Co's new head of publicity (Sherwyn had become Editorial Consultant) he had plans for a photo of Sherwyn to appear on the cover of *The Missing Millionaire* (new title for *The Unquiet Gentleman*) which was to be released in late May in Ripple's new *Discerning Yarns* list. Writers could no longer afford to be anonymous. They must become personalities. Sherwyn should appear with a pipe, but not in a book lined room but against a curtain of running water – universal symbol of profundity. So just as well that the wedding was kept quiet; the honeymoon would be in a Swiss ski resort no-one had heard of: the happy couple would return to live in the renovated dower house at Dilberne, where once the Dowager Duchess Isobel had spent her last days guarded by a security man whose closeness to her, some thought, was rather suspect. Sherwyn would probably write in a small flat in London where he could be close to the humming heart of cultural life – gone were the pre-war days of ivory towers, where Walter de la Mare's Listeners came to knock upon the moonlit door, where horses in silence chomped the forest's ferny floor. All that escapist, sub-occultist stuff that so entranced Sherwyn's father just didn't wash any more.

'Tell me, Elsie,' said Adela. She was pacing to and fro as she did when she was puzzling. Elsie was on her knees in front of Vivvie the better to tack-stitch the folds of satin she was draping over the slim skirt. (Syrie had decided on a trompe-l'oeil approach.) 'Do you think if we have arum lilies in the church people will think of funerals?'

'My sort of people will, Madam,' said Elsie. 'I don't know about yours. Arums at a wedding! The idea!'

Elsie's reply bordered on rudeness but she was a very good seamstress and Adela overlooked it.

'But May is simply dreadful when it comes to white flowers,' complained Adela. 'Only freesias really, and white tulips of course, if only the gardener had any forethought, but he didn't.' The month had been particularly bad: dry and cool and with a predominant north-westerly wind which seemed to make all the garden flowers shiver and sulk. 'On the other hand,' she went on, 'there are some simply splendid arums down by the pond. They make such a good display. Otherwise it looks as if one had to make do with Harrods. So common not to use one's own flowers.'

Syrie was doing the flower displays for the Dilberne wedding, including the church interior.

'Oh use the arums, who cares?' said Vivvie. 'It's my wedding, though everyone seems to forget it.'

Elsie Fletcher the seamstress, kneeling on the floor in front of Vivvie's belly, gave a little cry and dropped her box of pins.

'But it moved,' she cried. 'I saw it move. Something in there moved.'

Adela stood stock still. Once one accepted the impossible her daughter showed every sign of being pregnant. How had she missed it? She supposed because one so often averted the eyes. 'Indigestion,' she said firmly. 'Vivvie, best if you go and lie down. You ate far too much at lunch: you are so excited about the wedding you do tend to overeat. Elsie, that will be enough for today.'

Elsie put away her needles and threads and walked down to the village. 'If you ask me,' Elsie said to her sister, 'that girl's got a bun in the oven.'

'I thought something was up,' said Mrs Ashton. 'What with the short engagement and all. You'd have thought people like that knew better. She'll have to go into hiding.'

Vivvie went to her bedroom and lay down on her bed. Syrie had been at work here too. There was nothing familiar or comforting anywhere. The old dusty crimson velvet of the bed hangings had been thrown out and replaced by white gauze drapes. There were mirrors everywhere. and Vivvie studied herself in one of them.

Adela did a Coué exercise to steady herself – *every day in every way I'm getting better and better* – and went on up to Vivvie's room. She didn't knock. Vivvie was looking at herself in the mirror, full length, first this way, then that. She seldom looked at her body.

'Am I like the Van Eyck painting in the National Gallery?' Vivvie asked. 'The pregnant wife one?'

'Yes,' said Adela, 'that's exactly what you're like, only not so far gone, thank God. You and Sherwyn have been very foolish. I'm very angry with the dear boy. It puts us all in the most embarrassing situation. But don't worry. We'll whisk you away after the wedding and you can come back with the newborn when it's about three months old, keep out of sight for a little. With any luck your dress has enough drapes to get you through the wedding. Thanks to Syrie, whom you so despise.'

'But Mother–'

'Don't argue, Vivvie. This is all a great shock. Don't push me.'

'Village girls get pregnant all the time.'

'Yes but they're village. You're gentry. It's not what's expected.'

'It can't be Sherwyn's because we haven't done it. He's not interested, neither am I. I don't know how it happened. You don't get pregnant when you do it standing up. The stuff falls out. It's different for horses. Lily told me. But she must have been wrong.'

'I beg your pardon?' Adela was amazed.

'Sherwyn isn't the father. It can only have been the Angel Gabriel.'

Adela asked Vivvie many questions and then said: 'I see, pregnant by a passing stable boy, and you don't even know his name. Are you out of your mind?'

A Morning, Later In May 1923. Dilberne Court.

It was a fairly terrible wedding. It rained all day as it hadn't all month. Arum lilies glowed in the dim church, and made most of the guests think of the last funeral they had attended. Some fifty had been invited, for all the happy couple's efforts to keep the event as small as possible. Twenty came for Vivvie's side – mostly publishing friends of her parents, and of course Syrie Maugham and her husband Somerset, whom Sherwyn was happy to meet – and Sherwyn's father Edgar and stepmother, who had forgiven him now he had paid back all the monies owed, and actually had a novel finished and at the printer's. A handful of parishioners clustered round the church door. It was a Dilberne wedding, after all. Vivvie might not be of the direct line but she was still a Dilberne, and Jeremy and Adela, now being a Sir and a Lady, not a mere Mr and Mrs, deserved respect and support, though Vivvie was obviously no beauty. There would have been more but it was raining hard.

Vivvie, at five foot eleven inches, came down the aisle on her father's arm – he looked proud and pleased enough, well dressed and well fed at five foot ten – to the tune of here comes the bride, to the *Lohengrin* theme played by the local organist. Sherwyn, at five foot six and a half, followed with best man Mungo, five foot nine, and even he was dwarfed by Vivvie.

Someone in the congregation giggled into the silence as the ring failed to go on Vivvie's finger. (Mungo's idea of a practical joke, it later emerged, to switch rings with one from Adela's dressing table.) Father Harris carried on with the service but Vivvie burst into tears and scarcely managed the 'I do'. But it was not a ceremony that many cared to remember.

Vivvie didn't look too dreadful at all, swathed and hung about with satin. She might have looked pregnant but equally could not have been. A girl from Helena Rubinstein's London salon had come down and plucked her bushy eyebrows and arranged her hair in a flattering sweep across the brow which at least made her eyes look large and lovely. Vivvie, seeing such ministrations were inevitable and subdued by Adela's steely will and rigid jaw, had taken a dose of the tonic she gave Greystokes whenever he became restive, and sat calmly enough through the process. (She had taken quite a swig before the ceremony, as it happened, which may have been the reason both for her large-pupilled dark and lovely eyes and her bursting into tears. She was not normally so emotional.)

Neither Sir Jeremy nor Sherwyn had been informed of the pregnancy. Vivvie, according to Adela, must be seen as a virgin bride, as in proper circles in 1923 brides were. The thing to do was to get the girl married before anyone could change their mind. The baby was the legal child of whoever married the mother before the birth. The slur of illegitimacy was thus avoided.

The Wedding Reception

Silver braziers warmed the marquee. The rain began to abate. Scrambled eggs and oysters Rockefeller were served.

Sherwyn buzzed about the guests, Sir Jeremy was lordly, Adela was supremely gracious. Vivvie sat heavily in a corner and smiled: Greystokes' tonic, she noted, might sooth horses, but it sent humans charging about from one emotion to another, sometimes weepy, sometimes panicky, sometimes hopelessly placid. If you were in a placid stage that was that. As bearer of a baby by the Angel Gabriel, or whoever had sent him, it behoved one to smile and be placid and endure. She wondered if she had been soothing herself too much with Greystokes' tonic when the Angel Gabriel had appeared. Perhaps she should take a little less? Well, when she was on honeymoon she would have to do without.

Sir Jeremy rashly used the opportunity to button-hole Somerset and ask if he could see his way to signing up with *Discerning Yarns*. 'Me? A teller of yarns? I am well aware I am no lyrical writer, dear boy, but *yarns*? I think not. I am happy enough with Heinemann, no matter how much you and your lovely wife spend on dear Syrie.' And he wandered off to stand next to a brazier and shiver melodramatically.

Somerset had a reputation as being a poisonous bugger on occasion and Sir Jeremy felt able to overlook it. Writers could be tricky: he was fortunate that Sherwyn Sexton was both cordial and cooperative. He hoped that the involuntary giggle that had escaped from his own lips during the service had not been noticed. There was nothing to laugh about, after all. It was a sacred ceremony and if the groom was small and the bride was large instead of the other way round, what did God care? Would there be a place for a list to balance *Discerning Yarns*? Perhaps *Involuntary Laughter*? He must find Mungo and have a word with him.

Mungo was in conversation with Sherwyn. Both were standing shivering next to a brazier. Many of the guests had taken shelter in the morning room, unasked, and were no doubt grinding canapés underfoot into the zebra rug. No-one liked the oysters Rockefeller, fashionable bright green though they were. The old guard dismissed them as on a par with arum lilies at a wedding – nouveau riche, trade. The new guard saw it as a fashion too far, style before content and what did one do with the little sticks once the oysters were chewed – and chewed they had to be, at the very end of the season and so very large, and overcooked anyway.

'So what about the honeymoon, old chap?' Mungo was asking Sherwyn. 'Sorrento? Capri?' Mungo had apologised to Sherwyn about 'the ring business'. It had been a mistake: he'd had two rings in his pocket. He'd taken out Adela's by mistake, and fishing for Vivvie's had found it gone, fallen through a hole in his pocket. He did not go into detail as to why on earth he had Adela's ring in his pocket, nor did Sherwyn pursue the point. He was beginning to think that his mother-in-law's virtue was not her strong point.

'Barscherau,' said Sherwyn. 'A ski resort or something. Bavaria.'

'Oh dear,' said Mungo. 'Never heard of it.'

'That's the idea. I have a novel to write,' said Sherwyn. 'What I need after all this is peace and quiet.'

'Then you'll certainly get it,' said Mungo. 'The Alps, in May? Very strange. But I daresay there'll be a few mountain girls in plaits and dirndl skirts to keep you occupied.'

'Vivien has family connections in that part of the world,' said Sherwyn, stiffly. Sometimes Mungo went too far.

'And a long honeymoon, I daresay, since the birth can't be until at least seven months after the wedding and produce a very tiny baby at that. That takes us through until January before you can decently reappear. Can you stand it, old friend? Is even a fortune worth it? Have you tried the scrambled egg? Ugh! Little yellow balls of snot floating in salt water.'

Sherwyn, for all he practised aplomb, had actually dropped his glass of champagne. Staff rushed to clear it up.

'That's impossible,' said Sherwyn. 'Vivvie? Pregnant? You must be joking, Mungo. What's more, a joke in very bad taste. Are you drunk? I've never touched her. Would I, unless I had to? It would be like climbing a mountain. The very prospect terrifies me.'

'I thought she looked rather fetching today,' said Mungo, 'positively glowing with life and happiness. So you deny being the mountain goat. But who's going to believe you?'

'This is a very untoward calumny,' said Sherwyn. 'Pregnant? Vivvie's a virgin, what else can she be?'

'Not any more, my friend,' said Mungo. 'I looked down and saw that big, welcoming belly move of its own volition. That's why I fumbled with the rings. There's a bun in the oven all right, you sneaky bastard. Didn't she tell you?'

As the two men stood facing each other, Mungo in affected sorrow, Sherwyn in shock and disbelief, Sir Jeremy came up to them.

'What do you think, Mungo?' asked Sir Jeremy. 'Would we do well with a humour list? The proletarian masses need entertainment. We can't take ourselves too seriously. We've got the mystery list up and running. What do you think of *Involuntary Laughter*?'

'The times are ripe for a bit of mirth, sir,' said Mungo, smooth as ever. 'Why not?'

'What do you think, old chap?' Sir Jeremy asked his new son-in-law.

Sherwyn could think of a dozen reasons why not but he did not bother to utter them. He was rapidly working out the pros and cons of the new situation. Vivvie pregnant, but not by him. He could almost feel gears changing, interlocking, slipping into a different mode. It was almost exhilarating. He enjoyed the shock of the new: it was what he was good at. Vivien Sexton, his new wife, had deceived him, tricked him into marriage. He had every right to be indignant. But how he loved event: it was what made him a writer of fiction. He did what he could to bring about the unusual and exceptional in his own life: if that failed he took to the page and created more. Now fate had handed him a single shocking event on a plate, which would give rise to a hundred others, if he played his cards adroitly.

The sheep's eye story had been accepted by *Blackwood's* – Sir Jeremy knew the editor: not that that had anything to do with it – perhaps there could be a sequel in which the girl, made pregnant in Morocco, was desperately looking for a husband. Sherwyn would spend the honeymoon working such a story out. Vivvie had cruelly tricked him, of course she had. He was now, perforce, the legal father of her misbegotten child. He had every reason to be outraged. But so far as Vivvie was concerned Sherwyn occupied the moral high ground and she would be in no position to step out of line. The Ripple parents, like Mungo, would assume it could only be Sherwyn's child. Vivvie would not be believed if he denied paternity. He would not attempt to do so; being father to a Ripple grandson would have its advantages.

It might well be, of course, that Vivvie was more like her mother than anyone would believe; some kind of monstrous nymphomaniac rather than a heavenly one. How otherwise had Mungo gained access to Adela's ring, come to think of it? Sherwyn had assumed he was the only one to be at the receiving end of Adela's flirtatious overtures. But perhaps he was wrong? When he was back in London he would enquire further. At least there was a clause in the prenuptial so he'd go on getting the £20,000 if the marriage broke down as a result of infidelity on the part of husband or wife. It had been put there by Vivvie's lawyers to protect her interests – though she had promised him she would never invoke it. She had insisted, and indeed hoped, that Sherwyn would pursue his erotic impulses outside the marriage. He could see the clause might work in his interests as well – though the complications and scandal of a divorce from a nymphomaniac wife were best avoided.

As for Adela, she was the girl's mother. She must have realised before now that her daughter was pregnant – and had not seen fit to mention it before the wedding to give him a chance to pull out. Well, of course not. Just get the wedding over, and the family would not be tainted by the slur of illegitimacy. But it was still bad form. One could never be sure with the Ripples, he began to realise, quite who was conning whom.

It was perfectly possible that Sir Jeremy – what was all this nonsense about a humorous list? Discernment was one thing, but a serious house had no business dealing in humour – had not had his attention drawn to Vivvie's changing shape. At the best of times the poor girl huddled beneath dismal, shrouding clothes: how on earth had she managed to get herself impregnated? And at the best of times Sir Jeremy saw only what he wanted to see: he would not have been involved in the deceit.

Most importantly, Sherwyn had signed a mere one-book contract with Sir Jeremy, which had annoyed him at the time but he could now see it was perhaps as well. And that as a publisher Sir Jeremy was a rather annoyingly impulsive cove. But Sir Jeremy was staring at him, waiting for a reply.

'*Involuntary Laughter*,' agreed Sherwyn. 'Brilliant idea. Why not?'

In The Evening Of That Day

The bride and groom departed for the Alps, the Great Unknown. The wedding party under the marquee went on. The dessert course had been cleared away. Hot asparagus soup and rolls were being offered. Adela went down to the kitchen where Elsie Fletcher, the seamstress from the village – she had been roped in to help with the catering for the day – was washing out the great silver and glass bowls which had held the trifles, and plunging champagne glasses into soapy water (it was the days before detergent so they had to be rinsed in vinegar water to remove soapy residue and polished with a soft cloth – nothing was easy – before being returned to Harrods).

'I think all that went very well, don't you, Elsie?' said Adela.

'Yes, Ma'am, and didn't the bride look a picture.'

'Let us say she looked as good as she could. But the dress was magnificent. Thank you for your skills and ingenuity, Elsie. Not the slimmest of brides, of course. Overeating in anticipation of the great day, I fear.'

'I'm sure that's what it was, Ma'am. I'll say nothing to anyone, don't worry yourself. I'm fond of Miss Vivvie, and we're all glad down in the village she found someone to marry.'

'Quite so,' said Adela.

She took one of the six trifle bowls and studied it. It was made of cut glass, caught the light deliciously, and sparkling in the evening light and rimmed with real silver as it was, looked, and was, a really desirable object. Expensive too, and from Harrods.

'But oh dear, this one has a crack in it,' Adela said. Elsie was taken aback.

'It looks all right to me, Ma'am. It's not damaged. I've been very careful.'

'Oh no, see, it's quite cracked. It can't go back to Harrods like that. I'll have to declare it as wastage. Such a pity! Still, these things happen. Perhaps you'd like to take it home, Elsie? You could keep flowers in it.'

'Oh I couldn't, Ma'am, it's far too grand for me.'

'Nonsense, Elsie. It's in gratitude for all your fine work and loyalty.'

'Thank you, Ma'am. That's very kind of you. Not a word to anyone as long as I live.'

And Elsie put the bowl carefully to one side to take home with her after work, and Adela smiled and went back to what was left of the party. One by one guests were drifting away, by Bentley and Rolls-Royce, over smooth roads recently tar-macked to join up with the main road to London (Vivvie paid, helped by grants from Brighton County Council and the new Road Fund), humbler folk by charabanc to Dilberne Halt. Everything organised by Adela went swimmingly. But then she had, as they say, the luck of the Devil.

Adela then waylaid her husband Sir Jeremy, who was only a little drunk. She was wearing a pink and white beaded silk tulle dress as simple as Vivvie's had been elaborate, but then she had so little to hide. She came up to his shoulder; she looked up at him, so appealing, so small, so pale. The only flash of colour was from the Queen Alexandra ruby ring he had first put on her finger twenty years ago at Monte Verità. Sir Jeremy was touched. And still they loved each other – now more than ever.

'Such a day, darling,' she said, 'such a day! Our daughter married at last, and to a truly worthy mate.'

'I sincerely hope so,' said Sir Jeremy. 'He's a devious bastard, if a good enough writer.'

Adela then broke the good news to him; she was expecting; they were going to have a baby. She hoped he was as happy as she was.

Sir Jeremy peered at her through mists of alcohol. She had always told him that after Vivvie she was unable to conceive. Something had gone wrong in the unknown complexity that formed the female body. Women were strange creatures. One thing one day, another thing another. But surely bright young things had babies, not mature women such as his wife.

'I am happy if you are,' he said. 'But is it safe at your age?'

'Good Lord, darling, I am not as old as all that. It is perfectly safe.'

He had no idea how old she was, come to think of it. He could hardly ask her outright – that was unthinkable, and besides women were expected to lie about their ages. He could work it out, he supposed, but that too seemed an insult. It had been a long day and he was tired, unlike Adela, who was indefatigable. Now she was laughing merrily.

'An unexpected blessing, it is true. But Mother Nature often hands we women a last departing gift. It happens to the best of couples.'

'It might be a son, I suppose,' he said, doubtfully.

'Someone to take over from you. Ripple & Co could become Ripple & Son.'

'I am not a draper or a funeral director,' he said testily. 'I am a publishing house.'

He did not particularly want a new baby in the house. Having got rid of one child surely he deserved his wife's full attention. But who was he to stand in the Almighty's way? If God had blessed Vivvie's mother in her old age with a baby, as in biblical times He had Mary's mother Anne, who was he, a mere lower-case mortal, to argue with Him? He, Sir Jeremy Ripple, had other matters to think about. If the great and noble Lenin died, how long would the new order survive in a greedy and self-interested world? How could it stand up to the lies and slanders of the hundred-mouthed bourgeois press – all these scorpions!

Well, anything Ripple & Co could do to lead the working class forward, to help forge the unity and solidarity of the Party's ranks, it would strive to do. In the end victory would be achieved over the enemies of the working class. The Labour Party at home might have success at the next election, which would be a step in the right direction, for the reforms they planned were better than nothing, but all that was nowhere near true socialism, let alone communism: the struggle was universal and he knew what side he was on.

As for Somerset Maugham, what a stinker! Jeremy was still smarting from the snub. What was a novel at the best of times but a bit of a yarn with a social conscience? What Somerset wrote, everyone knew, was heavy on plot but light in discern-ment. Somerset was the last person entitled to put on airs. He needed someone with whom he could mull this over. But whom? Sherwyn would dismiss Maugham as being of no liter-ary consequence, a mere plot merchant; Mungo would make Jeremy look a fool for believing that when Maugham said that the novelist lived in a troubled world and it was his duty to acknowledge and contend with it, that he meant a word of it. Maugham was guided by money not principle.

Normally he could have discussed all this with Adela but all she seemed able to talk about was a new baby. A baby! But he was an old man; it was something of an embarrassment. Men of his age were long past the age when physical congress with a wife occurred. She was so damned attractive, that was the problem – and now how the world would snigger. Dignity would be impugned. His contemporaries would mock him; the up and coming see him as an old goat. Vivvie would go off and presumably get pregnant by Sherwyn – that was what marriage was about, after all, though it was hard to envisage and best if one didn't – and here would Adela be, emulating her, the generations hopelessly confused. In the meanwhile Adela was trilling on. It occurred to him that, for all her admirable qualities, she was just silly.

He shocked himself in thinking it. Adela, his pride and joy.

Sir Jeremy scarcely noticed when she told him the baby would be born in the autumn, that after all the excitements of the wedding she must be careful, she must look after her health and not get too tired, that she might spend the next few months abroad, spend the rest of the summer in the Alps and recuperate in the clean mountain air. Did he remember how happy they had been in Monte Verità? – oh, he did, he did!

'Whatever you think best, my darling,' he said. 'You must look after our precious bundle. What a delightful surprise. You breathe new life into an old man.'

Later On, In Dilberne Village

Meanwhile Elsie was down in the village high street sharing a late supper of wedding leftovers with her sister Mrs Ashton and Lily, who 'did' up at the Court. Mrs Ashton was a widow who had taken over the village shop when her husband died, and ran it very well. After his death her spinster sister Elsie moved in to live with her. Before the war Elsie had worked at Dilberne Court as parlour maid: during the war as a munitionette, and after that, her health much reduced and her skin a yellowish colour but her sewing skills unimpaired, scraped a living as a seamstress. The cut-glass and silver bowl she brought home that day was an unexpected bonus: she would be able to sell it to supplement her old age pension when it came along (5/- a week). She decanted a quart or so of leftover potato salad and mayonnaise and some rejected tomato salad into its clean, polished and uncracked beauty, piled it high with the green oysters Rockefeller which the wedding guests had for the most part left uneaten, and carried the lot home for supper, asking Lily to come round and help eat it.

When Mrs Ashton came home from the shop she insisted that the salad was put on individual plates, the oysters removed to a safe place, the bowl washed and polished and put for safety in her mahogany cabinet with the latticed windows. Mrs Ashton then asked her brother-in-law Sid the blacksmith to come round to put a value on the bowl. Harrods only hired out the best. Sid, who knew about metals and values, was quite impressed. The rim, he said, was hallmarked with the lion and Birmingham and dated 1895.

'A fine piece you got out of them toffs, Elsie,' Sid had said. 'Well done. And I should think so too after all you've done for 'em. In time it'll fetch at least fifty quid, so hang on to it as long as you can.'

Sid took the plateful of oysters Rockefeller down to his wife, but she scraped the lot out down at the end of the garden – any food so vile a green would do no-one any good at all. Sid was not too sorry.

Mrs Ashton brought home a few slices of best ham from the shop and they had a feast, washed down with cider. The potato salad leftovers were really good, although the mayonnaise had been made with olive oil which had a strange foreign taste, and it was peculiar to eat tomatoes out of season. Lily found an old cigar butt in her serving, after which the conversation became rather more critical of their benefactors than it had been at the beginning of the meal.

'The idea!' Elsie said to her sister Mrs Ashton. 'That bowl! Thinking she can bribe me to keep my mouth shut!'

'I hope you do,' said Mrs Ashton, severely. 'Poor Miss Vivvie. Least said soonest mended. She had no idea how to look after herself. Waiting for a train without even a coat, and snow on the way. Anything could have happened.'

'And it evidently did,' said Elsie. 'I saw that unborn baby move. Great kick it gave, and all but stretched the satin, and me a respectable person. They might at least have warned me. Enough to put you off dressmaking for life.'

'Worse than finding a cigar butt in your potato salad?' her sister enquired and Elsie said at least she doubted anyone had done it on purpose.

'Don't be too sure,' said Lily darkly. 'They're a funny lot, not like the old gentry. If you ask me, Lady Adela herself is pregnant. She as good as told me so. She said she couldn't face breakfast and then I caught her vomiting in the bathroom. Or at any rate bending over the basin. She shouted at me to go away.'

'Food poisoning,' said Mrs Ashton, firmly.

'It certainly is not,' said Lily. 'I help Cook and I should know. No, I reckon she's pregnant. She's not too old. My own sister got a bun in the oven when she was forty-five. It was her eighth. He wouldn't leave her alone though she begged.'

'Men!' exclaimed Elsie. 'All the same, high or low.'

'And I don't think it's Sir Jeremy's either,' said Lily. 'He's not all that often in her Ladyship's bed. Either in London or in his dressing room.'

'You have no business saying a thing like that, Lily, and I advise you not to repeat it. Whose is it, then?'

'She keeps the house full of young men,' said Lily. 'Could be anyone's. Mr Mungo's always hanging round. And if Mr Sherwyn's coming round she puts on more lipstick and draws dark rings round her eyes.'

'Under her husband's nose!' exclaimed Elsie.

'He doesn't notice a thing,' said Lily. 'He adores her. No, she's a real goer, that one.'

They ate on for a while in contemplative silence, broken only by a shriek when Elsie, who seemed doomed, thought she came across another shard of cigar in the salad, but it turned out to be nothing worse than a piece of potato skin which someone had failed to remove in the initial peeling. It is easily done.

It was a meal that stayed in the minds of the participants – if only because of both the silver rimmed bowl – which was to stay in Mrs Ashton's glass cabinet as an object of value and pride for the next seventeen years – and by the shock of a stubbed-out cigar butt found in the leftover salad – perceived by the three women, however vaguely, as symbolic of the humiliation of the have-nots at the hands of the gentry. And just as well that the meal was memorable, becoming as it did most relevant to the twins' enquiries, years later, into the nature of their parentage.

After The Wedding

Sir Jeremy and Adela's (well, Vivvie's) wedding gift to the young couple was a brand new yellow three-litre Bentley tourer, fresh from the factory – twin carburettors and a four speed gear box and a top speed of 80 miles an hour. It was in this splendid and well-upholstered vehicle that Sherwyn and Vivvie set out on their honeymoon, leaving the wedding party behind them.

As soon as there was no-one to observe them they both began to be happy. The sheer effectiveness and rumbling magnificence of the machine they drove, monarchs of all but empty roads, managed to dwarf all personal doubts and fears – Sherwyn forgot he was short, Vivvie that she was tall: they met as equals. (The roads might have been comparatively empty but they were far from safe – drivers were not tested and licensed and there were more than seven thousand fatal accidents that year – mostly pedestrians taken unawares.) But Sherwyn was a good and skilled driver and Vivvie felt he could be trusted. A man whose talent was keeping out of trouble would use the gift in all aspects of life. He would not fall off horses, have road accidents, take unnecessary risks, get food poisoning, choose the wrong hotel or the wrong publisher. She had chosen the right man. Driving, he looked handsome and alert under his peaked flat cap, his rather sharp nose seen in profile, the mouth, she could now see at her leisure, for she had seldom had the opportunity to examine him closely, having been fully occupied trying to forestall or respond to whatever he was saying, had permanently upturned corners, which was what gave him the appearance of always wearing a slightly ironic, somewhat cynical smile. This, Vivvie could see, would always give him an advantage in literary circles.

As for Vivvie, she wore a mannish brown tweed suit by Coco Chanel and a stern white blouse from Worth for the drive. The suit had a drop waist and by the time they had got to Dover needed to be let out a full inch. She had seemed, he thought, to keep the pregnancy small by effort of will alone. Once the wedding was over and she was out of the grounds of Dilberne Court she could at last breathe deeply and let her body do what it was so good at doing; namely, to grow and expand. He admired her for it. She removed the absurd little pill hat her mother had insisted on her wearing and let her hair fall loose around her face, so its imperfections were less obvious. He even felt affection for her. Perhaps an eventual divorce would not be necessary or desirable. She did not flap, or giggle, or chatter, or smirk, or snivel, or fiddle with her hair and clothes. She spoke only when necessary and then to the point. She was just large. The worst was over. The public scrutiny of their mismatch had been faced and overcome.

Neither felt the need to speak until they reached Dover. It took them some three hours to cover the 66 miles. Small country roads were not conducive to speed – things would get better, Sherwyn assured Vivvie, when they reached the long straight stretches of tree-lined roads of the Continent – roads which had carried so many armies to one fruitless war or another. They dined at the Castle Inn and caught the ten o'clock night ferry. The Bentley was loaded onto the deck by crane, and much complimented by all and sundry as she swung there, glittering in moonlight and floodlight mixed, and breaths let out as she was safely lowered and roped.

Sherwyn took care to say nothing of significance until both were preparing for bed.

'A few things I need to know,' he said.

'I can see that you probably do,' she said, calmly enough. And then: 'Wait until we're in bed.'

There were two bunks and Vivvie said she preferred the top one, and Sherwyn did not demur. He unpacked his own valise carefully to take out red and black striped silk pyjamas (Weatherill – a gift from Adela), undressed discreetly behind a screen and folded his clothes neatly on the shelves provided. She waited until he had finished and heaved herself up onto the top bunk without bothering to make use of the little ladder. She removed her outer garments decorously enough, but then dropped them unfolded onto the floor. Sherwyn tut-tutted to show his disapproval, but stopped short of getting out of bed to deal with them in a civilised manner. After that they both talked to the ceiling, in what was more like an examination of terms than an actual conversation.

Strange shadowy shapes moved across the ceiling as the ship slipped away from the lights of the harbour and made for the open sea.

'Let us begin,' he said. 'So whose is it?'

She considered.

'I don't really know. Can we settle for the Angel Gabriel? At any rate he came unannounced to a humble stable and lo! I was pregnant. He had a halo round his head so far as I know, but I suppose it could have been sunlight striking across his blonde hair.'

'I think Jesus was born in a stable, not conceived in a stable.'

'Yes he was,' she agreed.

'But you were not unwilling?'

'Good heavens no,' she said. 'It was all very – what can I say – gracious. My mother is very much against the explanation that it was divine intervention of some kind. She prefers to believe the baby is yours and that having an immature mind I am in denial. Could she be right?'

'I have no memory of any incident between us that might lead to a pregnancy,' he said. 'But blonde you say. At any rate not some kind of foreigner.'

'Not all foreigners are dark,' she said. 'I once came across a fair Norwegian. He was very blonde. And very foreign.'

'You must try not to argue,' he said, 'or we won't get on.'

They were both drifting off to sleep in their different bunks when he said:

'Very well. I accept it was the Angel Gabriel. Just see me as Joseph.'

'I was hoping you'd say that,' she said. 'I think we will have a perfectly satisfactory marriage.'

'I daresay we will,' he said. Sherwyn went to sleep wondering who would father the whitebait girl's child and if it might be The Uncertain Gentleman in the second book of the trilogy which now looked likely to happen. The difficulty was the first volume was already at the printer's, too late to change except at vast expense, and he was confined by what he had already written. Perhaps it wasn't such a good idea after all. But at least on this extended honeymoon there would be nothing else to do but write. He would not let himself be distracted by trivial diversions. He wondered what culinary delights Vivvie's Alpine village might have to offer, but feared they would be of the goulash, Weiner Schnitzel and sauerkraut kind. Though you never knew – some mountain goat cheeses were delicious. He fell asleep.

Vivvie for her part whispered a silent thanks to Greystokes. Everything had turned out very well, as the noble beast had prophesied. It was strange to be sharing so small and intimate a space with another human being, but she supposed it was what marriage entailed. She rather wished she had chosen the bottom bunk. She would have to get out of bed at some stage and didn't want to wake Sherwyn. But something inside her pressed on something else: pregnancy was a very mysterious process, but somehow at the end of it a new little baby burst into the world. Adela was then going to take it away and bring it up as her own, so she, Vivvie, could start afresh as a virtuous bride. It had sounded a good idea when Adela first mooted it. In many families in the land older sisters turned out to be mothers, mothers to be grandmothers. But supposing she grew to be fond of the baby? No, she didn't think that would ever happen. The Angel Gabriel's it might have been, but at the moment it felt like a rather uncomfortable and unsustainable growth clinging on where it wasn't wanted. And how on earth would it get out? She fell asleep.

The night passed without incident. In the morning, before setting out in the direction of Reims, Strasbourg and Baden Baden (Sherwyn: *'at least we can get a good meal at Brenners'*), through the Black Forest and on to Munich and then dropping down to Barscherau (Vivvie: *'I don't think it will be a matter of dropping down, as much as creeping up. We're talking about the*

Alps and in May. Though most of the snow should have cleared by now'). They breakfasted on café-au-lait, croissants and apricot jam in spring sunshine at the Meursualt Hotel in Calais. They consulted maps and compared them with Adela's written instructions, all of which seemed eminently sensible.

They were to make for Munich and then down to the Austrian border, the small town of Kufstein and then cut off to Barscherau, a village of a few hundred souls and a deserted Benedictine abbey, nestling in the arms of a mountain whose name she had forgotten. They were to stay at the Gasthaus Post until the baby arrived. Courtney and Baum had written ahead to make necessary arrangements for their arrival. They were not on any account to announce themselves as newlyweds: Sherwyn was there to finish a novel: Adela herself would turn up in July as the mother-in-law to supervise the delivery of the baby and depart a month or so later as its mother.

'Thus saving her only daughter from social disgrace,' remarked Sherwyn. 'I see – though I must say it seems a great bother to go to. Girls in the *haute bohème* don't worry so much about scandal. It's either a bottle of gin and a hot bath, or just go ahead.'

'I know so little about how the rest of the world lives,' she said, sadly.

To his surprise Sherwyn found himself vastly entertained rather than irritated by Adela's love of conspiracy, happy enough to be holed up in some mountain vastness with nothing to do but write for three or four months, oddly trusting of Gasthaus cuisine – of which he had heard good things from Mungo – and grateful that he would not have to be saddled with a child which was none of his. Adela would turn up when the snow was properly melted and the hills alive with the sound of birdsong, and the Alpine meadows full of flowers, and all would be well. It certainly made a change from Morocco and sheep's eyes.

Adela, it seemed, looked after everything that needed looking after, arranging anything that could possibly be arranged, so long, Sherwyn suspected, as it suited her advantage. It was hardly surprising that Vivvie was the way she was. Ah, the delicate Adela! Going to bed with Adela, which a man might imagine would be like going to bed with some faery child, all fluttering, delicate parts, one would have to be careful not to rub up against the steel inside, and end up like Keats' wretched knight at arms, alone and palely loitering after his encounter with the *Belle Dame Sans Merci*. Still, a man would like to at least try, and she would be turning up at Barscherau, a village too small even to be marked on the map.

Quite how Courtney and Baum fitted into the Ripple scheme of things he would investigate at his leisure. Vivvie had once suggested she 'owned' the village. It seemed highly unlikely. Vivvie was an agreeable fantasist who claimed her baby was fathered by the Angel Gabriel. But then it was also unlikely that Adela had given birth to this immense girl, yet apparently she had. The problem for the writer was making fiction stranger than life, not the other way round. But things had certainly looked up since Vivvie first appeared towering over him in his attic office in Fleet Street. After a few slow days on the road to Munich, past the Vosges mountains and Alsace, Sherwyn was able to let rip on a stretch of straight, well-tarmacadamed road, allowing the Bentley to hit her stride, as he put it, before swinging up through the zigzag roads of the Black Forest. Here the road was enclosed by dark fir trees and the sound of the engine was thrown back from a natural echo chamber, as Sherwyn repeatedly accelerated and braked for the sharp, uphill bends. Vivvie seemed to admire him greatly for his driving ability and he in his turn admired her for the way her head would bump into the canvas roof of the tourer when they encountered bad potholes, and still did not complain. He realised he had become quite accustomed to her height: it was only when they were in company that he became conscious of it.

Indeed, she made an excellent travelling companion. She didn't complain, wriggle, demand stops, chatter on, make little gasps or yelp when he had to make some unexpected manoeuvre – a cat or a child running out on the road, a bird into the windscreen, once a huddle of anti-motorists, armed with pitchforks, trying to bar the way – but remained interested, good humoured and alert. She seemed to regard her pregnancy as a piece of luggage she was doomed to carry round with her but was best ignored. She would, Sherwyn assumed, be relieved rather than distressed when her mother took the burden away.

When they eventually returned home, he with a finished novel, she with a stomach as flat as it ever had been, which was not saying much, they could buy something magnificent and suitable for a successful writer and his wealthy wife, possibly in the Cotswolds. They would entertain. His mother might come over from the States to visit. His father and stepmother would be welcome so long as they showed due respect. He himself would spend time at the Savage and the Garrick and take a flat in the Albany to concentrate on writing. Vivvie could spend time with her horses and if she had the occasional visit from the Angel Gabriel or one of his cohorts so much the better. She would be discreet. He would father his own children when and where he saw fit. He was, after all, a bohemian, a great writer. At heart he lived in a garret, like Baudelaire, like Verlaine; or in a studio, like Holman Hunt, like Modigliani. God, he missed Rita.

May & June, 1923. Barscherau, Austria

I can't tell you how happy Sherwyn and Vivvie were for those two months. They shared a big feather bed together without either making a sexual move towards the other. She was bulky and soft and growing bulkier by the day. He was shorter, bonier and more crisply limbed than she, but in the dark and warm seemed to fit naturally enfolded into her, as a plum stone inside a plum.

Barscherau still looks much as it does in the picture postcard that was reproduced some fifty years later to sell like hot cakes to the legions of tourists – a tiny picturesque Alpine village perched on a mountainside above the road from Oberammagau to Kufstein. There are flowering meadows in the foreground complete with grazing cows leading down to an azure lake – or however you want to describe that rather shockingly repro-duced blue – snow-capped peaks in the background, and just above the village, still to be seen, the ruined domes of an aban-doned abbey established in 1524 by nuns fleeing from the worldliness of Venice. The nuns had brought with them enough stolen artworks to glorify God with a splendid church in the wilderness. In 1786 the Emperor Franz Joseph I's men had made a rather inadequate job of destroying the place, leaving it to the moth and rust of centuries, not to mention the ice and tempests of the mountain, to do the rest. The abbey remained a magnificent partial ruin, even housing a Mediaeval painted wooden Madonna of sufficient mystery and history to keep the abbey on the tourist trail in later decades.

When Vivvie and Sherwyn were there in 1923 Barscherau's population had fallen below a mere couple of hundred, only to leap to many hundreds then thousands during the late thirties after the building of a ski lift, a score of chalets and a smart hotel. And all on land which was to be eventually owned, by virtue of Vivvie's great-grandmother's much disputed will of 1884, by Vivvie's twin daughters Mallory and Stella. The estate was still badly administered by the London lawyers Courtney and Baum, by then a crotchety and stubborn firm of wily old lawyers, experts in inheritance law, but willing to overlook the odd discrepancy in cheque signing, knowing that few would be interested enough to check up on details of why or how the money rolled in.

Anyway, here they are now, Sherwyn and Vivvie, installed in three rooms in the Gasthaus, a sprawling generous looking wooden house, white painted, window boxes just waiting for red geraniums, and a heavy, gently sloping roof. When they throw open the shutters in the morning it is to the steady drip of melting icicles, snow turning from white to the palest of greens as the grass breaks through, a clear bright sky and lung-fuls of crisp, invigorating air. The lake is a deep, clear blue, speaks of unplumbed depths, and reflects white mountain tops. They spend their virtuous nights encased top and bottom in a massive white feather quilt. There is a beautiful ornamental tiled stove in a corner of their bedroom and the wooden furniture might be rough hewed but it is serviceable, and the table in their living room stands up well enough to the pounding of Sherwyn's typewriter. For breakfast there is fresh baked bread and coffee, butter and plum jam and bright yellow cheese slices made grey with caraway seeds, and eggs – the hens have started laying as the mountain sun grows warmer – for lunch, more bread and even stranger cheeses and apfelstrudel and cream – and for supper goulash, goulash, goulash, mostly beef, but sometimes mutton or goat, onions and potatoes with a dollop of sauerkraut to keep everyone healthy. It is horrible. But Sherwyn, ever practical, has brought oriental spices in the back of the Bentley and teaches both Vivvie and Frau Bieler the landlady how to curry the various meats, using cumin, coriander, turmeric, ginger and garam masala to this end. They have no more complaints.

The Gasthaus Post is run by Herr and Frau Bieler, an amiable pair in their fifties, he the great-great-grandson of the Bieler who built the place. Visitors are rare – mostly government inspectors or public officials, the occasional party of hikers, and the odd antiquarian (usually odd in both senses of the word) following up rumours of a unique wooden Madonna in an old abbey somewhere in these parts. The Bielers deny the existence of such a thing, even to Vivvie who likes to walk up to the old abbey and has actually seen it, large as life, a crude wooden statue of a woman with a serene rather beautiful expression, with dark Asiatic features, a big belly and a cross carved into her forehead, sitting under the only corner of the abbey still with a partial roof – sitting on a marble plinth beneath a delicately painted if weatherworn frescoed dome, or third of a dome. 'But I've seen it,' says Vivvie. 'I like to walk up there. Why do they deny it?'

Sherwyn says it is something to do with the terms of her batty great-grandmother's will, and no doubt the Bielers are under instruction, but from quite whom who is to say? One of the conditions of Vivvie's inheritance is that the statue in the old abbey is not to be sold. Surely Vivvie knows this?

'I know practically nothing about my inheritance,' says Vivvie, who has been putting this moment off for some time. 'Mama likes to keep me in ignorance. But now I am a married woman perhaps we can all have a proper discussion about these tedious financial things and find out why I am the only one to sign cheques some of the time but not all of the time.'

Sherwyn, who finds money anything but tedious, agrees that it would be a good idea indeed. If he can intervene in the management of Vivvie's estates so much the better. Barscherau, he can see, but does not say, could be usefully turned into something of an alternative Chamonix, a fashionable centre for winter sports. But he's on his honeymoon, unerotic though it may be: he is in the middle of a second novel in which his hero Rafe Delgano is turning into more of a languid connoisseur than he had appeared in the first – though still handy with a gun, a knife and a garrotte, the latter to be used of course only on the most bestial of villains – and it absorbs him. Sherwyn is more relaxed and cheerful than he has ever been before – the effect of mountain air and scenery or perhaps just the sudden cessation of the money worries that have plagued him all his life.

'These things can wait, my dear,' he says, amiably, 'until we get back home. Then I promise you I will be a whirlwind of activity and investigation and provide sound financial judgement.'

It is midsummer's day, and finally warm enough for the cows to be let out to grass. The sound of cowbells is thrown from one mountain peak to another, and is the prettiest sound imaginable, the one described by Johanna Spyri when her heroine Heidi moved from the city to the village of Dörfli in the mountains. But Vivvie cannot concentrate. She is suddenly anxious. 'My mother has always seen me as intellectually impaired,' Vivvie says, 'and at the moment I certainly feel that I am. How is this baby to get out? It seems so large and my openings are so small.' She asks Sherwyn if he would drive into Kufstein and take out some books on childbirth from the library.

'They'll be in German,' he warns her. 'Best wait until your mother is here.'

'Yes, but where is she? She said the baby would be born in July and July is nearly here.'

He wonders if in Adela's absence he should suggest Vivvie finds a doctor but decides against it. Childbirth is an entirely natural process – did not African mothers give birth in the fields and go straight back to work again? – and if Adela's plan was to work the fewer witnesses there were to the circumstances of the birth the better. Adela was no doubt sitting out the season in Cannes, or somewhere else agreeably smart and warm, nursing a fake pregnancy.

'Not that I mind,' says Vivvie. 'I may decide to keep the baby. I have grown quite accustomed to it. Indeed, I may have quite strong feelings when the time comes for Mama to take it away. She will only hand it over to nannies to look after, and I could perfectly well do the same. I am not the moral imbecile she thinks I am. A shotgun wedding is not the same as being an unmarried mother. And I have you to look after me, Sherwyn.'

He feels unaccountably pleased at this show of trust.

'Indeed,' she says, 'I daresay the time will come when pregnant brides are two-a-penny.'

'I have no doubt you are right,' he says, temporising, thinking hard, rearranging circumstances in his head. If the girl keeps the baby, what will Rafe Delgano do? 'But this is now and that will be then. Just remember that one can become unaccustomed as easily as accustomed. And that your mother is a very determined woman.'

'I know,' she says sadly.

The gears slip and change again. Vivvie will not be pregnant for ever. A baby must come out of her one way or another, sooner or later, a baby that he had envisaged – as much as he had envisaged anything – as being raised by Adela, and presumed by everyone, including Sir Jeremy himself, to be her husband's offspring. He himself, having been Vivvie's fiancé, and therefore the most likely suspect, would be free of blame. The possibility of an Angel Gabriel wouldn't even arise: Vivien was too unreliable a narrator to be taken seriously. But how complicated all matters to do with the Ripple family turned out to be. None of them believed in simple solutions.

But if Vivvie were to raise the little by-blow herself he would be its legal father, and would be required to look after its welfare and education. He would be expected to meet it mewling and puking over breakfast tables, and later over dinner tables, behaving as if it were his own, and God alone knew what it would grow up to be. It might be all shame and embarrassment as he could see that Vivvie had been to her parents. For all he knew the Angel Gabriel was a black man.

Perhaps she had offered herself to a black man with the same kind of careless abandon she apparently offered her spiritual self to her horse? There had been no talk of rape or violence: in fact there had been very little talk at all. Adela might know more about the putative Angel Gabriel than she was letting on. Vivvie's defence that she had not known she was pregnant until just before her wedding day – she had been told by a servant you could not get pregnant if you did it standing up – had always seemed a little thin. That Adela had not even noticed her daughter's condition was less hard to believe for she noticed only herself. And was it possible that Adela was herself pregnant (what was all that business with Mungo and the ring about?) and meant to emerge one day onto the social scene as the envied young mother of a young child? But no – he was a writer: this was the stuff of fiction, not reality. He went too far; he was in danger of being carried away by his own over-complex plotting. Adela was a good mother making a noble sacrifice to shield her only child from disgrace. That was all there was to it.

But a legal baby! A little lovechild, and none of his own. He was too young. Babies were so ageing. He was not father material, any more than Vivvie was mother material. The sound of the cowbells took on an ominous note. Rafe Delgano would lose his followers if he was seen to father a child. Sometimes, and he is well aware of it, Sherwyn Sexton cannot tell the difference between himself and Rafe Delgano.

'But one does have to ask oneself,' says Sherwyn to Vivvie, 'whether one has the strength and energy to face up to your mother once she has made up her mind.'

'Now I have had a little rest here in the mountains,' says Vivvie, 'I might just have the strength so to do. Let her say and do what she likes. She is not me. I will keep my baby.'

And in thus declaring herself, I am sorry to tell you, she signs her own death warrant. Look, all this happened a long time ago. Sooner or later we all join those who live in the past. And she's only a character in a book.

The Morning Of Thursday July 3rd 1923. The road to Kufstein

A couple of weeks later Sherwyn drove off to the nearest big town – Kufstein – in search of oil and fuel for his car and a book on obstetrics in English, if possible, for Vivvie. He had a strong sense of turning a new page, starting an adventure. He would take it where it led him. The world unfolded before Rafe Delgano, who, unusually for him, had not been to bed with a woman for quite some time. What went on in the bed, according to the manners of the times, tended to fade away into a row of dots rather than give any explicit detail, but the point was generally taken that Rafe acquitted himself manfully and the maiden ended up in love, and docile.

The road to Kufstein was fast and good, remade in 1860 to further the Emperor Franz Joseph's rather nutty military ambitions, and almost deserted save for the occasional lumbering peasant with cart and a group of brave and sportif young persons enjoying a cycling holiday. He built up what he felt was a good head of steam. Then a brand new Audi Type K shocked him by overtaking: Sherwyn let him go. The war was over.

The road wound up to above the tree line, curled down again to blue lakes and green meadows, with their scattering of timbered mountain chalets with red flowering window boxes, brilliant at this time of year, and their stacks of firewood, much diminished, he noticed, after a hard winter. It was all so charming, so peaceful. Questions had been asked in the House, he was aware, on the subject of Austria's possible rearming in defiance of the Reparations Commission, and a suspicious relationship with the Škoda works in Czechoslovakia, but there was no sign of trouble here. He felt elated. London and its politics seemed so far away. Perhaps he should move Delgano out of Morocco and into Austria, land of Sachertorte and apfelstrudel, and statues with fig leaves over male parts, so much more indecent than the real thing? More cake, less sex. Cakes had certainly become very popular in England. But no, Rafe's savoury gourmet self in the exotic spice lands of the Near East was currently much appreciated by readers so why try and mend what was not broken? And the seduction of fair complexioned girls with blue eyes in dirndls and plaits might cause offence, whereas almond eyed, dark skinned murderous beauties were fairer game. Oh, Rita, how he missed Rita. Rita would have to put up with Vivvie's existence as his wife. He was fond and protective of Vivvie, but as one might be of a sister. She would surely recognise that.

Any day soon the delicious, delicate and dangerous Adela would tear herself away from Cannes and turn up in Barscherau. He would make her an egg curry. She would appreciate that. Not too heavy a dish for so light and lithe a person. Vivvie was happy enough with goulash but it could get tiresome. Vivvie would come to her senses after she'd given birth and realise how unfair it was to land him, Sherwyn, with a baby which was none of his own, and hand the responsibility and the cost over to Adela. They would go back to real life in England, he as a famous writer and Vivvie as a respectable young bride, able to ride Greystokes free of encumbrance. In time the secret might out, and the child's big sister be revealed to be its actual mother, as happened often enough in the working classes, if rather more rarely in the upper, but by then time would have blunted the sharp edges of scandal. All would be well. 'Blunting the sharp edges of scandal.' A good phrase, he must not forget it.

A herd of cows was crossing the road. Sherwyn slowed the Bentley and stopped. The cowbells suddenly sounded strange, a warning cacophony rather than a soothing melody. It was probably only the way rock cliffs were throwing back the sound of the bells, but it made him wary. There was something he had overlooked. But what? Something strange was going on. The Bielers seemed pleasant enough but were too like actors in a play. Mein host and his frau, in traditional costume. He jovial and kindly, she bustling and domestic. Peasantry were easily bribed, everyone knew. But why? To keep quiet about who gave birth to whom, and where? Possible. And what role did Courtney and Baum play? They presented themselves as old and decrepit but they were quite capable of chicanery. Sherwyn must be careful. He must warn Vivvie. She might have more of a fight on her hands than one thought. Strange how a chap could get to feel so protective of a small, heaving lump beneath a swelling belly, hammering with tiny feet and hands to get out. Not the little one's fault about the Angel Gabriel. In truth he, Sherwyn, rather enjoyed his current role as Joseph. Writers were all Josephs in spirit, as he might claim in his autobiography one day, shepherding dark truths to the light of day. Priests were beginning to fail in their role as moral arbiters to the outside world, scientists had already failed – no matter what

H.G. Wells had to say on the subject: look at the aerial bombardment they had made possible – and writers would have to take their place.

The stream of cows reached the track on the other side of the road and the cowbells sounded perfectly normal again. All these were the fears of an over-active imagination and the effect of sound waves bouncing back and forth between rock walls. The cutting ended, the valley road ran beside the river and he was in Kufstein, where there was a newsagent, a railway station, a cathedral, a library, lots of people, a few of them in regional dress, and an intentness and busyness which quite shocked his eyes.

Sherwyn found a week-old copy of the *Times*, fuel enough in cans at the back of the Fachgeschäft to satisfy the Bentley, though the store keeper grumbled at so heavy and sudden a loss of his stock – and he was even able to buy a new dipstick for an Audi Type K which fitted the Bentley well enough. The tip had snapped off his the last time he'd been measuring petrol. He could find no medical books in English in library or bookshop, though the girl in the library ran after him to tell him in her charming broken English accent that there was an English doctor practising in a village called Kiefersfelden just across the border in Germany who might be able to help him.

He thought the girl – she said her name was Greta – dimpled and smiled up at him in such an interested and interesting way that she might be up for something more intimate than a mere conversation about the existence of medical books. She was tiny and had the thickest of thick yellow plaits on each side of her pretty little head, and her smocked dirndl was lower cut than anything English girls dared wear. Perhaps he was altogether wrong about the kind of girl fiction readers appreciated. At any rate the writer owes it to himself, and indeed his readers, to follow opportunities through without fear or favour to see where they might lead. He must take the risk in order that others may lead quiet lives. He was about to ask Greta to step inside the Bentley and show him the way to Kiefersfelden but a stern lady in black called her back into the library, and Greta sighed and shrugged and went back to her work. Sherwyn's faith in humanity and his own special place in it dipped. Fate, which had begun the day promising so much, had changed her mind and turned her back on him.

Lunchtime, Thursday July 3rd 1923. Kiefersfelden

But, as it turned out, fate was only teasing and it was as well that Greta was not beside him, for when he arrived in Kiefersfelden he ran into Adela. It was a shock. His grasp on reality, never strong, faltered, and, some might say, failed. It was as if he had started a new chapter in the novel of his life. She was leaning against the wall of an elaborately decorated Gasthof, all wooden shutters, Lüftlmalerei and geraniums, smoking a pink Sobranie from a long ivory holder. Smoke curled above her head and drifted into vast pale blue skies. Sherwyn brought the Bentley to an abrupt halt, with a squeal of brakes there was no-one else around to hear, for the village seemed deserted. Only a couple of hens ran squawking for safety. They would have to become accustomed to the automobile age, or suffer death. He managed to think this, a Rafe Delgano thought which he must remember to use when convenient, even as he contemplated her reality, or lack of it.

Sherwyn stepped out of the Bentley. He was wearing his long brown leather coat with the silver buckle which Vivvie so admired. 'It makes you look like a romantic hero,' she had once said and now he wore it whenever he could. The morning air was crisp and sharp and the mountain shadows deep and it felt the right thing for a chap to wear.

Adela wore a mink coat, bulky round the shoulders but falling down to slender ankles. It was colourless: she seemed to be hiding inside it, as if she were some tiny furry Alpine creature evading predators. Her pale hair was tied up in a sweetly disordered knot on the top of her head, so that fetching tendrils fell around her brow. She smiled up at him, as so few women could. She was usefully tiny. Her lips were sweet but her teeth were thin and sharp. He had a vision of Vivvie's teeth, strong, solid and reassuring, but preferred Adela's.

'Adela, it can only be you! A pink Sobranie. But why, how? This is the ends of the earth.'

'I'm your mother-in-law, darling, and mother-to-be of your child. Why should I not be here? And what have you done with poor Vivvie?'

'Safe at home in Barscherau. Her village.'

'Our village, darling. She must be very near her time, Sherwyn. Should you leave her alone?'

'I am looking for books on obstetrics, as it happens. And an English doctor by the name of Harold Walker.'

'Ah, dear Harry! But how clever of you to have searched him out! One simply has to have an English doctor when in foreign parts. Look at what happened to poor Victoria, Crown Princess of Prussia.'

'What did,' he asked crossly, 'if it's relevant?'

'Ah, so relevant. They made her have German doctors, not English, for the royal birth, which was why the Kaiser was born with a withered arm and the whole world went to war. I'm so glad to see you, darling. We can go all go together in a proper car: I expect all Harry has is a pony and trap. We don't want poor Vivvie to face the event alone.'

It seemed that Adela had taken the train from Munich to Kufstein in search of an English doctor for Vivvie's delivery – 'I *care*, darling, I *care*. She is my only daughter' – but found the town to be intolerably provincial and without charm – 'perhaps you haven't noticed, darling, but then you are on honeymoon!' She was laughing at him. He hated her. 'I ran the English doctor to ground here in Keifersfelden – such impossible names they have here – but such a darling man, a real scholar, he reminds me of Sir Jeremy – and he found me this divine Gasthof across the border, where they make their apfelstrudel with butter not lard and the Eintopf is quite bearable, beef instead of goat, and real beds, not feather swamps in cupboards. So I stayed. But it will never be home. And how is dear Vivvie bearing up?'

'Perfectly well,' he said. He hoped he spoke coldly enough for Adela to notice. How had Vivvie survived her mother?

'Of course she is. Strong as a horse. Indeed, I sometimes I think she is a horse. Sir Jeremy insisted on being present at the lying in, as if he was in some kind of foaling box. I'm sure that's why Vivvie turned out the way she did. Strong of neck and fetlock, or whatever it is that horses have. And such good childbearing hips. But impossible to dress, impossible, no matter how much one spent. You're not going to demand to be present, I hope, Sherwyn.'

'Good God, no. Women's work.' The idea horrified him. Blood and gore. One would rather not think about it. Adela prattled on, quite mad, more herself than he remembered, but then she was outside her normal setting, and he had grown accustomed to peaceful peasant ways, a slow rural life. She was probably always like this, self obsessed, butterfly minded, languidly vicious, and he just hadn't noticed. Poor Vivvie. But the baby had to go, even into the clutches of this fiend in angel form. What other choice was there?

The page turned. They were in the Bentley in search of Dr Walker, a quarter of a mile up the rutted track to Madron, when she complained of heat and shrugged off her mink. It was impossible not to notice that her arms and shoulders were translucent and slim, and that the little hands were perfectly manicured – the nails and the lipstick brightest red, matching the common geraniums in the window boxes, a touch of vulgarity that seemed almost deliberate, a kind of 'take me, I'm anyone's' gesture in defiance of all propriety, as a bad girl would suddenly bare her breast, presenting the lure of the unattainable suddenly attainable. Another good Delgano phrase he must remember to remember. When the hand crept up under his romantic hero coat and pressed its fingers gently against his trousered parts, as Vivvie described them, they twitched in automatic response. Sherwyn was outraged, but kept on driving as if nothing had happened. But it had. A new paragraph had begun. Forget Delgano, he suddenly knew what it was to be Mungo, thus no doubt so assailed. He, Sherwyn, was just one of many. She was a predator, fearsome: the fur coat was her wolf's clothing. He was the lamb, the helpless little furry thing. He was not accustomed to it. He was usually the predator: the one who pounced on the unwary. He brushed away her hand and Adela laughed, her little trilling superior laugh.

'I know, darling,' she said. 'An outrage! Your own mother-in-law, a nymphomaniac. But you started it. You fathered a baby on my innocent child.'

Another shock. He had got so used to assuming that the Angel Gabriel, or some equivalent, had done the fathering, he had quite forgotten that as he had been Vivvie's fiancé he would be held responsible for all eventualities. In the circles in which Vivvie moved, a shot gun wedding suggested an unseemly carelessness, a passionate intensity of the kind married adulterers engaged in; not romantic young lovers, who were all sighs and stolen kisses. The Thames, in living memory, floated with the bodies of shamed girls. And what did she mean, that he 'started it'? He remembered vaguely being drunk when he first encountered her at some ridiculous office party, all detail lost in the mists of time. But 'started it'? Vivvie had 'started it', by proposing to him in the first place. He should have known better than to listen. The Ripple women were all mad. But here he was, married and trapped, stuck up a mountainside with two of them, one improbably enormous and refusing sexual congress, one improbably tiny and propositioning him, the two of them forcing him into a fictional role over which he seemed to have no control and certainly had no understanding. How could it possibly benefit Adela to be behaving as she was? Drugs? Possibly. But that was a plot point too far. The hand was back, exploring. What would Delgano do? He laughed aloud. A whole flurry of dot, dot, dots, no doubt, to spare the blushes of sensitive readers. Everyone knew, nobody said: what an odd world it was. 'Don't be bitter, darling, I do so love this coat. Such soft, fine leather. It's all perfectly simple. Vivvie is to have a little brother or sister, not a son or daughter, and will share an inheritance – morally mine, in any case – which I can control for another twenty years. Vivvie, as you must understand by now, is incapable of managing money. Someone has to develop Barscherau and you're so busy with your fiction.'

As a plot point it seemed implausibly thin but the little soft mouth with its little sharp teeth followed where the hand had led and Delgano's parts, unleashed, sprang to life to meet it. Sherwyn pulled in to the side of the road.

Teatime, Thursday July 3rd 1923. Kiefersfelden

What a busy day, and not over yet! Dr Walker's home, once found, was a chalet on the edge of the village. The window boxes needed watering, the woodstack replenishing, the shabby shutters repainting, and the skinny guard dog, leaping and noisy at the end of its chain, could have done with feeding. The doctor had no books on obstetrics in English, let alone German. He apologised if he was still in his dressing gown and slippers but they had taken him unawares: he had a deadline to meet. He was writing a book on the uses and abuses of clinical spinal anaesthesia for Ripple & Co's new medical list. Adela said yes, she knew that, he was one of her husband's band of writers: indeed, indeed, she had once met him, it must have been in 1903, on Monte Verità, when she had briefly been with the Ascona community.

'Good Lord,' said Dr Walker. 'You!' and he sat down abruptly. He gazed at Adela with what Delgano could only describe as lascivious eyes, while the young Mrs Walker – a plump blonde little thing – ran round serving coffee with whipped cream and large slices of Sachertorte from none too clean porcelain cups and saucers. At least three little children all with runny noses ran about the room, along with cats, dogs and hens, stirring up books, papers, crumbs and toys. The doctor – at least fifty, Sherwyn reckoned, and safely unappealing, with balding hair, broken glasses and dandruff – explained he had been studying neurology at the Preyer Institute of Physiology at Jena – 'the Germans are so far ahead of the English when it comes to pain relief' – when he'd met and married little nurse Maria from the Tyrol, and now lived in happy domesticity in the shade of Madron Peak, finishing his book. He no longer practised medicine on moral grounds; what was doctoring but a hidden conspiracy against humanity, a plot to ensure the fittest could not survive?

Sherwyn thought the safest thing to do was cut and run; the doctor, though he might have been to a good school, was a recusant non-conformist and spiritual failure too mentally wayward to be trusted with the little *bâtard*'s delivery. A local doctor or midwife would be a better bet. But Adela took no notice of Sherwyn's nods and winks towards the exit and seemed delighted with the doctor – how lucky she was to have found so highly qualified, charming and experienced a doctor in so unlikely a place, and an old friend of her husband's at that, and entreated him to attend Vivvie in the hour of her need, and so on and so on. The doctor seemed hypnotised. Sherwyn marvelled. The little mouth seemed to have so many uses.

Still the doctor hesitated. They were right to look out a physician. A midwife could not meet the needs of the woman in labour.

'The mother wants to please the doctor, who is the father figure, and so relaxes: the midwife represents the mother, with whom she is in competition. And so she tenses.' Dr Walker went on to say that there were two pathways to pain: the physical and the emotional. The spinal injection blocked the physical pathway, but it was the doctor's presence that soothed the mother: thus suffering was halved. 'But it's twenty years since I myself have attended a delivery. Things can go wrong.'

It occurred to Sherwyn that the good doctor had been struck off for incompetence or malpractice or both, which was why he was hiding here in Kiefersfelden, but Adela was determined to get her way. She let it be known that Ripple & Co were eagerly awaiting Dr Walker's study on the perils of spinal anaesthesia, undoubtedly a timely and seminal work. The doctor perked up a little: so interesting an area, so little understood! He was a twilight sleep man himself – scopolamine and morphine induced amnesia, so mothers remembered nothing at all about the experience – though they had to be strapped down during labour: they struggled and shrieked so – but times had moved on. Hypno-anaesthesia was seen as old fashioned, but studies proved it safest of all. Was their daughter easily suggestible? He peered at his visitors through spectacles which hung from one arm and seemed not to have been cleaned or wiped lately.
'Not that I'd noticed,' said Adela. 'If I told her to do something she'd always do the opposite. Let's stick to the twilight sleep.'

Sherwyn thought that, on the contrary, Vivvie was extremely suggestible – why else the Angel Gabriel? – but he held his tongue. Contradiction seemed impossible. Adela's mink coat gleamed and shone in the little room, her tiny red tipped fingers fluttered. The doctor himself seemed mesmerised. Maria suddenly leapt to her feet and ran round the room after her children, wiping their noses with savage hands still sticky from Sachertorte. Hens squawked, cats squealed, dogs bared their teeth, dead flowers drooped across small windows and blocked the light. The Alpine paradise suddenly looked and sounded if not like hell, like purgatory. The doctor looked as if he was beginning to think so too. Perhaps his imagined sensual heaven with young Maria was not working out as he had hoped. He capitulated. Of course he would attend to Vivvie.

Notes were taken and arrangements were made. Adela would send a telegram the moment Vivvie went into labour. Dr Walker would be notified within the hour, and would set out in his pony and trap for Barscherau. Adela was not to worry her angelic little head. The doctor had never known a woman deliver in less than six hours and he would be there within three. Maria opened her mouth to protest but shut it again, unwilling to risk disturbance of the domestic peace in which her husband's memory would conflict with hers. Sherwyn suggested he simply drove Vivvie into the public hospital in Kufstein for the birth but Adela said such hospitals were not safe places: they were full of germs and 'ordinary people'. Dr Walker agreed, and Sherwyn found himself overruled.

He was only a man: what could he, Delgano, know about these female matters? He would leave it to those who did. He was happy to be back in the Bentley with Adela. She was so certain, so, well, upper class. She behaved as if the incident in the car had not happened, which seemed to Delgano to be the height of aristocratic sophistication. She was, after all, the niece of an Earl, Delgano was the son of a market trader. Unlike most detectives in literature – Lupin, Sherlock Holmes, Lord Peter Wimsey – he had been to board and grammar school, and was the more easily socially abashed – though seldom sexually. Readers liked him the more for it. He was a wounded class hero. Delgano belonged to the future, as Sir Jeremy never tired of saying; was not this the age of the common man, whether worker by hand or brain? When it came to virility at least, an unshaven working class had the edge on a wrung out, neurotic bourgeoisie, and Delgano typified it, glorified it.

Adela prattled on about how lucky Vivvie was to have a mother who had tracked down so accomplished a doctor to attend her in the hour of her need. Delgano did not quarrel with her. She even enquired how Sherwyn was getting on with the book, and it took Delgano a second or so to remember who exactly this Sherwyn was. When they arrived back at the Gasthof, he watched her lips as she asked:
'So will you stay the night, darling? Such a successful day! One really needs to celebrate.'

Sherwyn returned long enough to drive out Delgano – both of them, he decided, were suffering from some kind of shell shock: what Mungo would call, after Freud, a dissociative hysterical state – to decide that neither could be held responsible for their actions. Did Adela expect him to climb up to her window under cover of darkness? It would be thorny – he might fall. He certainly could not go straight to her bedroom – horrified peasantry would bar the way. Rafe Delgano would scatter them, biffing and bashing, on his relentless way to the three dots of celebration. But he was Sherwyn: he was the writer, not the actor. He hesitated.

'Oh come on, darling.' The little fingers tugged at his leather sleeve. 'What one starts one must carry to completion. Don't worry about Vivvie. She's not the kind to wait up.' Sherwyn followed. He would not be being disloyal to Vivvie: she had given him his freedom, even though she had probably not envisaged him being free with her mother. And after all he was a writer, and a writer must be true to his public, and see all experiences through to the end, even though enjoyed by Delgano's body, not his own. He, Sherwyn, would not have succumbed to Adela's blandishments so easily. There would have been no twitching of parts.

The respectable peasantry looked inclined to bar the way as Sherwyn tried to follow Adela upstairs, mink coat and Bentley notwithstanding – a small crowd had gathered outside to admire it – but Adela quickly explained that this was her husband, Sir Jeremy Ripple, who would be staying overnight before going on ahead to visit their daughter in Barscherau, and apologies were many and varied. It was a relief to Sherwyn to see an actual bed with sheets and blankets, and not the pile of down and feathers in a cupboard where he had grown accustomed to sleeping with Vivvie. Adela had no intention of sleeping. She was little and tiny but remarkably lithe for her age: she made no sound, had no conversation, offered no directions. He could have been Delgano, could have been Sherwyn, could have been Sir Jeremy himself, it probably made no difference to Adela. Perhaps that was what nymphomania was, a *furor uterinus*, accompanied by an absence of emotion. One day, one day, when all this was over, he would get back to Rita. Only he could see that it would never be over, he was married to Vivvie, had slept with his mother-in-law in his father-in-law's name; there would be no end to it. He was in Adela's power for ever, a secret that could always be told when it suited her to tell it. He plunged on and on, but never came. The mouth had been the best of it.

He left the bed as Delgano, sleek and confident, leaving Adela still asleep.

'Frühstück, Herr Ripple? Kaffe? Wurst? Strudel?' asked the landlord's daughter. He accepted coffee – more whipped cream – and drove back to Barscherau before Adela woke. A hen had chosen to sleep in the car overnight, fluttering in through an open window no doubt. It objected vigorously to its ejection and Sherwyn had to remove dust and dung before he could drive off. There was no sign of Delgano. Sherwyn drove home as himself, grateful to occupy a single body and mind, anxious about Vivvie, anxious about impossible plot twists he had apparently brought upon himself.

Friday July 4th 1923. Barscherau

Sherwyn came home not with medical books but with news that he had encountered Adela, and had not been home when expected because of having to spend the night in Kufstein waiting for a delivery of fuel from Munich. Vivvie imagined he had probably spent the night with some dirndled girl of easy virtue but that did not concern her. Wives had a right to sexual jealousy: platonic lovers – for this was how she was beginning to see herself and Sherwyn – did not. She had begun to see how painful human relationships could be: she had strong feelings about the baby and it was not yet even a human. What would she feel like when it burst upon the world? Burst was probably an unfortunate word: it was what she feared she was about to do. She had once seen a mare from Greystokes' harem give birth, and the foal stuck a leg out of the mother and nothing happened, and nothing happened and then the rest of it exploded out as the mother's flanks seemed to implode. The foal lay there for a little and then staggered to its feet and everyone watching cheered. The mare looked behind her, seemed interested but oddly impassive, as if it was all beyond her. Vivvie supposed you just let it happen, and Nature knew best.

She'd had a dream in which a little boy's leg stuck out of her for a bit and then the baby fell out, and the child – a cheery little fellow with fair curly hair; he must have been about three – staggered to his feet and ran about. Vivvie had felt very proud.

It was the prospect of Adela's arrival – in the next day or two, Sherwyn said – that disturbed Vivvie. She should be happy to see her mother again but she found she was not. Indeed, the very thought of her made Vivvie feel awkward, unnaturally large and unmanoeuvrable, like some uneasy Mount Everest plonked in the way to annoy normal people. Her mother moved and thought so lightly and quickly and despised so much: she was bound to turn up and say the wrong thing to Frau Bieler, whom Vivvie now liked and depended upon. Adela would sneer at the poor woman, probably openly, for her broad waist, the bare strong arms, the full skirt, the puffed sleeves, and the unstylish white smocked bib she always wore. 'Ignorant peasantry,' her mother would be quite capable of muttering, but loud enough to be heard, when throwing out the bilberry infusion and horse chestnut paste that Frau Bieler had so carefully made up for Vivvie's varicose veins, and worked so well. And it seemed a doctor from England was to come and help with the 'delivery' – as if the baby was something evil: '*Dear God, deliver us from evil*' – which was absurd, since Frau Bieler had brought fourteen of her grandchildren into the world.

As for handing her own baby over to Adela, the more she thought about it, the less she liked it. Adela would only hand over his care to a nurse. It was going to be a boy she was sure of it; she could almost hear Greystokes lifting his nose and whinnying *boy, boy, boy* – and the Angel Gabriel was not likely to be the agent of someone who would beget a girl. Vivvie acknowledged that she was not a very practical person and might not be a fit mother for a baby boy, but if she were to stay where she was Frau Bieler would probably agree to do the child rearing and Vivvie could stay where she was, amongst the mountains and the geraniums and the feather beds, breathing God's fresh air and not London smogs or Sussex fogs. After all, she had money of her own – Sherwyn had promised to look into that side of things – and some of the Barscherau inhabitants even curtsied as she went by. She could do as she liked – so long as her mother didn't come along and argue her out of it.

And her poor husband, Sherwyn, working so hard to finish his novel. Adela was bound to upset him as well. Sherwyn behaved so much better when he has being admired than when he felt others were being critical. Probably most men were the same. She had been so peaceful and happy and comfortable with Sherwyn: and now a shadow was falling over them all, deep and black, as when the sun goes down behind Mount Untersberg and the ravens swarm and the dangerous little dwarves come out. They pretend to be your friends but they're not. Vivvie shivered, suddenly cold. But Frau Bieler came in all excited because her Ladyship Adela was coming at last, *die glamouröse Dame!*

That night, when she and Sherwyn had supper together, it seemed to her he had somehow changed, though she could not quite put her finger on what it was. He picked at the Schweinebraten with Knödel and cabbage salad of which Frau Bieler was so proud, as if it was somehow not quite good enough, and even pushed it aside so Vivvie had to finish it for him. She asked him if anything was the matter but he said no, he was just rather tired, and then perked up and read her what he had been writing during the day. He wondered if it went too far for contemporary tastes and Vivvie said it certainly did. Sherwyn's readers did not want to know exactly what went on behind the door after Delgano closed it – a row of little dots was enough for her, and surely everyone else. He didn't want to find his work consigned to the forbidden erotica rooms of the British Library, did he? Where on earth did he get all these horrid ideas from?

Sherwyn looked at Vivvie when she said this as if she were some kind of enemy. But why ask her if he did not want her to tell him? And after supper in front of the fire Sherwyn collapsed again and stared into space. He seemed to her to be exuding a different kind of energy and that energy was perverse, and depressed. He no longer looked her in the eye. It was something he had said to her mother, or her mother to him, probably about the baby. Whatever it was, Sherwyn was no longer good father Joseph to Vivvie's Mary. So mothers destroyed one's dreams.

Saturday July 5th 1923. Barscherau

On Friday night Sherwyn slept like a log and Vivvie very badly. Unplaceable but implacable strains and pains ran up and down her body. She would have tossed and turned all night only she couldn't: she was too heavy. The baby held her pinned in her middle as if she were a dead butterfly in a display case. She longed to struggle up like a newborn foal finding its legs but she was too weighed down, like a butterfly drenched in a rain storm. A vulgar cabbage white, she thought, nothing special. Nothing collectable, or only by cruel schoolboys, the kind who liked to tear the wings off flies. She would never be compared to the beautiful wood white or the delicate green veined Orpona, as her mother sometimes was. A thing of rarity and delicacy. Her father often spoke of the proletarian butterflies who were going to emerge from peasant chrysalises, but she didn't see it happening to the Bielers and rather hoped it never did, though according to Sherwyn, Vienna was now known as red Vienna, and part of the Comintern, and any time now even the Bielers would be singing *The Red Flag*. Another reason, Sherwyn said, not to bring Delgano to Germany, but to keep him in Morocco, currying sheep's eyes. She fell asleep, and when she woke Sherwyn had gone.

Frau Bieler said Sherwyn had left early for the Fachgeschäft in Kufstein to collect a new dipstick for the Bentley. No, he had not said when he would be back. Vivvie remembered well enough Sherwyn mentioning that he had managed to buy a new one two days before, designed for the new Audi much esteemed on these parts; they had even been overtaken by one on the road to Kufstein – 'the advantage of a militaristic past: the roads are always good'! – but suitable for a Bentley, and she said as much to Frau Bieler. She then wished she had not. It smacked of disloyalty, and was none of her business where Sherwyn had gone. She had given him his freedom and must stand by it. She had suspected she was pregnant when she married him: she deserved her punishment, and punishment it was. Yesterday's high spirits had oozed away: they belonged to some other person. Sherwyn was no longer Joseph. Adela was welcome to the baby, her shame and disgrace, the uncomfortable, unwelcome lump, more than welcome. How could she have even dreamed otherwise? She would concentrate henceforth on horses. She understood horses. Babies she did not, let alone men.

'Men will be men,' said Frau Bieler, in English, coming back to bring Vivvie coffee and whipped cream. 'Not to be depended on.' Both women by now had a smattering of the other's language. 'You are near your time. It happens. The dipping of the stick.'

What could the woman possibly be implying? A dipstick was a simple dipstick. They broke. And *her time, her time*. It was terrifying, her 'time'. Frau Bieler's comments were unnecessary and crude. And if it was her time, why wasn't her mother here, looking after her? Where could she be? Vivvie pushed away the coffee – she felt sick – and for some reason complained that the room was dirty and the windows needed cleaning. It wasn't in her nature to complain. She could see she was behaving very oddly but she couldn't help herself. Vivvie was put in mind of her tabby cat Tibbles, who when she was about to have kittens, acted as if she were possessed, ignoring her cat basket and insisting on making a home in Adela's lingerie drawer, all silks and scents and lace and it was all lick, lick, lick until Adela found her and picked Tibbles up by the scruff of her neck and flung her out of the room. Fortunately Frau Bieler did not take offence but smiled indulgently, took away the coffee and brought Vivvie a bucket of hot soapy water and a cloth.

Vivvie cleaned the windows as best she could, hoping that sanity would return. It seemed very important suddenly that the windows sparkled. But cleaning? She did not normally clean – others did that. When she got back home she would ask Mungo to what extent he agreed with Freud that pregnant women were consumed by penis envy – wasn't it possible that men were equally consumed by womb envy? – and that this ended up in a lot of unnecessary and compulsive activity and human distress. Men took to women to feel better, while women took to cleaning. If only men and women could be rational! Her mind seemed to be working very slowly. It was as if Sherwyn hadn't unlocked the Bentley brake properly and the wheels were having difficulty turning round. Then she remembered that Mungo knew nothing of the pregnancy, just that she and Sherwyn were on an extended honeymoon in the Alps, and if anyone was pregnant it was Adela, so she'd better stay quiet. How difficult life was, Heaven alone knew, but how clean and shiny the windows. She was surprised when there was a whoosh and the contents of the bucket ended up on Frau Bieler's wooden floor. Then she realised the bucket was still full and the water must have come from inside her. Her knickers were sopping wet. She shrieked aloud. She was making a terrible mess. She was coming to bits. She was bursting. And she wanted her mother.

Frau Bieler came running, looked and called out so everyone could hear, '*Mein Gott! Das Fruchtwasser abgegangen!*' So one had waters, and they broke. If only one had at hand the medical books she had instructed Sherwyn to find. Well, Vivvie would make do with Frau Bieler as midwife. Frau Bieler had delivered fourteen of her own grandchildren and not lost a single one. Childbirth was an entirely natural process and it seemed that, was one to take the pregnant Tibbles as an example, one could be guided by instinct. She had a pain. It was like a ribbon tightening round her midriff, starting in her back and moving round to her front. At least she wasn't trying to have her baby in Adela's lingerie drawer. Vivvie felt quite sane again. It was a great relief. Whatever happened, she would not give her baby away.

The Morning Of Saturday July 5th 1923. The Road To Keifersfelden

And so it was that Vivvie came to give birth to twin girls. Sherwyn was with Adela at the time, posing as Sir Jeremy Ripple. He had gone into Kufstein to buy yet another dipstick – the tip had snapped off at once – it must be a major failing with all these big tourers – but on the way Delgano murmured in his ear that there could be no harm in dropping by on Adela, if only to dissuade her from submitting Vivvie to the eccentric and none too clean Dr Walker's care, and even perhaps to warn her that Vivvie was having second thoughts about giving the baby away. Not, Delgano suggested, that that was necessarily a good idea. Adela might be right and Vivvie incapable of sensible motherhood. She was a very strange girl, emotionally retarded in some way, seeming in denial of her own pregnancy, going so far as to attribute it to some vague supernatural being, talked him into marrying her and then deliberately foisted a little bastard upon him.

'What should I have done?' Sherwyn asked.

'Signed the contract,' said Delgano. 'Then run. Run like the devil, and never looked back! Now look what you've got yourself into. And this business with the mother-in-law, madness, but she's there waiting I bet, all pink and perfect and having breakfast in bed, so you might as well.'

At which point Sherwyn took a left turn to Keifersfelden. If Vivvie had reacted better when he'd read his work aloud to her the night before he might have gone straight on to Kufstein and purchased the new dipstick. But she hadn't reassured him at all, just seemed rather cold and disapproving. It wasn't her kind of thing, he could see, but she was hopelessly bourgeois. His mind was doing its overexcited thing again; click, click. Cogs were moving, shifting, falling into place.

There was a way out, Delgano was suggesting, there always was. Get the baby out of the way, and then behave so badly that Vivvie had no choice but to divorce him. He could afford it – the prenuptial settlement was generous – how anxious the family must have been to take Vivvie off their hands! And anyway Sherwyn would by then be so far into his publishing career he would have no further need of Ripple & Co any more. Delgano, his creation, was talking sense, Sherwyn realised. A writer arrived at the truth through his own characters.

As Delgano had predicted, Adela succumbed to the pleasures she had no hesitation in offering. Men and women were alike, as Sherwyn was later to write, in that the more they had the more they wanted. He added 'Use it, or lose it' but struck that out. Too crude, too vulgar. That was in his 1946 book *Delgano Lets Live*. Delgano, like his writer, had moved to Paris in 1942, as an undercover restaurateur working for SOE, famous for his pâtisserie.

Sherwyn had started writing as a neutral, anonymous observer of life, not as one who had any special or painful experience of it. Most writers between the wars, before the cult of personality, were recognised only as a familiar (if you were lucky) name on the spine of a novel. To expose anything too emotional, let alone personal, in one's writing was unliterary, distasteful and shaming. Women's stuff. The stiff upper lip ruled. After World War II everything changed: the writer became valued for the degree to which he was prepared to expose his emotions and his knowledge of the indecorous. Sherwyn was one of the first to abandon three dots and open the bedroom door. In the mind of the reader, Delgano and Sherwyn quickly became one. And after the publication of Mungo's *Vice Rewarded* Sherwyn saw no reason that it should be otherwise. The more he was Delgano the tall lover, the culinary connoisseur, the less Sherwyn the dwarf, the better. Sherwyn hoped to reclaim himself in time as a literary rather than a commercial writer – though as it happened he never got round to writing the great novel or memoir which would have established himself as such. It had begun to seem too much like hard work.

Anyway. Or alternatively, so it goes.

Later That Morning. Barscherau

It was a swift and easy birth. Frau Bieler and her daughter Greta acted, perforce, as midwives. Vivvie lay on the kitchen table with a couple of pillows. They gave her brandy to keep her cheerful and took some themselves to give them courage. They congratulated themselves that at least no doctor from the town had arrived on the scene. Such a one had come up from Kufstein a year or so back to assist at a neighbour's delivery but had injected her with the fashionable potion for twilight sleep, and her screams had been heard down the street, and the next day her wrists were raw where she had struggled against the cuffs. But at least she had no memory of the occasion at all. Which was all right for her which they supposed was something. But not for the neighbours or her poor husband.

They talked while they worked. They hoped the baby would be a boy – it didn't matter much what a boy looked like. It mattered a lot for a girl. Sherwyn was a good-looking man in spite of being on the short side so they reckoned Vivvie must be quite wealthy for it not to matter.

Frau Bieler said they behaved in bed like brother and sister and outside it as well. It was possible Herr Sherwyn was not the baby's father. Greta said the Burgomeister at Kufstein had said they were not to pass on rumours, hadn't the cheque for the booking been issued by the same London lawyers to whom everyone in the locality paid their land dues? Frau Bieler said she didn't care what the Burgomeister said.

They wondered why the English milady, who had been meant to arrive with the young couple, had not turned up to be with her pregnant daughter when the time came, and why the English husband with the big car had left her alone at such a time, but who knew how the minds of foreigners worked? They had paid good money for their quarters, been perfectly pleasant, and caused no trouble, at least until now. The Bielers would charge extra for soiled sheets and towels.

Vivvie smiled when she could and groaned when she couldn't, and thought it was like her monthly pains but rather more so. They kept putting brandy to her lips and an infusion of angelica root and she sipped and let the women's voices pass over her. There was a slight problem when the head wanted to come through and couldn't, but Vivvie's body, which seemed to have very little to do with her any more, decided to thrust it out, and did. The women seemed very excited and pleased. A little girl, perfectly formed. Vivvie asked what she was called before falling asleep. Angelica infusion can be quite strong.

'Stella,' said Frau Bieler, surprised, but pleased enough to be asked. In England, it seemed, the midwife named the baby. Stella meant star. The baby was a lovely little thing, its head quite unsquashed, as could happen if a labour was quick. The afterbirth slipped out and was wrapped in paper and burned. The baby was washed, swaddled and put to the breast. Frau Bieler and Greta had coffee and cake.

Vivvie woke and groaned again and Greta checked to make sure all was well. Then she cried out in alarm. An infant foot had appeared from between the massive thighs. Twins, and this one a breech birth. Greta ran round and called in Frau Auerbach from next door to help. They gave Vivvie more infusion from the angelica root potion. Frau Auerbach swore by Frauenmantel and Alraun or mandrake, so they boiled some of that as well.

A thigh appeared. Vivvie shrieked. Nothing happened. Vivvie fainted and couldn't push. Greta said, 'I've done this with goats,' put an arm in and pulled, but not too hard so as to break anything. Another leg burst out and then the body – a girl – and finally the head. A really large baby. Twins they might be, but not identical. This one even played dead for an anxious moment – probably the effects of the mandragora root, which can render a person sleepy – then breathed, lived, opened its mouth and announced its arrival with a cry of rage.

Frau Auerbach was given the privilege of naming the newcomer and chose to call her Mallory, a name which signifies unfortunate. Because this she was. Mallory too was washed, swaddled and put to the breast, but tended to bite while she sucked, having been born with one front tooth already formed. Stella sucked easily, sweetly. Mallory never elicited the same cries of enthusiasm as Stella. She did not smile for quite some weeks, unlike the elegantly formed Stella, and kept her initially squashed head and frowning brow for quite some time. But at least both babies were born alive and healthy, and both were to live into the next century. Mallory was always to have a slight limp because her swaddling, done by Frau Auerbach in the Alpine fashion – swaddling prevents the infant, accustomed to the confines of the womb, from startling itself by its own sudden movements – was a little too tight and resulted in a degree of hip dysplasia. Indeed, she was so busy doing it she did not realise that part of Mallory's afterbirth remained in Vivvie's womb. None of these women, after all, were trained in any way.

Frau Bieler swaddled Stella, and did it more loosely and so the baby was to walk easily and dance freely all her life.

When in later life Stella consulted their horoscopes (how Mallory sneered) she came back and told her sister that they were Gemini butterflies. Mercury in Gemini in the first house. 'Oh,' said Mallory, 'then I suppose I'm the vulgar cabbage white and you're the lovely wood white.' They were both in their twenties at the time and living in what the army had left them of Dilberne Court. The cabbage white was wreaking havoc in the vegetable garden. The wood white could turn Dilberne woods on a June evening into a shimmering, magic grotto. Dark green shadows and a host of pale lacy dancers. Mallory spoke without bitterness. Like her mother, she was brave in facing harsh truths. She accepted the injustice to which we are all born. That's what comes of having your transiting moon making a square to the planet Pluto – like mother, like child – if that's the kind of thing you believe in. Your author half does, if only because it comes in so useful when writing novels.

Anyway. On, on. Poor Vivvie has to die, and all Adela's fault.

Sunday Morning, July 6th 1923. Barscherau

The Bentley pulled up outside the Gasthaus Post the next morning, with Adela in her mink in the passenger seat, and Dr Walker and three of Adela's cases in the back. Another five filled the boot, which male Bentley owners complained was unnecessarily large but women passengers seldom did. The suitcases were calf skin and from Aspinal. Adela did not travel light. Sherwyn had hoped to get back to Vivvie by Saturday evening but one way and another there had been delays. Adela had decided she might as well move in with the young couple in Barscherau since the food was reasonable, and the Keifersfelden landlady was beginning to look at her oddly – heaven knew why – and Dr Walker must take a preliminary look at Vivvie and bring up his twilight sleep equipment and leave it – '*a special bed with straps and cuffs, why? A simple birth! But she supposed he knew what he was doing!*' so they might as well take the good doctor along for the consultation, and perhaps dear Sherwyn wouldn't mind dropping him back afterwards and she could have a good chin-wag with Vivvie – this business of her looking after the baby was a nonsense – tittle tattle about shot gun weddings would do Sherwyn's literary career no good at all – and then Dr Walker had to be persuaded yet again: he seemed reluctant to visit Barscherau – and then Adela had to collect all her luggage, and all Sherwyn wanted was to get back to Vivvie and his writing and the smooth running of the days.

When they did get back, Vivvie was sitting up in a truckle bed in the big front room with two cradles at the end of it, and a wet nurse – Frau Auerbach's daughter Berthe – suckling baby Stella in a rocking chair beside it. Baby Mallory grizzled alone. Dr Walker was recognised by Berthe as the doctor who had delivered her sister's baby and she leapt from her chair in gasping alarm, which set Stella off, and marred any touching scene Vivvie had envisaged. Frau Bieler hurried him off to his room. Adela embraced her daughter, but was obviously shocked. Twins. Girls, non-identical from the look of them. Now what? She went to her room.

'Man proposes, God disposes,' said Sherwyn, and sat down beside Mallory's cradle and rocked her until she calmed down and slept, and sang a lullaby the while.
'Such a weeping and wailing and rocking of cradles
And rocking a baby that's none of your own.'
'What's that?' asked Vivvie.
'A song my mother used to sing. She called it St Joseph's lullaby. I can't think why it came to mind.'
'I can,' said Vivvie. 'Your own mother was such a gadabout. Why else do you think your father gave you a stepmother who looked like a horse?'

He would stay married to Vivvie. They would keep the twins. Too bad about Adela, who would just have to return to Sir Jeremy with the news that she had had a miscarriage: he was doing her a favour: she would have to grow old gracefully, side by side with Sir Jeremy. No 'rocking a baby in somebody's cradle and none of his own' for Sir Jeremy, poor old man. At least he, Sherwyn, had been sufficiently careful with Adela to be sure she could not get pregnant. There must be an end to complication, however much they might suit Delgano.

Food and drink were brought to Vivvie: she felt sore underneath and rather tired but otherwise perfectly well, had been told not to set foot to floor for three weeks for fear of going mad, and had decided never to part from her babies. Berthe had agreed to come with them, bringing her own baby, when she and Sherwyn went back to England, he with his finished novel, she with her twins. It didn't matter in the least what gossips had to say. See, she was perfectly capable of making plans, even though her mother was there in the next room, sulking.

She loved both twins equally but Mallory rather more so because she alone had a squashed-up face, and a vague look of the Angel Gabriel – had he perhaps been a stable hand? It had been hard to remember detail when everyone was so keen for her to do so, but now the babies were real and no longer a dream it might be possible. She would tell Sherwyn. Stella looked more like Adela, which bothered Vivvie a little. One didn't want a child who would grow up to tell you what to do all the time.

Sunday Night, July 6th 1923. Barscherau

That night all ate in the kitchen, since Vivvie was lying-up in the front room. Adela looked out of place, still wearing her mink and complaining of the cold though the night was warm, almost hot, and the stars shining so brightly and beautifully in a clear sky.

Sherwyn was looking rather ravishingly handsome, if not so tall as many, or so thought Berthe, Frau Auerbach's daughter, who was eighteen and lived next door, but it was not her place to say so. Berthe had a year old child of her own, but since the carry-on the day before had been acting as wet nurse until Frau Sexton's milk came in – twins, after all; and the mother might not have enough, one of them being so difficult and greedy. Berthe's mother had rashly named that little later one Mallory, which was unlucky, meaning 'unfortunate'. At least she, Berthe, had been named 'bright' by the one who brought her into the world. Sherwyn had taken off the glorious leather coat she so admired from her upstairs window as Sherwyn came and went, but was wearing a smart white shirt and a red spotted cravat, dashingly knotted. Berthe thought perhaps Vivvie's mother, Lady Adela, as she insisted on being called, was after Sherwyn from the way she looked at him, but she couldn't be; she was an old woman in spite of all her jars of this and pots of that and the silk knickers. Berthe had had to help her unpack, even though one of the babies was crying. Berthe thought that if Frau Sexton meant what she said, and would take her with her back to London, she would probably go. She would send money back. Her mother had been as far as Munich but she herself had hardly gone to the end of the road.

She kept having to slap down the English doctor who was making stupid attempts to nibble her ear – disgusting, horrible old man who didn't even notice his glasses were broken, not to mention dirty. He'd been the one who'd attended her big sister Trudy (meaning 'strength', chosen by Frau Bieler, who brought her into the world) and given her the twilight sleep after which she was never quite the same again. Berthe was surprised he had the nerve to show his face in Barscherau again. And everyone knew about poor little Maria who'd had to marry the English doctor, and then had two more in a single year, and a twilight sleep with all three – not that she'd ever been up to much anyway. What could one expect? Did not 'Maria' mean 'sea of sorrow'?

For supper the guests had Wiener Schnitzel and Tiroler Gröstl followed by strawberry strudel and whipped cream: the rest round the table made do with Käsespätzle and apfelstrudel. Adela scraped the lovely crust of the Schnitzel before picking at it and sawing away with her knife as if it were tough but it was not. Like all Frau Bieler's cooking it was excellent. She caught Herr Sherwyn looking at Adela as if he didn't like her one bit. 'Twins, eh? I think they'll come back to London with Vivvie and me. We'll stay at the Albany for a bit, though I'm not sure babies are quite their thing.'

'Indeed they are not,' said Adela. 'It is out of the question. You have no idea at all about babies, and your wife even less.'

'We'll take Berthe back with us,' said Sherwyn. 'She has all the wisdom of the untutored peasant.'

'She's an ignorant, impertinent chit of a girl,' said Adela, throwing down her fork so that the cream made grease marks all over the table. 'And just look how she's making up to the unfortunate Dr Walker. The girl's uncouth.' It was fortunate that Berthe's schoolgirl English was not good enough to understand fully what was going on, though since she was considered clever she was allowed to study at the boy's gymnasium in Kufstein.

'My wife, my children,' said Sherwyn.

'That's what you say,' said Lady Adela, in a harsh and ugly tone of voice which made everyone at the table uneasy. Dr Walker took off his spectacles, wiped them with his napkin and put them back on by their one remaining arm. Now it seemed to Berthe he could see through them, or more or less.

'Ah. I thought you were the grandfather,' said Dr Walker. 'But I see you're too young. You're the father.'

Then Adela's face, which had gone quite crimson, faded quickly back to its normal pallor, and she smiled sweetly round the table at everyone and turned to Sherwyn and said:

'We could split the difference. You take one, I take one.'

'I know which one you'd take,' said Sherwyn. 'No. Or only if I have first pick.'

'That wouldn't work,' said Adela, 'I'd be back where I began.'

'Exactly,' said Sherwyn. 'Face it. Go back to Sir Jeremy and grow old.'

Which Berthe thought was rather cruel, even to someone as nasty and skinny as Adela. Sometimes when she looked at Sherwyn he seemed much taller than at others, and more broad shouldered. But they ate by candlelight not lamplight because

203

of the presence of guests, and in the flickers sight could be deceptive. Or perhaps Berthe saw what she wanted to see. Mind you, she really liked Frau Sexton even though she was peculiar, and Berthe wouldn't want to do anything that might upset her. One of the babies started to cry in the next room and she had to leave the table. Dr Walker tried to follow her but Frau Bieler, who noticed everything, called him back and forestalled him.

Later On Sunday Night, July 6th 1923. Barscherau

Berthe drowsed by Vivvie's bed into the small hours. It would have been more sensible just to go to bed – one had been made up for her in the attic – but she was too tired. She'd fed baby Mallory at around eleven o'clock. Mallory had been born with a single front tooth showing and though the baby fed well, with strong and powerful gums, the tooth could dig in and tear. Not that it was the baby's fault. When finally Mallory settled, baby Stella woke and was put to the breast. She sucked steadily and sufficiently, then smiled – though they'd say that was wind – had her back patted and went back to sleep. The mother slept the while, propped up in bed, occasionally stirring or spluttering or doing what people did when they slept. It must have been after midnight when the lamps were extinguished in the kitchen and she heard the cat being turned out. After that the household slept.

An hour or so later she was disturbed by Vivvie's moaning and heaving, though she still seemed asleep. Berthe thought she'd better check and, pulling back the quilt, found blood oozing out freely from beneath its padding. She thought perhaps she should get help. The doctor was the obvious choice, but she had no intention of knocking on his door in the middle of the night. She didn't want to disturb Frau Bieler who had worked so hard and cooked so well; Herr Sexton was not the kind to involve himself in female matters. Frau Ripple was the next choice: why should she sleep soundly when others did not?

Berthe found her way upstairs by flashlight to the room where she knew Lady Adela slept and tapped on the door. There was no reply so she opened the door and shone the torch into the bed recess. There were two heaps in it. One was Lady Adela and the other, so far as she could make out, was Herr Sexton. The room smelt strongly of brandy. Berthe retired to the staircase, recovered from the shock and then banged and battered upon the door. Lady Adela eventually appeared, wearing her mink but nothing else.

'Your daughter is bleeding to death,' said Berthe. 'You need to go.'

'Everyone bleeds after childbirth,' said Adela.

'Not as much as this,' said Berthe.

'Go to your room, girl,' said Lady Adela. 'I'll see to it. I'll call the doctor if I think she needs it.'

So Berthe Auerbach climbed to the top of the stairs and fell into bed and slept and woke to the sound of babies crying, her own mother shaking her, and pandemonium in the house downstairs. The dogs were barking, the babies were crying. Lady Adela was staring into space. The doctor was on the phone to the medical examiner in Kufstein. Frau Bieler and Greta were washing out piles of bloodstained quilts. Herr Bieler was in the front room, mopping up blood from the floor where Vivvie's truckle bed had been – the legs of Mallory's cot were inches deep in it: Stella's were spared: the wooden floor must slope quite badly. Herr Sexton was moaning and dashing away tears over a lifeless Vivvie laid out on the kitchen table, big white marble limbs naked under a cloth, but eyes closed and at peace, which was more than her husband was.

'For God's sake someone shut up those babies,' he shouted, being at the end of his tether, though it only set the dogs off again. Frau Auerbach from next door had had the sense to fetch Berthe down and she now put one baby to each breast and the twins fell silent as they sucked, and at least everyone could think.

But it was a gruelling and horrid scene, not easily forgotten by anyone involved. Vivvie had died from a postpartum haemorrhage while she slept. Dr Walker accused Frau Auerbach of not having checked that both afterbirths had been delivered, and she accused him of having sent her eldest daughter mad with his twilight sleep and shouting ensued. Berthe marvelled that one body could produce so much blood, pigs were bad enough but at least you could eat them afterwards. She hated thinking about her poor sister. Dr Walker denied having been called for.
'Even if I had been, there would have been nothing I could do.'

He was probably right. Ergometrine as a drug for childbirth was not synthesised until 1935, after which a swift dose of it would have cleared away the retained placenta and Vivvie would not have bled to death. But this was 'before which' not 'after which', and 'before' has a multitude of risks, though thank God they diminish with the passage of the years. But Dr Walker could perhaps have done something to remove the clot with a suction pump – he had any amount of surgical equipment in the boot of the Bentley – or just lifted her legs, plunged in his arm and removed it by hand. It might have worked. It might not have.

'You should have gone to look and fetched me,' he said. 'She was your daughter.'

Frau Ripple wept a few dainty tears and said she had gone to look but the girl had been exaggerating, only a few drops of blood and she had no medical training so she'd gone back to bed. In the morning she'd heard one of the babies crying and had gone to see what she could do, the girl being nowhere to be seen, and found poor Vivvie dead in a pool of blood. Her own daughter. Imagine the shock.

The medical examiner came and forms were filled in. The English doctor was able to get a lift back to Kufstein in the examiner's pony and trap. The body went with them. Everyone fell silent – even Frau Auerbach; who now the doctor was gone seemed able to stop weeping. Herr Sherwyn went to his room and typed. Milady went to her room and revarnished her nails. Greta took in the washing – it had already dried, being a hot, windy day – and folded everything away. Berthe suckled the twins. Frau Bieler was able to make everyone a nourishing goulash soup with beef and paprika and dollops of sour cream. Most ate without speaking. There seemed little to say.

But that night there were tears and angry sounds all over the house. In the morning an ashen and angry Herr Sexton left in the Bentley for London without taking either of the babies. Two days later Adela departed for Keifersfelden, taking both of them with her. She dropped them off at Dr Walker's house. Thus they spent the first three months of their life with Maria, she of the vale of tears, who was still nursing her youngest. Adela herself stayed quietly at the Gasthof until the end of September, when she hired a nanny and a nursemaid in Munich, and departed with the babies for London.

Sunday Afternoon, July 13th 1923. Barscherau

Vivvie was buried in Barscherau in the grounds of the old abbey, where the Black Virgin reigns. The whole village climbed up the mountain to be with her, and to strew flowers on her coffin to mark her passing – small neat bouquets, which the undertaker provided. Courtney and Baum dealt with the funeral expenses, and sent an expensive wreath all the way from Munich.

Sir Jeremy was too busy to attend – Trotsky had accused Stalin of centrism, Stalin, Trotsky of factionalism: the Central Committee was in uproar. Sir Jeremy's new magazine *Workers Arise* was in crisis – but he sent a representative of Ripple & Co, to be with Adela at this dreadful time. She must come back to him as soon as she could.

At least Adela was there, brought by pony and trap from Keifersfelden, climbing up the mountainside to say goodbye to her daughter when it would have been so much more practical for everyone for the interment to have been on level ground in Kufstein. She left the mink behind but looked very stylish in little black fur bootees, a flowing black dress with rows and rows of expensive pearls, a little black cloche hat, and smoked a black Sobranie from an ebony holder throughout the ceremony. She spoke to no-one, not even the Bielers, who had done so much for Vivvie, and all but turned her back on poor Berthe, who was having to live on sage infusions to dry up her milk.

'In your mercy look upon this grave,' said the priest, sprinkling the large coffin with holy water, and what more beautiful place than this could there be to be buried, if only Vivvie were there to see it, 'so that your servant may sleep here in peace; and on the day of judgment raise her up to dwell with your saints in paradise.'

'Amen,' said the congregation.

'We pray for our sister now but let us pray also for ourselves, so weak and prone to sin, and also for our enemies.'

'Amen,' said the villagers, though they could not see that they had done much wrong. But no-one can be free from guilt and certainly not foreigners who have won the war. Perhaps he was talking about them.

When the first clods of earth landed on the coffin, Adela left.

I think I have been rather hard on Adela. A girl can't help her nymphomania,
any more than Sherwyn can help his inner Delgano. A writer inhabits his characters and vice versa. It's been rather drastic for me inhabiting the skinny, slight Adela. I was more at home with Vivvie in her bulk, solidity and wayward thoughts. But Vivvie's gone off now, unto the black unknown. So I say, but actually it's not all that unknown. I see it as a great Hieronymus Bosch lake, misty, where characters go after the writer writes 'THE END' and they're left writerless and rudderless.

Thousands and thousands of them, more and more over the years, fictional personae, heads bobbing about in the great lake, still talking, protesting, gesticulating, arguing. By God, they're a noisy lot. There I see Madame Bovary in her midnight blue cloak with the paler blue lining, the one she wore to run away with her deceiving lover, forever lamenting. There's that rather mean looking Nick Dunne, the husband in *Gone Girl*, with his shifty eyes and crumpled shirt, forever protesting. There's Paddington Bear, spooning marmalade. A celebrity's a celebrity, for a' that. No class distinctions down here in the character pool. Come to think of it, it's a bit like a horror film: all those shapeless, faceless bodies, characters yet unborn, floundering about in the depths, waiting to take form. Can there be no end to it?

Anyway, the funeral is over. The girls grow up in Dilberne Court, and later in Belgrave Square as the Misses Stella and Mallory Ripple: twin daughters (non-identical, as many take care to point out) of Sir Jeremy and Lady Adela Ripple.

PART THREE

Lunching

May 2nd 1926. Simpson's-in-the-Strand

Mungo had the beef – great thick reddish juicy slabs of it carved in front of him, deep brown gravy sweetened with port, turnip puree under a crackling golden canopy of Yorkshire pudding. He was lunching with Sir Jeremy, who was beginning to show his age: his hair now so thin it seemed better to go beardless. Mungo declined the roast potatoes, though the waiter, in black frock coat and white apron down to his ankles, assured him they were the house special, rolled in flour and seasoning before roasting to give them the famous Simpson's crust.

'I'm "banting",' Mungo explained to Sir Jeremy. 'Dieting. Olive says I must.'

Olive Crest was Mungo Bolt's new wife, aged twenty-two, lively and fashionable daughter of a department store tycoon from Baltimore, Cyril Crest. Mungo was doing well, had resigned from Ripple's and started his own advertising agency, Bolt & Crest. So far Bolt's, as it was called, handled only small accounts – diet pills, cough medicines, sewing machines and the new zip fasteners – but had smart offices in Grosvenor Square and high ambitions. Mungo wanted to take on the Ripple account – the Book division, at any rate, which, thanks to Sherwyn's Delgano thrillers, was flourishing, if not the Vivien Political List, which was not. Vivien's List, called after Sir Jeremy's deceased daughter, was the magazine publishing side of the Ripple empire and limped along, ever virtuous, with the weekly *Breakthrough*, the monthly *Workers Unite*, and for some reason the quarterly *Health, Energy and Breath*. But Sir Jeremy was not convinced. If Mungo would take over Vivien's List he might think about it, but the fiction list was doing perfectly well on its own. Vivien's List just needed time, in any case. It was on the right side of history.

'Time is money,' said Mungo.

'You're just a born capitalist, my son,' said Sir Jeremy. 'Not your fault. It runs in your blood as socialism runs in mine.' He chose the turbot with lobster sauce. His digestion wasn't quite what it was. Adela was now a vegetarian. She was quite right. Meat was murder. No, he didn't want a poached egg with the fish but he'd have some spinach.

'What's the matter with eggs?' asked Mungo.

'Theft,' said Sir Jeremy, sadly. 'But not as bad as murder – Adela says so.'

'Well, I'm sorry you can't be tempted, Sir Jeremy,' said Mungo, and pointed out that while working as head of publicity at Ripple's, it had been he who had put Delgano on the map.

'Sherwyn's novels don't need advertising,' said Sir Jeremy, 'they sell themselves.'

'Nothing sells itself,' said Mungo. 'Except possibly armaments. And careful that Delgano doesn't turn out to be just a flash in the pan. He's doing all right in the women's market, but what about the men's? A cook, for God's sake!'

'A gourmet,' said Sir Jeremy. 'Quite different. What exactly have you got against poor Sherwyn?'

Mungo grunted and did not say that he greatly resented Adela's switch of interest from himself to Sherwyn. God alone knew what had happened when they were all there up that mountain. He feared the worst. Adela would not let a mere matter of being pregnant get in the way of her carnal appetites. Rumours about Adela and Sherwyn abounded in the literary world, but never reached Sir Jeremy's ears, nor would he have believed them if they had. Sherwyn was his son-in-law, and Sir Jeremy loved his wife.

Mungo was not sure if he loved his wife. Olive was turning out to be very bossy. He had wanted to call the agency just Bolt, but it had ended up called Bolt & Crest, and Olive had insisted on his taking on the zipper account – *A Zip in Time Saves Nine Buttons!* – which was nothing but an embarrassment. Zips might go down well in the US but never in England. And he was a married man, and there was no longer Adela to turn to: she was absurdly taken up with her little daughters and also apparently Sexton. Mungo smiled brightly at Sir Jeremy.
'Nothing at all,' he said. 'I daresay I'm jealous. I always wanted to be a famous writer and here I am, an ad man, trying to sell zippers. "*He who unzips and runs away, lives to unzip another day.*"' But Sir Jeremy didn't see that as funny. Mungo gave up on the Ripple account. Let the old man go to hell in his own way.

The wine waiter came at last. Mungo ordered a 1920 St Estèphe. He was paying. Sir Jeremy ordered a glass of Riesling. The German wine industry had picked itself up: the mark was stable again.
'One way of paying off reparations,' said Mungo and Sir Jeremy frowned at such cynicism. He liked to see the best in humanity. Fortunately the wine came, the red in a glass so large it caught the tip of one's nose.

'A bit new,' he said, 'but it should be all right. Nothing much came out of France during the war.'

'Except death and destruction,' said Sir Jeremy cheerfully. 'But that's all behind us now. One world, one communism, and there'll be an end to war.'

'There's basic human nature to contend with,' said Mungo. 'Hate, fear and greed. The death wish. Thanatos.'

'You and your Freud,' said Sir Jeremy. 'Nihilists all.' He deplored the state of the nation, the antics of Trotsky in Russia, the fact that Baldwin's government and Labour weren't behind the imminent general strike. But at least if it happened the population would be politicised at last.

'And sales of *Workers Arise* will creep up,' said Mungo. 'What about a slogan like *The working class can kiss my arse, I've got the foreman's job at last*?' He sang it to the tune of the *Internationale*: Sir Jeremy didn't think that was funny either.

Mungo enquired as casually as he could after Lady Adela and the twins.

'All flourishing,' said Sir Jeremy. 'My wife gets younger as I get older. Everyone remarks on it. As for the twins, one is so pretty and sweet, as one would expect of her mother's daughter, and Mallory takes after me and is very clever. A little definite in her opinions, perhaps, and only three. They're not identical, you know. Her mother says she will grow up to be a union organiser. I hope so. The workers of this country could do with a better class of leader. Watery socialism will never work.'

The country was in uproar, divided. A general strike threatened – transport, dockers, printers, miners. Churchill wanted to arm the soldiers. Baldwin said it was 'more difficult to feed

218

a nation than to break it'. The King said 'try living on their wages before you judge them'. But mine owners had to cut wages. The Germans were suddenly back in business, flooding the market with cheap coal, not to mention Riesling. Mungo held his tongue.

And who but Sherwyn walked into the restaurant, with his redheaded artist floozy on his arm. She was wearing a pale mink coat very much like the one Adela sometimes wore. Mungo choked on his treacle sponge. Sir Jeremy was irritated and pushed away his crème caramel.

'Three years since I lost my daughter,' said Sir Jeremy, 'but even so! Why can't he just get remarried, like anyone else? She's so, well, obvious.'

Sherwyn came over as Rita took her seat in a far corner of the restaurant. Sherwyn nodded to Mungo cheerily enough and wished him luck with his new project: he hailed Sir Jeremy with enthusiasm.

'Father-in-law! Publisher! Those about to die salute thee!'

'What an idiot,' was what Mungo thought. Sherwyn was wearing one of those film director's long brown leather coats with a high collar. Mungo looked down, and yes! – built-up heels on the brown and white co-respondent shoes. What on earth did Adela see in this upstart author? He, Mungo, had been good enough to father Adela's twins – he doubted the old man had it in him – then suddenly she was crawling all over Sherwyn. Everyone went along with the pretence that the twins were Sir Jeremy's seed. At least Sir Jeremy had the wherewithal to rear and educate them decently. And Mungo could hardly say a word. He had Olive to think about.

'About to die?' Sir Jeremy looked confused.

'Oh, nothing in particular,' said Sherwyn airily. 'Just I'm off to learn engine driving. My nation calls me! Three hours' instruction – all a fellow needs, apparently – I hope to God they're right. But *adversa virtute repello!*'

That's not going to please the old man, thought Mungo, smiling steadily on. Is it possible Sherwyn is thinking of switching publishers? Possibly to someone who understands the value of advertising? And isn't it, Mungo thought, just a little tasteless to be talking about death so casually? And then Sherwyn asked after the twins – my twins, thought Mungo – as he'd bought gifts for them from Morocco – in such a way that Sir Jeremy couldn't help but ask the bounder round.

He just wants an excuse to get to see Adela, thought Mungo. It was difficult carrying on an affair under the boss's nose – as he knew only too well. There was no denying that the redheaded Rita – over there already sipping champagne – was a real looker. What on earth did all these women see in Sherwyn? He'd inherited a lot through his poor dead wife, of course; that always helped. But even Vivvie – the elephant, as Mungo always thought of her – had been after Sherwyn from the beginning. He felt an unexpected pang of sorrow for poor Vivien, struck down on her (understandably very much extended) honeymoon, far away in foreign parts. And the baby too. He'd seen the poor little thing churning away inside its mother's belly, magic in a way, and under a wedding dress, all promise, no fulfilment. Sherwyn hadn't seemed all that upset when Vivvie had died. Well, it was hardly surprising. At least he was free to philander at will. Rita the redhead was certainly a dish – in a bouncy, bosomy kind of way. His own Olive was a nice looking girl, if a little pale and thin. One day when he had time he would write his own novel, which would knock anything Sherwyn could write into a cocked hat.

Sherwyn went back to his table. Mungo paid the bill. Sir Jeremy walked back to Fleet Street and Mungo took a cab to Grosvenor Square.

Midday, September 3rd 1931. 17 Belgrave Square

The twins were eight. They stood hand in hand upon the kelim rug in the nursery. They had no clothes on. They were staring into the cheval mirror examining their reflection. It was the same mirror Sir Jeremy had stared into and decided he was a fine figure of a man back in 1922. Much of the Art Deco furniture from Fleet Street had ended up in Belgrave Square, to Sir Jeremy's and everyone else's relief. (Cousin Rosina had died in 1927 of what was spoken of, if at all, as a growth, but was actually cancer, and left her property to Adela.)

'Why do they say we're twins when we don't look at all alike?' asked Stella, who was a fairly normal eight year old, apart from being so exceptionally pretty.

'Because we're non-identical,' explained Mallory, who like her mother Vivvie had an intelligence quotient too high to be considered normal, and an unfortunately squashed-up face in which her chin seemed to be forever trying to reach her brow. 'We come from two eggs not one. And please don't ask me who laid the egg.'

Stella didn't, though she wanted to. No matter how often Mallory tried to explain the facts of life to her, Stella stayed confused. Men and women sticking bits of each other into where they pooed and widdled? Why would they want to?

Mallory was to be believed in most things, just perhaps not this. And it was not the kind of thing you asked your mother about.

'You mean we have two fathers?' she asked her sister.

'No,' said Mallory, 'that can happen, but it's not likely. No, we're no different from ordinary sisters, just born at the same time and we shared a womb. That's the bit where women grow babies.'

'I'm glad I shared with you,' said Stella, graciously.

'Thank you,' said Mallory. The twins got on extraordinarily well, considering how different they were. 'Of course if we did have different fathers because our mother had two different gentleman friends in the same month then that would be why we're so different. I might be royalty.'

'Ooh, do you think so?' asked Stella hopefully.

'Me, not you. You're mother and father mixed. I'm perfectly possibly mother and the Prince of Wales mixed.'

Mallory took measurements and wrote them down in a notebook she kept at the bottom of the toy box.

'I'm two inches taller than you,' she said, 'and half an inch more round the ankle and wrist. Your legs are the same length, but one of mine is half an inch shorter than its pair. We have no busts, and we're fairly straight up and down, not in and out, as we will be when we start really growing. That's called adolescence.' Their second cousin Rosina's library had come to Belgrave Square, and there were many books in it on physiology, particularly as it related to the maturing of Aboriginal women as compared to their European sisters. Mallory would pore over them while Stella sat entranced by books like *The Wind in the Willows*.

'How do you know all this?' asked Stella.

'Because you have the looks but I have the brain. People look at you and try to please you. They look at me and try to forget me. Everyone thinks you're nice because you tell lies to save their feelings. People think I'm nasty because I want to know the truth. You know how to get round people but I know how things work.'

'Isn't there some way we could share?' asked Stella.

'You mean both of us have one leg a quarter of an inch shorter instead of my having half an inch? Not really. No. Pity. But it's very nice of you to offer.'

'We can't be as one, but we could act as one,' suggested Stella. 'We could swear an oath.'

Which is what they did. They took the razor blade from the utility knife that Mallory kept hidden in the wardrobe for emergencies, and cut into the sides of their thumbs and mingled their blood and swore on the collected works of Tennyson (which Mallory considered to contain more wisdom than the Bible) to work together all their lives to find out how they were born, and to whom, and why. Adela would have had a fit, and the fact that they were spoiling the kelim by dripping blood upon it wouldn't have helped. Mallory's hand slipped and she cut into the artery on her wrist by mistake. Morna the nanny from Galway was down in the kitchen preparing the twins' lunch, Adela was in Harrods – having for once left Stella behind, for once – helping Igor Kubanov the equestrian to purchase knee boots, and they were alone in the nursery. Mallory didn't panic but wrapped a handkerchief tightly round her wrist and held her hand above her head, in the meanwhile continuing to proclaim the oath.

'Let us swear an oath together, Stella and Mallory combined, While in Belgrave Square we sisters live and lie reclined...

Let who conceived us, how conceived us, be the truth we seek
to find.'

Mallory would have worked further on the metre but the circumstances were beginning to seem rather drastic. The kelim
rug, a present from Uncle Sherwyn a few years back, was quite
soaked. Fortunately the blood stopped flowing of its own accord.
'Fill the nursery bucket with warm water,' said Mallory, 'and
bring as many towels as you can find.' Stella ran to do as she was
told. Morna would be back very soon. Mallory sloshed the
water all over the rug, so lots of the blood ran out onto the
parquet floor.

'Put the towels on the floor and tread up and down on them.'
Stella did. Mallory ran with the sopping towels to the window
that looked out over the front door and dropped them on to the
balcony below. She would retrieve them later. The two bloody
handkerchiefs followed.

'Just as well there's lots of red already in the kelim,' Mallory said.
'No-one will notice.' And nobody did. Stella thought her sister
was wonderful. She herself would never have thought and acted
so fast. She said as much.

'Yes,' said Mallory. 'But you might have charmed Morna into
not telling Mama which would have been just as good.' Mallory
was always very fair. They agreed that they made a good team,
and by the time Morna came in with lunch (fish in white
sauce, potatoes and mashed parsnips, followed by rice pudding
with golden syrup – the blander food looked and tasted, the
better it was for children) they were sitting up at the table
peacefully waiting: Stella, with an air of blonde Madonna-like
serenity about her, and Mallory lowering as usual, though she
couldn't help it, it was just the way her brow leaned down
towards her jaw.

They lived quiet nursery lives.

'I worry about them,' Morna would write to her mother in Galway, 'but at least they have each other.'

Mallory would keep a paper screw of white pepper from the downstairs dinner table in her pocket, together with a little bottle of Angostura bitters borrowed from her father's drinks cabinet (walnut burr, as sold to Lady Adela, though she and Syrie Maugham were to quarrel over the price) to enliven the nursery meals. Mallory would offer some to Stella who would recoil in horror, preferring her food both unadulterated and guilt free. The bottle was kept behind the leg of a chest of drawers.

Every now and then, often at weekends when Father was away at Dilberne Court with the horses, one or other of the Uncles would appear, say very little, but gaze at the girls with wondering eyes, then leave behind spectacular gifts which the recipients rather tended to despise. The kelim rug got spattered with oil paint as well as drenched in blood. Adela had not wanted it in the nursery in the first place but Sir Jeremy had insisted, saying it was a present to the twins, brought back from Morocco by their favourite author, and the twins should have it.

'I don't worry about Stella,' Adela said. 'I'd trust Stella with anything, even a Lalique vase. But Mallory! Even a simple thing like a rug – she'll only end up tripping over it and breaking her leg.'

Sir Jeremy sometimes wondered if something couldn't be done about Mallory's limp, but Adela said no. It did the girl no harm, was not painful and wasn't likely to ward off suitors. 'She'll have to learn to be a lot more pleasant if she's ever to find one of those!'

Sir Jeremy said: 'You used to say the same thing about her big sister, as I remember, and poor Vivvie did very well in the end. Got Sherwyn Sexton, of all people!'

Adela was well into The Change by now – though no-one would have known it what with the cucumber slices, the monkey gland masks, the ice treatments and her pretty little daughter Stella trotting along by her side – and found she sometimes couldn't concentrate properly. When Sir Jeremy did something like referring to poor Vivvie as the twins' big sister, she could get confused and have to change the subject quickly. One way and another Vivvie seldom got mentioned in the twins' hearing. Once they'd had a sister much older than them but she'd passed away.

Though once they'd been lunching with their parents, learning table manners (Morna wasn't very good at it, apparently) when Vivvie's name came up. Greystokes, long dead, had sired a horse which had won the Oaks. A winner for him at last!
'Your sister would have been so pleased,' said Sir Jeremy. 'If only she had lived to see it. But she died in childbirth.'
'Boy or girl?' the twins asked.
'A dear little boy,' Adela said quickly.
'I never knew that,' said Sir Jeremy. 'What a pity!' He wasn't much interested in children: women's world.
'Such a painful time for me,' put in Adela, 'losing poor Vivvie like that. And I was so pregnant myself, and abroad at the time, and so upset. I'm sure the shock didn't help.'
By which presumably she meant Mallory's limp. All their big sister's fault. After that Mallory recorded every mention of Vivvie in a little diary especially kept for that purpose. She kept

it under a carpet in the splendid dolls' house given to them by Uncle Mungo.

'Is he a real Uncle?' Stella asked Morna the nanny, their surrogate mother.

'Ask your mother. She's the one to know,' Morna replied: an unsatisfactory answer which Mallory carefully recorded in the doll's house diary.

Morna kept out of Lady Adela's way, and Lady Adela kept out of hers. Both knew upon which side their bread was buttered. Morna had a good room in the nursery wing at the back of the house, and could ask her boyfriend in – he was in the Horse Guards – whenever he was off duty. Which was more than she could do in Galway, where it was marriage or nothing. She ate well, albeit by herself, and slept in a warm bed, had Saturday night off and seldom had to venture into the rest of the house. She was fond of the children – Stella was a sweetheart, though Mallory could be difficult – and Morna wanted nothing to change.

But Morna did like to disapprove: indeed, it was one of her main pleasures in life. The twins rarely saw their father, who got home late every night and was off at weekends to see to his horses down in the country. The mother gadded about and spent money, yet worried about the cost of heating the nursery. The Ripples entertained every Wednesday – writers, publishers, politicians – though at least she got caterers in to see to it all. And the people who visited the house! Firebrands, revolutionaries, socialites, beauticians, masseurs, the endless stream of painters, decorators, interior designers – Syrie Maugham and her crew. And then of course the Uncles:

Morna, ever suspicious, looked for resemblances to them in the twins, but saw none. Stella was obviously her mother's but fortunately taller, more solid and with more colour in her cheeks – but Mallory was a child out of the blue, a changeling, an elf child, belonging to neither alleged parent, let alone one of the Uncles. All Mallory wanted to do was read and write and play patience while she waited to grow up, so Morna let her just get on with it.

There were other Uncles too over the years who came and went – wasn't Adela too old for this kind of carry-on? – but Sherwyn and Mungo were the only ones who'd drop by, leave presents, stare at the twins, say very little and go away. Always separately and often on a Saturday, Morna's night out. Well, how Lady Adela chose to live was her business, so long as she didn't mind going to hell, not Morna's, and if Sir Jeremy wanted to look the other way that was his business.

But little Stella had to be forever dressed up to be taken out by her mother to some charity do or other, or some smart restaurant lunch, or only to Bond Street for beauty treatments – Adela said a girl was never too young: but *eight*? – or to Harrods to be bought some pretty new frock or other. As a result Stella spent most of what spare time she had admiring herself in mirrors, whereas Mallory made herself so difficult on outings that Adela preferred just to leave her at home. When she was three she'd have tantrums and her mother would come back with her ankles black and blue. Which suited everyone.

If all was not perfect inside the house it was certainly better than outside. Wall Street had crashed, the pound had devalued, unemployment was double what it was when the twins were born, hunger stalked the land, though you could never tell such a thing within Harrods where Adela did the shopping. You could buy anything from an elephant in the Pet Shop to caviar and yak butter in the Food Hall. But sales of *Workers Arise* slumped. The workers had arisen in the General Strike and much good did it do them.

Sir Jeremy tried to woo A.J. Cronin, he of *Hatter's Castle*, onto his fiction list but failed. Readers went on preferring to buy books about middle-class detectives rather than suffering workers, though Zola did all right in France. Understandably, perhaps. France was a republic; England limped along behind as a regressive monarchy. For some reason Mallory's limp seemed to Sir Jeremy to act as a metaphor for the whole nation – limping along when it could be struggling upwards into the new Marxist-Leninist dawn. He didn't seem able to forget poor Vivvie falling off her chair at his investiture ceremony. It had seemed at the time some kind of omen. A better man than he would have been true to his principles, refused the knighthood, not consented to kneel before the monarch. He'd felt obscurely to blame for what had happened next.

And he should never have let Adela go off on her own to have the twins in Austria where the doctors were known to have such odd ideas. As it was Adela hadn't been able to save Vivvie – all that had happened was that he had lost a grandson and was landed with two daughters in his old age – one of them with a limp as a result of the shock to their mother of Vivvie's death. He hadn't been paying proper attention – he'd been fairly taken up with Phoebe at the time: a lamentable episode of which he was not proud. But probably the older a man got the more there was with which to reproach himself. There was no escape. And it pleased Adela to have a title. Fortunately money was not such a trouble to her these days. Rosina's will had left her well provided for – some compensation for the unfairness of her grandmother's will, which had so exercised her in her younger days.

He was so lucky in Adela. Other men had a far worse time; they had wives who looked old, felt old, talked and behaved old. Adela seemed to be perpetually beautiful, youthful, gracious, kind and capable – above all capable. Other women talked about the servant problem all the time – Adela just got on with it. She could not bear too many servants about the house. She said Morna was bad enough but at least she kept herself to herself, did what she was told and took proper care of the children. But other live-in staff? No. They gossiped, they broke things, they stole things, they were never properly trained, they took time off for funerals – especially if they were Irish as they so often were these days, and came from large families. As she told Sir Jeremy she'd rather make do with a couple of dailies and a laundress, and bring caterers in for dinner parties or anything special. The rest she'd do herself. She could peel a carrot or wipe a basin as well as the rest of them.

Sir Jeremy could almost believe his wife was a proletarian at heart. Rumours were coming through from the British Embassy there of 'a famine' in Russia but it didn't seem possible with Stalin in charge. People were so ready to believe bad news coming out of the USSR, so reluctant to believe the good. Most likely just the kulaks at it again, sabotaging the Great Idea, spitting in the wind against the mighty onrush of historic necessity.

February 15th 1937

The twins were thirteen, rising fourteen. Sherwyn took Rita out to lunch at the Georgian restaurant in Harrods. It was not a place the literati frequented, and Rita had insisted on it. Rita's reason, he found, was that 'Sybil would never go there'. Sybil was E.L.T. Mesens' wife, and worked as a buyer for Dickins & Jones, the department store, and was much feared in artistic circles. Sherwyn found this amusing. E.L.T. was a surrealist painter who ran the London Gallery, and with whom Rita was having an affair under the nose of C.R.W. Nevinson.

'Too many initials for comfort, Rita.'

'Yes but I love him.' E.L.T., C.R.W., what difference did it make to her? '*But I love him!*' was Rita's perpetual cry, and it had done her quite well. She was beginning to make quite a name for herself as a painter, being a source of both scandal and erotic delight for the truly talented, who did what they could to foster what little talent she had. Sherwyn even had a painting by Rita over the mantelpiece of his Orme Square house, where he lived with his wife Marjorie McShannon, the American actress who had starred in the film of *Black Eyes*, adapted from the novel *The Eye of the Lamb* by Sherwyn Sexton. Zukor at Paramount had put the kibosh on the original title; dark eyes now referred to Marjorie's fabulous eyes, and Delgano ended up as a Chicago gangster – but that was the way the film industry was – you took the money and ran; and Sherwyn ran, taking Marjorie

McShannon, that pocket Venus, with him. The film had made good money for a while, though the gangster seam had eventually run out and in the next novel Delgano had to be seized by remorse and return to Europe and haute cuisine.

The Marjorie marriage, as Sherwyn now thought of it, three years in, was not going too well. Rita for example would go to bed with a fellow at the drop of a hat, but for Marjorie it had to be a specially trumpeted occasion, for which you almost had to make an appointment, and certainly shower, shave, bring flowers, woo and pursue: he'd be so infuriated at the end of it that actual sexual performance became difficult. He was sure Marjorie discussed his prowess or lack of it with her girlfriends: if she gossiped about her previous film star husbands – blow by blow, to the delight of the yellow press – why not about Sherwyn the bestselling writer?

Sometimes he longed for those few blissful months when he and Vivvie had lain side by side like spoons in the Barscherau cupboard that served for a bed, plum and plum stone, bodies at one but no sex. Life was simple without sex. On the other hand Rita was looking particularly lovely. In her late thirties, perhaps by now, but her eyes still alive and her mouth still generous and as ready to laugh as those fond eyes were ready to weep.

Harrods had whitebait on the menu – he'd checked before he booked. It was February when all the little small fry which swam in great shoals up and down the river estuaries of England could be harvested before they grew into vulgar, bony herrings. It was an annual ritual for Sherwyn: he always thought that first whitebait story had brought him luck. It was the kind of thing Rita understood, and Vivvie would have too, and which Marjorie most certainly would not. It had been a story written at the worst of times, before his genius was recognised, when he was poor as Knut Hamsun was when he wrote *Hunger*, when his shoes let water and he could not pay his restaurant bills or his gambling debts. But now was surely the best of times. With one fell swoop he had switched his destiny, married Vivvie and so set the wheels in motion; all the cogs fell into place and the fame and fortune he deserved were his. And here he was, living with a film star and lunching with his mistress, who was sobbing into her sardines on toast – chosen to keep him company in his whitebait: she refused it herself: 'All those little eyes looking at you! At least they cut the heads off sardines before expecting you to eat them!' – and wondering what Rita would say if he asked to take her back to her studio in a taxi. He thought the current studio was in Fulham – not too far from Harrods. Sherwyn wondered if she still had the purple crushed velvet sofa she used to say she kept in memory of him. He was due at a film première at seven o'clock with Marjorie. There would be just about time if they didn't take too long over lunch.

'You don't really love E.L.T. Mesens,' said Sherwyn, 'let alone C.R.W. Nevinson. You just want a little excitement when disturbed *in flagrante* by Sybil and there's some terrible row.'
'You don't know Sybil Mesens,' said Rita darkly. 'She'd just want to join in with Mesens. and me. Then she'd tell Nevinson all about it and he'll be so upset. He's very neurotic at the moment. He's soon going to be fifty and thinks no-one takes him seriously any more. He had his heyday as a war artist and landscapes just aren't as exciting. Yet he will insist on painting them.'

'His chance will come again,' said Sherwyn. 'What about me? No-one takes me seriously any more. I go out to dine with Marjorie and heads turn: once it was for me, now it's for Marjorie.'

'You're jealous,' said Rita. 'You're so used to being top dog.' That surprised him. Could it be true? He certainly felt that the attention the public gave Marjorie was absurd. He, Sherwyn, was acclaimed for his talent and achievement. All Marjorie had to do was waft around and look pretty.

No, it was not jealousy. It was justified resentment. Quite different. He told her so.

'You always had your eye on the main chance,' said Rita. 'That much was always obvious. Writers are so different from artists. Painters just seem to want to destroy themselves.'

They almost quarrelled. Sherwyn said she shouldn't worry. Another war would come along and C.R.W. Nevinson would be saved by the bell, and absinthe would run out so E.L.T. would be saved from a nasty death. (He was wrong. The absinthe never runs out.)

Rita said war was impossible and Hitler was only taking back what had been stolen from the Germans after the last war. That really irritated Sherwyn. He was becoming quite a patriot, to his own surprise. His current intended, the delightful Elvira, model and bookseller, talked politics quite a lot. It must be her influence. Sherwyn complained that Rita was a dull-witted socialist, Rita that Sherwyn was a reactionary little Englander. 'The country is in a very serious mess,' declared Sherwyn. His voice rose. Ladies who lunched looked in his direction. Hats of all shapes and sizes turned to him – velvet parrots, jaunty feathers, discreet turbans and coquettish little veils, floppy brims – though how anyone ate in them was a mystery.

'Sherwyn, do keep your voice down. Ladies hate to have attention drawn to them.'

'You could have fooled me.' But he lowered it and the hats turned away. 'The nation is torn between bourgeoisie-hating socialists – like my own dear prosperous bourgeois publisher – and now apparently you, my dear.'

'Sir Jeremy's a communist. Don't you even know the difference?'

'There is precious little, other than that "communism" uses a strong magnetic force to draw every appeaser, every fruit juice drinker, nudist, sandal-wearer, sex-maniac, Quaker, "Nature Cure" quack, pacifist, and feminist in England to its side. The socialist magnet has a slightly weaker draw. As for thesis, antithesis and synthesis, have you ever known a decent working man take the slightest interest in Marxism? Hence the grand old socialist sport of denouncing the bourgeoisie, at which your initialled bed companions so excel.'

'No-one can accuse you of doing that, Sherwyn. And you can only be quoting Elvira. How suggestible you are!' Good, at least she was jealous.

'Had you not noticed how socialist writers, propagandist writers, dull, empty windbags the lot – '

'Name them!'

'Shaw, Wells, Nesbit, Blair, Sinclair, Tressel, starting with that bore William Morris. Will that do? Hypocrites the lot. Lashing themselves into frenzies of rage against the class to which they invariably belong. If not by birth by adoption.'

'I was right. You are eaten up with jealousy. You want their reviews. I daresay they want your money. Writers are worse than painters. Can we not talk politics? I was only saying what everyone else is saying.'

'I would expect no more of you, my dear.' Nor did he. He calmed down. He really must learn that Elvira was an exception. She was not like other women. She had a brain. He was waiting for his *navarin d'agneau aux navets* and Rita for her *coquilles à la crème*. Sometimes he thought her costermonger origins showed. Few people ordered fish for both courses. First fish, then meat, was what was customary in the middle class. He had a half bottle of Fleury, she had more champagne, simple girl!

'I have no children. Men never love me. They only want me.' Time for more tears, it seemed, and a soupçon of self pity. Then she said, surprising him, 'How clever of you to have reproduced yourself. How are your twins?'

Of course. The twins. Sir Jeremy's and Adela's, alleged children of The Change. Rita knew well enough they were Vivvie's, not Adela's – Sherwyn had come back from Austria and told her the whole story, or at any rate the bits that didn't include his nights with Adela. But apparently she assumed that he, Sherwyn, had been the one to impregnate poor Vivvie. He had been her fiancé, after all, why would she, any more than Adela, think otherwise? Vivvie's Angel Gabriel story had always been absurd.

It got so difficult as years passed and one got older to remember exactly who knew what and who didn't – things slipped out. A great recommendation for telling as few lies through life as one could manage. He should have kept quiet in the first place.

Rita's hand crept over onto his, where it lay on the table. You could always tell a woman's age by her hands, but Rita's were inscrutable. They were never her best feature at the best of times, always on the large, rough, working-girl side, but so unlike Marjorie's little white paws he found himself grateful for their touch. They were all promise. He wished Marjorie would let her hand stray to his every now and then, or his to hers, but she'd have had her fingernails painted some new colour and only tell him to be careful not to smudge them, and put him right off. Perhaps he could take Rita home and comfort her? He didn't like to see women cry.

Sherwyn did not bother to deny paternity. It would take too long. He told her he liked to see the twins once or twice a year. For their last birthday he had brought them both back a string of pearls from Italy.

'Doesn't Sir Jeremy find your interest in them rather strange? If he believes he's the father? You do live a complicated life, Sherwyn!'

'He takes good care not to complicate his own. If there are boats to be rocked, Sir Jeremy is not going to rock them. I am his prize author. I don't get literary reviews but I keep the firm in business. He trusts his wife, unlike your friend Nevinson. If Adela has gone to the trouble of presenting him with twin girls and says they are his why should he doubt her? They keep her happy and he wants her happy. As for me I am the husband of a disgraced dead and gone daughter, the twins' brother-in-law, his ex-son-in-law but two.' Before Marjorie, Sherwyn had had an unfortunate two-year marriage (including divorce) to a dress designer who had turned out to have lesbian tendencies.

'It keeps the family in touch but not too much in touch. I drop by, see the twins, smile at Adela who smiles back, and go away again. It suits everyone.'

In truth, he visited the twins to keep an eye on them, to keep his faith with Vivvie as a Joseph to her misbegotten babies, but he was not going to tell Rita this, or anyone. It behoved him as an Englishman to keep quiet about such irrational behaviour. Rita asked if the twins were happy with the pearls. In her experience, she said, young girls rather despised pearls. Sales at Dickins & Jones were right down. It was impossible to tell cultured pearls from the real thing so how could you know if the gift was priceless or shop-girl?

Sherwyn said he would never give the girls cheap pearls. They had been most appreciative of them. They'd looked lovely on Stella's neck, delicate translucent little things, but rather hopeless on Mallory, who didn't have much neck at all.
'Yes,' said Rita. 'I hear they're very different. Of course twins can have two fathers, if the mother has two lovers around the same time. The first one out belongs to the first lover, the next one to the second. One can only hope Stella is yours.'
'I didn't know that,' said Sherwyn, surprised again. 'But Vivvie was hardly the kind to have lovers – though how can one ever know anything about women? For all I know Vivvie took after her mother. Everyone but Sir Jeremy knows Adela is a nymphomaniac, and she's anyone's.' He felt bad. He was traducing Vivvie. Horrible how easily one slipped into this kind of disagreeable banter. He never let Delgano do it.
'Yes, tell me about the fabulous Adela,' said Rita. 'I always thought you rather fancied her.' And she complained that he'd

always had a thing about titles at the best of times. He was such a snob. A pity the real aristocrats were always out of reach for someone like Sherwyn. He hadn't been to Eton, only St Paul's.

Sherwyn asked for another half bottle of Fleury. She had more champagne. The main course was very slow in coming. Emboldened by her hand in his Sherwyn told her about the nights he had spent with Adela, which was why he hadn't been there when Vivvie gave birth and so couldn't tell her which twin was born first. He was ashamed even to remember the occasion, he said, which was true enough. His conduct was the product of high altitude, he said, summer in the Alps, a temporary insanity.

'And abstinence,' said Rita. 'I know what that does to men. But Sherwyn, really, your own mother-in-law! How could you!'

'I know, I know,' he said. 'But it was all so long ago: mists of time, all that. But Adela will keep quiet. I try not to meet her eye. Nor does she want to meet mine. I know where too many bodies are buried.'

'Supposing she had triplets! Supposing there were three of you. Do you think

Mungo could have got to her? He always wanted what was yours.'

That Sherwyn hadn't thought of. Nor was it a pleasant thought. Mungo was hardly a candidate for the role of the Angel Gabriel, certainly not one to whom he, Sherwyn, would have been willing to play Joseph. Lucifer, possibly. Sherwyn had assumed Mungo kept turning up with trashy presents for the twins because he was still trying to get back into Lady Adela's knickers. Or more likely these days – since Adela was beginning to look tiny and withered up, not tiny and delectable any more

– to annoy Sir Jeremy for years ago turning down Bolt & Crest as his agency. Boring Olive Crest had long departed the scene, sensibly enough; no doubt having discovered that Mungo was a vindictive man who bore grudges. Crest Zippers were doing just fine, though, under the slogan *For Speed and Comfort Just Zip & Unzip! Buttoning's Such a Bother*. Vulgar. It was a possibility of course. Mungo was certainly capable of any villainy. He had been buttering up Sir Jeremy for as long as anyone could remember and had probably been going down to Dilberne Court, one step ahead of Sherwyn every inch of the way.

Really, he thought. Surely Harrods could do better than this. He wanted to eat fast and take her home to bed and dry her tears and shut her up. When at last the food came the *navarin* turned out to be greasy mutton on a bed of mashed turnip and swede; her *coquilles* were rubbery.

'Let's go home and have something at my place,' she said. 'We might as well have gone to Dickins & Jones. The food is better.'

Sherwyn, gratified, asked for the bill. While they were waiting a large lady came up and asked him if he would be kind enough to sign his book for her. She had bought it, his latest, *Delgano and The Parisian Affair*, in the bookshop on the second floor, and recognised him from a book reading. He thought Rita would be impressed by this evidence of his fame but she sighed and took off her mink and ordered a strawberry ice, which came at once, and settled down to eat. He got rid of the large lady as soon as he could, inscribing on the title page his signature, date, place, and the message 'Patience and shuffle the cards' which always seemed to be popular with readers, suggesting as it did that some day Fortune would change their life for them as it had his.

The strawberry ice seemed to have sweetened Rita and he got her home to her studio – the rent paid for, he gathered, by E.L.T.'s wife Sybil – which was agreeable enough, smelt as ever of paint, turps, anthracite and old knickers, and yes, there was the crushed velvet purple sofa. Sherwyn acquitted himself well enough. Indeed, Delgano would have been proud of him, and he was in Leicester Square, washed and shaved, to meet Marjorie by seven.

The film was *Fire Over England*, with Flora Robson as Queen Elizabeth and Laurence Olivier and Vivien Leigh as juvenile leads. Marjorie said of Olivier, 'So handsome! So brutal!' and of Leigh, 'Not nearly as pretty as everyone says' and of Flora Robson nothing at all. Sherwyn thought perhaps he might try being more brutal.

Saturday Morning, March 11ᵗʰ 1938

It was a Saturday morning, and an eventful day for Adela. It was her fifty-third birthday which was bad enough. War clouds were gathering over England, someone had said on the radio, but there was little sign of that in Belgrave Square, other than that a lad had delivered four gas masks to the front door at eight in the morning when he should have gone to the back, which was easier to open. The front door always stuck. Adela had called and called for Morna to open it but the woman had refused to hear, as so often these days. Morna would have to go. She was idle and rude. The twins would make a terrible fuss but it would have to be done. However, not today. Today was going to be busy. She would ask the music teacher to stay for lunch – a darling lad, so like Tarzan the Ape Man it was amazing that his fingers were so small and deft – she had said as much to him, and he had said 'If I'm a Johnny Weissmuller then be my Maureen O'Sullivan. Those beautiful grey eyes!' so he was certainly interested, deserved lunch. His name was Carlo. When she'd looked in the mirror this morning she'd actually been rather pleased. She didn't look a day more than forty.

Sex was the most effective beauty treatment of them all, not that this was anything one could say aloud. Sir Jeremy, thank heavens, had always been most attentive, though he was rather falling off these days. He was twenty years older than she. Not

244

of course that she envisaged anything more than lunch. Igor was coming to dinner and it would be just him and her. She had said to Sir Jeremy that the last thing she wanted was her birthday celebrated – people kept looking at one and wondering how old one actually was – and he must go down to Dilberne Court for the weekend as usual. She had never understood this love of horses; horrible, smelly, enormous, oafish things, pooing whenever and wherever the fancy took them. Odd how her life had drawn her to the horse-mad. Perhaps it was something to do with her stars? First Sir Jeremy, now Igor, and of course poor Vivvie and her Greystokes.

And of course Sir Jeremy had insisted on being there when Vivvie was born, as if they were all in a foaling box, and she'd always thought it was something to do with the way Vivvie had turned out. They said men turned to litigation when the sexual drive left them, but Sir Jeremy's had turned to horses. But it could be useful. It gave her her weekends free. The Dilberne stud farm had become racing stables, the Grand National was only two weeks away, Mayfair Lights was a keen contender, and the owner Frank Darling would be down to keep an eye on his darling. The least Sir Jeremy could do was to be there too.

Mayfair Lights was the grandson of Greystokes, long departed this life. Like Vivvie, poor Vivvie. Adela tried not to make the same mistakes with Mallory as she had with Vivvie; let her go to school and tried to focus on her good qualities not her bad, as Mungo had always advised, being so keen on Freud. Freud had suggested that girls who had a low opinion of themselves ended up with an unbalanced 'id' and a reduced 'superego' which drove them to promiscuity.

'Freud, Adler and Jung,' Mungo had said, 'were all of the same opinion.'

'Oh, fried, addled and hung,' she had replied, thinking herself rather clever. 'You complain I'm promiscuous but my "id" is in perfectly good order, as you may have noticed. If anything I'm rather vain.'

Mungo had come back with some nonsense of her having had undemonstrative parents and been orphaned at too early an age. She was still fond of Mungo but really he had to go. At least Sherwyn hadn't forever been bringing up her past as Mungo loved to, if only, Sherwyn said, in compensation for the inadequacy of his parts: 'Big nose, small willy.' Sherwyn could be very catty, but was well endowed. Part, if not all of his attraction. But then she seemed to be so easily attracted to men.

Those early years were not ones she cared to think about: when as a young orphan everyone thought she was dead and she had been obliged to earn a living pretending to be a spiritualist and healer. But she had even ended up at the Prince of Wales' sickbed, when his appendix had burst in the nick of time of its own accord, and he was saved from the death everyone expected. The smell of the putrid organ had been atrocious. But Queen Alexandra had given her a ruby ring in gratitude and she still wore it on special occasions. It had brought her luck. She had worn it on their wedding day when lightning and thunder had split the skies on Monte Verità. Those were the days! She might wear the ring for lunch today. She would choose the pale pink jumper with her white skirt; the jumper was a little tight but that was all to the good: her breasts were as full of promise as they ever were, little perky mounds with pronounced nipples: the deep red of the ruby would flash invitation and promise.

There may have been some truth in what Mungo said about belief in the self. Adela had done what she could to build up Mallory's confidence and Mallory showed no signs of being at all easy with her favours the way Vivvie had been. And this was in spite of the misfortune of Mallory's looks – even worse than Vivvie but at least not so enormous and much, much quicker of thought and tongue. No-one would mistake Mallory for the village idiot. Vivvie had been smart enough, just reluctant to speak before she thought and determined to speak the truth. Mallory had no such ambition. If anything, unlike Vivvie, Mallory was turning out to be a man hater and a bluestocking, insisting that the North London Collegiate inspired by the famous bluestockings the Misses Beale & Buss was the only place for her:

'Miss Buss and Miss Beale,
Cupid's darts do not feel.
How different from us,
Miss Beale and Miss Buss.'

Mallory went all the way over on the No 13 bus to Hampstead every day just to study science. She obviously took after her Aunt Rosina, who had been something of an academic and probably, as so many of these women were, a good friend of Sappho. Stella was happy enough to be home tutored: a stream of young tutors came and went, some of them good-looking and all of them in the end half in love with Adela, *la belle dame sans merci*, and just occasionally, and very prudently, a few of them gratified in that love.

Looking back, Adela's determination to pass off the girls as her own did seem something of a madness, but it had happened and she had carried it off. Sir Jeremy never seemed to doubt that the girls were his and had been proud of this last evidence of his manliness, fathering children at his late age. And Stella had always been such a pleasure to show off. And even Mallory, the ugly little brain box, could at least make people laugh.

At around ten Harrods' green van came round to deliver her special birthday dinner in its cold box. Oysters, blinis with caviar, soured cream and chopped egg, fillet steak and vegetables prepared for cooking – Igor wouldn't mind helping with the cooking: there would be just the two of them and a little domesticity would be fun – followed by trifle. The image of Johnny Weissmuller's Tarzan rather appealed to her, and she saw herself as a miniature version of Maureen O'Sullivan: he was so big and she was so small...

Adela put the oysters aside and decided she would serve them for lunch after the piano lesson; oysters and caviar was perhaps overdoing it for dinner. She had been having this on-and-off affair with Igor since the handsome young White Russian refugee out of royal St Petersburg had been employed by Sir Jeremy down at the Dilberne stud.

That was before Sir Jeremy discovered communism and was merely on the side of refugees everywhere. Igor was now an Olympic gold medallist, winning the equestrian event in Berlin in 1936, and now show-jumped in events all over the world, but always visited when passing through London. He was a fine-looking man, tall and slim-hipped, olive-skinned but with a shock of blonde hair, now rather thinning and fading but whose didn't – though compared to young Carlo with his broad shoulders he did seem a little, well, flimsy. But one never knew about the parts men protected and hid so assiduously: tall and slim-hipped translated in Igor's case into agreeably long and enquiring: in Carlo's, who was to say what broad shoulders implied? It might turn out to be short and stubby?

Well, she could only find out. She had always been plagued by a really terrible curiosity. She got on perfectly well with Mallory, able to ignore the girl's deformities, but found Stella less interesting, a perfect mannequin but hopelessly innocent. Yes, Carlo for lunch, Igor for dinner. The twins would be safely in the nursery wing. Sound did not carry. First the oysters, then the caviar. One wasn't going to get away with it for ever, but who cared? She shivered in anticipation.

Adela was in this pleasant mood of self analysis and expectation mixed when the twins came into the morning room to wish her a happy birthday and bring her a birthday gift. Good Lord, Stella had grown so tall. She positively towered over Adela. She was going to be as tall as Vivvie, only at least slim and elegant, with these long, long, perfect legs. Mallory just stayed short and squat. How old were the girls? Fifteen, sixteen?

The parcel had been beautifully wrapped in pink crepe paper and pale blue ribbon. She suspected this was Stella's doing. Stella favoured pastels, Mallory strong colours – lots of black and red

– she herself stuck to whites, greys, fawns. It looked like a book. It was. Sherwyn Sexton's latest novel – *Delgano's Archipelago*. (11/8, Sherwyn would say. He had worried about the proportion a lot but gone with it in the end. It sounded right.)

'I know you love him, Mama! He's such a good writer, isn't he' That was Stella.

'I wouldn't go as far as to say that,' put in Mallory. 'But we thought you might enjoy it.'

'Is he our father, Mama? Do tell!' said Stella.

'What an extraordinary question, girls!' Adela laughed merrily. 'What on earth are you talking about? Your father is Sir Jeremy Ripple.'

'Why can no-one ever call him just Jeremy Ripple?' asked Stella. 'Why does he always have to be Sir Jeremy?'

'Your father is a very impressive and important man,' said Adela, though she had sometimes wondered herself. Remarkable how that investiture occasion seemed to have threaded through all the years, since Vivvie had fallen off her chair and embarrassed everyone so much. 'You are lucky to have him as such a father, a man knighted by the King himself.'

'And we know you're not our mother,' said Mallory, 'we worked that out years back.'

'This is complete madness,' said Adela. 'I shall get very angry with you in a minute.'

'Like any man rightfully accused of infidelity,' said Stella, and she no longer looked straight at Adela, but down at her feet, 'anger will be the first reaction of any woman accused of having stolen some other woman's children.'

Stella is no longer any use to me, thought Adela. Anyone who sees me with her will believe that if I'm old enough to have given birth to this tall towering creature I must be well past my prime. I suppose it had to come. I earned some fifteen years of youth by starting afresh with Vivvie's children, but now I'm back to where I was. Well. So be it. But how am I going to work it so these children don't tell Sir Jeremy? He'll be none too pleased to find out he's been fathering children who are none of his own. But perhaps he won't worry too much, what with Germany about to invade Austria. He's been so angry about the mood of appeasement that has struck the country he's been hardly able to concentrate even on Mayfair Lights' chances of winning the Grand National. She herself thought the Austrians were the same as the Germans anyway, apart from a few details like what they ate for breakfast and what kind of bed they slept in, so what was all the fuss about? She told the girls she wouldn't listen to another word of this pernicious nonsense and set them to opening oysters. She would show them life was not so easy as they thought.

But she couldn't help asking them what made them think she was not their mother, as they struggled and groaned and risked hands and eyes with slipping and breaking table knives. Adela did not lead them to the drawer where the oyster openers were kept.

Mallory said that when they were eight they had made an oath but it had taken them many years to realise all they had to do was ask. She quoted it.
'Let us swear an oath together, Stella and Mallory combined, While in Belgrave Square we sisters live and lie reclined…
Let who conceived us, how conceived us, be the truth we seek to find.'

Adela complained that it was hardly up to Tennyson's standard, and Stella said she'd realised that at the time, but they'd been only eight.

'After all this money spent on your education!' Adela said. 'Me not your mother! Who, then? I was here at dinner the other Wednesday sitting next to your father's hero, Herr "Bert" Brecht from Germany, whose play Fear and Misery of the Third Reich your father means to translate –'

'Get translated,' put in Mallory, the pedant.

'– and he said to me that a child belongs to the person who looks after it not the person who gives birth to it. He was talking about the nation and the German worker, no doubt, but there was a lot of truth in what he said. Have I not looked after you, reared you, at considerable expense to myself?'

They considered this.

'Very well,' said Mallory, charitably, 'we accept you as our mother,' and Adela breathed a sigh of relief. This at least simplified matters. 'But who is our father? Sir Jeremy is simply no use. Horses! Uncle Mungo or Uncle Sherwyn? Both behave as if they were, bringing us presents and asking about our education and our boyfriends. We don't have those, we are too young but they don't seem to comprehend that.'

Who indeed, thought Adela. When she'd told Sir Jeremy back in 1923 that she was pregnant, it had not been a lie. But by whom she could not tell. It could indeed have been Sir Jeremy, it could have been Mungo. It could have been Sherwyn's, all on that one occasion, the investiture party, when people drank far too much because of Syrie's inedible nibbles. Syrie should have stuck to interiors, not branched out into food. She'd been with Sir Jeremy the night before: his knighthood had made him very eager; Mungo a very quick celebratory get-together when she'd been dressing at home before the party and Sir Jeremy was already boringly at a meeting; and then Sherwyn at the end of the party though he was so drunk he might not have even remembered and certainly showed no sign of doing so thereafter – but that speech of his, what was it? – *Oh delicate damsel, I swoon, I swoon,* had been so unexpected and he the gatecrasher, the interloper, the romantic knight in shining armour, she'd thrown caution away. She must have drunk far too much herself.

And then she'd miscarried the day after Vivvie's wedding: the strain of the event had been too much: Vivvie pregnant, and by Sherwyn! She didn't tell Sir Jeremy, it would have been too, too shaming. Everyone would have laughed and said of course she was too old to carry a baby. And of course she wanted Vivvie's, she had lost her own. It was very strange, being a woman and propelled by instincts she knew nothing about herself. Sometimes she wondered if it could be the effects of emminin, the pill she'd been taking since Vivvie's birth to control her migraines. It worked for the migraines, and had been pre-scribed by a Harley Street physician, and was derived from the late pregnancy urine of Canadian women and contained the ovary-stimulating hormones of the placenta which didn't sound very nice – but anything to stop the crucifying head-aches. If she stopped taking it they came back. But what else might they not do?

Sherwyn had once accused her of nymphomania which she had strenuously denied. She was no kind of whore, she was not sex-mad. It was no kind of compulsion which made her both so attractive and so attracted by men. She just enjoyed sex and men sensed it. Other women could be happy with one man in their entire lives. But times were changing. There was hope for even Mallory yet. Intelligent women were not the source of horror that once they had been, pitied for being brainy because they were destined to be neurotic and unhappy because having babies would never be enough for them. She found herself fond of Mallory as she had never managed to be with Vivvie.

Sometimes she felt bad about Vivvie. She had gone into the room in Barscherau in the middle of the night and found Vivvie passed out in all this blood and just shut the door and gone away and called no-one. Sherwyn had to have time to get back to his room and he couldn't have done that with the whole house in uproar. And there was nothing anyone could have done anyway. Vivvie had been delivered safely. Now she had a postpartum haemorrhage. Blood everywhere. One of those know-it-all peasant women had not checked that both placentas were out. The twins had not shared a placenta. Anyone could have noticed even then that they were not identical. These days Dr Walker might have had Ergometrine in his little brown emergency bag but not back then, in 1923. She had to claim the babies as her own. There was no way out. Sherwyn could never have coped with them. He was far too selfish.

She had cut both men, Mungo and Sherwyn, out of her life. It seemed that the best she could do for the twins was to attribute them both to Sir Jeremy and herself. As Vivvie's young sisters they would inherit, and she, Adela, would manage their estates until they reached their majority.

'I've done the best I could,' she said to the girls, 'in the light of my own nature. What else can any of us do? As to your Uncles, for them to be real uncles your mother and father would have to have siblings, and we have not.'

'We're not idiots,' Stella said. 'We worked that out.'

'Last time I was down at Dilberne,' said Mallory, 'I asked the old women in the village shop whose sister made our sister's wedding dress, and they said yes, Miss Ripple was pregnant when she was married.'

'Servants' gossip,' said Adela. 'A long time ago. And they're not very bright. How would they remember?'

'You gave them a glass and silver bowl with old potato salad in it,' said Mallory, 'and they assumed it was a bribe to keep quiet about it. How could they not remember? She still has it in her cabinet: she washes it out once a month and polishes the silver because the cottage is damp and it's prone to tarnish.'

'They have it wrong,' said Adela. 'I was the one who was pregnant.' *Oh, what a tangled web we weave, when first we practise to deceive*, Adela thought. She was going to be exhausted before this day was out. 'I didn't want that getting about. I'd just found out that your sister Vivvie was pregnant: it was a dreadful shock. She was engaged to your Uncle Sherwyn. I didn't want that getting about either.' She explained that brides in those days were meant to be virgins and went into hiding if it became evident that they were not. There was all kinds of skulduggery over dates and premature births and so on. Sherwyn and Vivvie went into hiding in Bavaria, so he could finish his novel in peace.

'They must have loved each other very much.'

'They did. And then poor Vivvie died giving birth and her little boy too. Puerperal fever.'

'Did they name the baby?'

'Of course. Arthur. After my cousin Arthur. He was an Earl, you know, and was brought up in this very house.'

'So you keep telling us.' That was Stella the beautiful. She could be very catty.

'And it was a month or two before I could bring you two back to your father. Death can keep one very busy, especially when it's in a foreign country. Your Uncle Sherwyn was too upset to be much help. If your Uncle Sherwyn turns up with gifts it's because he still feels guilty.'

It didn't sound totally plausible but she thought they had accepted it, and then the front door bell rang and it was Carlo the music teacher with the Tarzan shoulders. and just as well because now how was she going to explain Mungo? People were such a bother. The girls for asking questions. Sherwyn and Mungo for not fading away when required.

Mallory had her lesson first. Adela could hear from the kitchen. It sounded both delightful and determined. Mallory was a dab hand at Rachmaninoff. When Stella had hers she struggled through an early Mozart sonata which sounded pretty enough. She also sang a little Handel, and Adela felt very proud. One way and another the twins could only bring her credit. She laid the table for two and cut bread as thinly as she could. When the lesson was finished the twins would go back to the nursery wing where Morna would have prepared steamed plaice, cauliflower cheese and parsnips as ever.

The lesson seemed to be going on rather a long time and Adela could hear the sound of girlish giggling. She went into the library and found Stella on the piano seat gazing up at the music teacher with loving eyes, trying to sing Handel, *Did You Not See My Lady, Go down the Garden Singing*, while Tarzan the music teacher had his hand down her chest and was rubbing her nipples. Stella was now giggling so much her voice quavered and faded into breathlessness. Both seemed to be enjoying the experience very much. Adela threw Tarzan out of the house.

Adela felt old, jealous and helpless, taken advantage of, humiliated. Carlo only wooed her the better to woo Stella. Something she had not foreseen; the daughter must always be more fanciable than the mother. As the daughter grows up, the mother grows old. Stella was sent weeping back to her steamed plaice and parsnips and Adela scraped the oysters into the sink.

Then she called Courtney and Baum and found some ancient, boring person there, who turned out to be the original Mr Baum himself, and told him to arrange for the twins to be sent off to the best finishing school in France. He said he could recommend one in Lausanne in Switzerland where his grand-daughters went, but had brought them home because of the international situation and he feared the lights were going to go out all over Europe. Adela said what nonsense, nothing was going to happen. Hitler wouldn't dare: people must not be intimidated but go about their business as usual. Otherwise he had won. If Mr Baum was Jewish he might be well advised to bring his family home, but these were good English, Christian girls, and would be perfectly safe.

She instructed him to arrange their passage to the *Académie St. Augustine*, a finishing school which royalty attended, and to do it forthwith. Then she went to the nursery and gave Morna her notice to quit. The girls were grown up now and her services were not needed. Morna threw a dish of cauliflower cheese against the wall and it dripped down onto the kelim rug. The children wept profusely. Morna packed but stood at the door saying she would be back for her wages. Adela said she would deduct the cost of cleaning the rug and doubted there would be anything left to pay. Morna said the rug was nothing but an old rag, Mr Sherwyn was a mean bastard, but went back into her room and slammed the door. It was the girls who packed, saying they couldn't wait to be finished and get out of this madhouse. Adela locked the door between the nursery wing and the main house, went up to her bedroom, took another emminin in case the migraine returned, and fell asleep.

Saturday Evening, March 11th 1938

But the day was not yet over. Igor let himself in at around six o'clock, as was his custom through the side door of the mews entrance at the back of the house, and up the unused side staircase which Inspector Strachan had insisted on being built when Robert, Earl of Dilberne was Minister of Trade and in danger from Irish terrorists and might need a quick getaway. Adela had always felt that perhaps Isobel, his wife, was more in danger from Inspector Strachan.

Igor took off his riding boots – he was seldom without them – with some difficulty, and joined Adela in the bed. It seemed to him the least he could do. He did not like to see women upset. Some complained that she was not as young as she used to be, but he was not as disturbed by age as so many of her compatriots seemed to be. So far as he was concerned many a good tune was played on an old fiddle. When she felt better they went down to the kitchen for supper.

Adela explained how badly the girls were behaving, how important it was to send them abroad to finishing school to learn how to become ladies and at least learn some discrimination. The music teacher! A scurrilous lout, louche as a rat, and poor little Stella bewitched. Adela had never been so angry.

'A mother in defence of her brood,' he sympathised. The caviar was excellent. It reminded him of home, long ago. He had left St Petersburg as a lad in 1917, a White Russian émigré from Soviet persecution, found work in riding stables, excelled in equestrian circles, been accepted into society – '*a Cossack, don't yah know!*' – and indeed, being so charming and present-able, into many high-born beds. He'd been a gold medallist in the 1936 Berlin Olympics, after which nothing was too good for him.

The girls met him.

'But he's so stupid,' Mallory lamented. 'What do they all see in him?'

'Darling,' Stella said, 'his looks, his length,' which shocked Mallory – Stella had picked up too much that was vulgar in her shopping and beauty parlour sprees with Adela. But Stella was probably right. It was certainly what their mother saw in him. Morna always reported back on the state of their mother's bed and how it wasn't always their father in it.

'Lausanne will be safe enough, won't it?' Adela asked Igor. She felt a little bad about her decision. She needed confirmation. Sir Jeremy would only say it wasn't safe if she asked, but was so up in arms about 'Herr Hitler and the fascist onslaught' his judge-ment could hardly be trusted.

'I should think so,' said Igor. It was a long time since he had been a mere White Russian refugee; now he was just a splendid equestrian on a splendid white horse. 'I was in Lausanne only last year for the Longines Cup. A very civilised place, and a triumph for me, I may say.'

'Such a dreadful day for me,' said Adela, 'and then I had to fire the nanny. I should have done it years back. She's set such a bad example to the twins. Table manners, bad language – you know how it is with servants.'

The steak was fillet and she served it with leeks in white sauce. She made the sauce herself while he watched. Such tiny, competent little hands. Even just watching them sent a shiver up his spine.
'You did the right thing,' he said. 'You always do.' He had once seen a servant creeping about the bedroom in the early hours when they were meant to be away, but had thought it better to keep silent.
The front door bell went.
'Bloody hell,' she said. 'You'd better not go. I will.'
'Send them packing whoever they are,' he said. 'I am supremely happy.'

But she didn't. It was Sherwyn Sexton, slightly drunk, and she asked him down to the kitchen. Igor and he knew each other from here and there. Igor's position as passing lover was abundantly clear. No Sir Jeremy in the picture, Igor with his boots off and Adela had flung her old fur coat on over her negligee. Sherwyn said he knew the mink from of old and Adela said: 'Oh, that old thing,' and Igor assumed Sherwyn too was a former lover, which made things easier between them. Whatever it had been, it was over. Sherwyn asked for bread and cheese and was given it, and Igor opened another bottle of champagne. It made a splendid pop and Igor and Adela giggled complicitly. It seemed the girls had telephoned to ask for help. They complained that they'd been locked in without food or drink. Their mother had gone mad. Stella had kissed a boy and so Adela was sending them off to stupid Switzerland to boarding school, one which nobody had ever heard of. Mallory was meant to be matriculating in June, a year early. Physics, Chemistry, Biology, Applied Maths, Latin and Greek, what hope did she have now? Their mother had then fired Nanny, who had looked after them since infancy, and upset her very much. Their father was away in the country: he cared about his horses more than he cared about his own children. They had rung Uncle Mungo but the girl said he was in Japan selling zips. *Unbuttoning's Such A Bother*. So they'd called their Uncle Sherwyn. He was to come round at once.

So he had and here he was. What did Adela have to say?

At which Adela laughed merrily and said the girls were quite hysterical; it was inevitable, alas, their stage of psychosexual development being what it was; they'd had a perfectly good lunch and to do without supper would calm them down. Mallory was too fat anyway, there was no point in paying for a nanny – had Sherwyn any idea how much servants, even the worst ones, charged these days? – for grown up girls, and the sooner they were at school the better, especially Mallory – whoever would want a scientist wife, a cordon bleu cookery course would stand her in far better stead, and Lausanne was a perfectly safe place, Igor had said so. Would Sherwyn like wine? Champagne and cheese simply did not go. Probably better if Sherwyn didn't see the girls, he'd only stir them up.
Sherwyn went down to the wine cellar and brought back a '29 Latour which must have cost Sir Jeremy quite a penny.

Around midnight Sherwyn said he really must be getting back to Elvira. Adela said she couldn't think why, and Sherwyn said:

'Because for once in my life I am happy.'

Adela said: 'You're such a bourgeois at heart, Sherwyn.'

Sherwyn said there was a lot to be said for early nights.

'You didn't think that once, Sherwyn,' said Adela. 'Years back, you and I, the night of that fabulous party. We were celebrating me being Lady Adela. Three in the morning at least. The caterers had gone home leaving such a mess. You helped me clear up.'

'You're sure you don't mean Mungo? He was around at the time.'

'No, I don't mean Mungo,' said Lady Adela crossly. 'I mean you. You'd said that lovely thing to me. We were under my mink. It was brand new from Harrods, a present from Sir Jeremy. This very one I'm wearing now. I use it as a dressing gown.' Even in her agreeably drunken haze she realised it was an area where she would be wiser not to go. She must be very careful not to get cross or say anything that couldn't be unsaid.

But the men seemed to have forgotten about her. It was annoying. They were getting on well together, talking about all that old hat esoteric stuff, Gurdjieff and Ouspensky and the fourth dimension and life after death. But so many millions of men had gone off and been killed and not a single one proved to have come back from the dead, you'd have thought people would have learned. It was what everyone did these days instead of religion. It was irritating. It reminded her of her stupid youth and Monte Verità. She should never have married Sir Jeremy, he was so old and boring.

'Well, I'm sorry,' said Sherwyn. 'I simply don't remember.' Nor did he. He could see it might have been possible. Another drunken fuck at a drunken party. But Adela? Surely not. The boss's wife? Mind you, he'd been pretty furious with him at the time. He thought vaguely there might have been someone called Phoebe, yes, Phoebe, big bouncy girl, Sir Jeremy's secretary. She'd typed his first Delgano novel: nice girl. Yes, possibly Phoebe. But not Adela, who was making it up. She simply had to be the centre of attention. She was looking very cross.

He returned pointedly to the conversation with Igor, and the four ways of self development talked about in esoteric circles. It seemed safer. Delgano had got involved in a theosophist group in Indonesia: Sherwyn wished he'd had the opportunity to talk to Igor earlier; Igor could have filled in where Sherwyn had to simply guess. But Adela was not going to let it go.

She even pulled at his sleeve to interrupt and say that before her day fell to pieces the girls had given her a copy of *Delgano's Archipelago* for her birthday.
Sherwyn asked her how old she was which made her angrier. It was not a gentlemanly thing to ask, he knew, but it served her right.
'I forget,' she replied brusquely. 'Since everyone round here seems to forget so easily. The girls, by the way, are convinced you're their father not their uncle.'
'That is not possible,' said Sherwyn. 'But let us not go into all that.' No, it wasn't possible, he thought. Vivvie was not forgettable. Unapproachable all those months in the goose feather bed. It might have been the case with Adela; way back then. He had drunk a great deal in those days. He needed another drink now. Elvira could wait. He was confident enough she would wait. Elvira was like Vivvie in that respect. She made no unnecessary problems.

'Go into what?' asked Igor, sensitive to some change in the atmosphere. Difficult to go into anything, Sherwyn thought: the air in the kitchen already being so thick with alcohol fumes, Adela's non-stop pink Sobranies, and Igor's snuff, evil antisocial stuff from Georgia which he'd refer to affectionately as his burnuthi. But Adela seemed deaf to Igor. Sherwyn was her prey.

'Men are so forgetful,' said Adela. 'Apparently they even forget about fathering babies.'

'Tell me more!'

'Oh, go away, Igor! Sherwyn made me pregnant that night. Do you mean men even forget when they make a girl pregnant?'

'There's not exactly some great thunder flash,' said Sherwyn. 'Life goes on as ever. But if I did I most sincerely apologise. So drunk I forgot.'

'Oh you're a great and convenient forgetter.'

'What was it, a boy or a girl?'

'A boy.'

'Oh dear. Is he going to come through that door any moment and declare he's my son? You're old enough. Or perhaps he's Igor here?'

'You beast, you beast! You callous beast. I miscarried.'

'How convenient.'

'Fathered a boy on me, fathered twins on poor Vivvie. I shall never forgive you for that. You took advantage of her. She was such an innocent. I can look after myself, but Vivvie! My daughter!'

'Hello, hello,' said Igor, and was ignored.

'You forget you murdered your poor Vivvie,' said Sherwyn. 'You let her bleed to death and stole the twins. I don't forgive you for that.'

'I say, I say!' said Igor.

'Well, you didn't want them.' Adela was weeping bitterly, though Sherwyn didn't believe a single tear. 'You were happy enough to see those babies go. What else was to be done? I did it for your sake. I loved you. I've always loved you.'

'Thanks very much,' said Igor with a sniff and sneeze. 'What about me?'

'And you loved me, Sherwyn: "*I swoon, I swoon*". What a fool I've been!'

'Yes,' said Sherwyn, 'a greater fool no woman has ever been.'

They fell quiet. Adela snivelled, and huddled into her old mink. Igor broke the silence, and talked about thunder flashes and fathering babies; a strange experience he'd had when a pretty virgin lad with blonde curls, working in Sir Jeremy's stables. He could only have been about sixteen, an émigré youth fresh from Russia, an orphan in a foreign land preyed upon by gross and ignorant stable hands. All he had to comfort him was his love for Greystokes, a handsome dappled grey he was allowed to ride every morning. Together they would gallop the length of the downs in glorious countryside and he would practise the Cossack skills of his forefathers, and find life worth living. He owed his Olympic medal to those early morning rides with Greystokes.

'Greystokes?' Adela was asking. 'Greystokes?'

'Wonderful beast,' said Igor. 'I was down at Dilberne only this morning to take a look at his grandson Mayfair Lights out of the filly Bejasus.'

'Vivvie and you? Greystokes?'

'I don't know what her name was, just that she had incorporated the female spirit of the horse, large limbed, smooth, storm

266

clouds gathering, an apparition of beauty.' Pause, snuff, sniff, sneeze. 'She even had a mane, a reddish mane. A long, long time ago. I know you have no time for forgetfulness, but yes, men forget. On those wondrous mornings I would lean from the saddle and gather little mushrooms as the ground flew past. Yes, that is how I honed my skills. Now Mayfair Lights is to win the Grand National. I pay my homage.'

'Blonde curls,' said Sherwyn. 'Blonde curls. A stable lad. The Angel Gabriel.'

'Yes, men forget. But I do not forget those soft, welcoming eyes. Greystokes' eyes. I lost my virginity to those eyes. Then the storm broke. But the lightning flash came after I had left the stable. Nothing can have happened. I went home and cut off my curls and after that I was safe.'

'The conception comes after the act,' said Sherwyn and then beneath his breath, imploring to heaven, 'A Cossack. Now Mallory is explained. And I have been St Joseph to this oaf!'

'But after that I became a disciple of Gurdjieff. There are more things in heaven and earth.'

Adela sprang to life. She beat upon Igor's breast with her little fists.

'My daughter, my daughter, you raped my daughter! I shall never forgive you.'

'I did nothing of the sort,' said Igor, with dignity. 'I communed with her and she with me. Together we loved Greystokes.'

'Hold on a moment,' said Sherwyn. His friend Igor was having to shield himself from Adela's blows. The woman was totally out of control. 'Make up your mind. One moment the twins are mine, the next his. Shall we just blame the Angel Gabriel? Vivvie always did.'

'Bloody horses,' said Adela. 'They've ruined my life.' In this mood, she was frightening, capable of anything. He tried to divert her.

'It's true I fucked someone that night. I thought it was Phoebe but it might have been you. I admit it.'

'It was certainly you in the mountains,' Adela said, 'in the days when you were loveable. And who the fuck's Phoebe?' She was beginning to calm down a little.

'She worked for Sir Jeremy. She was his secretary back in the old days. We were rivals for her affection and I was winning.' Oops. Bad mistake. Delgano would never have made it.

'She still is,' said Igor. 'Phoebe. If she's the nice fat one down at the stables this morning. She stays in the village most weekends. They do bed and breakfast. I stayed there last night. They have a cut-glass bowl in the cabinet. Very beautiful. The bowl, not so much the girl. The rim's solid silver. It looks very valuable. I wonder no-one's sold it.'

Adela's little fists had stopped flailing. But she was ashen white. Sherwyn thought she might faint. Then she opened her mouth and started screaming, great large animal shrieks from that tiny soft mouth as if some hidden part of her was communing with the devil in a language only the devil would understand. There seemed very little the men could do. Igor went upstairs to collect his boots and they left. Adela was still screaming.

'I don't think you should have said that,' said Sherwyn, as they turned from Belgrave Square into Upper Belgrave Street. They were both quite shocked.

'Eezveenete,' said Igor. Sherwyn supposed he was speaking Russian. He took it as agreement.

'One rule for the ladies,' said Sherwyn. 'Another for us.'

'Da,' said Igor. Sherwyn understood that. A simple 'yes'. Igor's hand was rather familiarly upon Sherwyn's arm. Sherwyn shook it off.

Coda

August 29th 1939. Harley Street

'Why on earth would Adela want to poison me?' asked Sir Jeremy. 'I offered her a divorce but she didn't want one.'

Phoebe sat at Sir Jeremy's bedside and took shorthand notes. She took them down at the rate of a hundred words a minute. Sir Jeremy was dictating an article on how the British ruling class would decline to bomb German factories because the Cabinet had declared them to be private property. The hypocrisy and mendacity of the imperialist classes knew no bounds. 'Isn't that so, Phoebe?'

Phoebe smiled placidly, put down her pencil, took Sir Jeremy's hand and squeezed it affectionately. The bouncy girl Sherwyn remembered had turned into a sensible-looking sturdy woman of the stoical-personal-assistant kind, with a pleasant face, brogues on her feet, in a knee-length black skirt and white blouse damp under the armpits. Luckily, Phoebe showed no sign of recognising Sherwyn as her suitor of long ago.

They were in the London Clinic. Sir Jeremy sat in a hospital bed propped up by pillows. It was a hot day. He had been admitted ten days before suffering from mushroom poisoning and had, they said, barely survived. His liver and kidneys had been severely affected but he had won through. Enquiries had apparently traced the source of the poisoning to the death cap mushroom, by way of potato soup in a thermos ingested by Sir

Jeremy at the office. There had been little time lately for long lunches at Simpson's or Rules.

Sir Jeremy looked thin, pale and decidedly older. But a nurse, or perhaps Phoebe, had combed and smoothed his hair and in his white hospital gown he looked tidy, composed and almost impressive. He boasted of having lost half a stone.

'It's an ill wind, dear boy. And why assume Adela is the guilty one?' he said.

Sherwyn refrained from saying that having arrived back from France to find Phoebe ensconced with Sir Jeremy at No 17 Belgrave Square, Adela might well have seen it as the last straw and perhaps added a sprinkling of powdered death cap to the potato soup Phoebe had prepared for his lunch. Sherwyn had used that plot in *Delgano's Archipelago*, which he believed Adela had read. He doubted that Sir Jeremy had. These days the actual reading of books was left to those who ran the money-making side of Ripple & Co, the fiction and biography lists, while Sir Jeremy got on with the political tracts and little magazines.

'Perhaps it was just an accident. Perhaps a genuine error. Perhaps someone mistook a death cap for a field mushroom. They look a bit similar.'

'Far more likely,' said Sir Jeremy, 'to be a political opponent or a disgruntled employee. I have made enemies, as how can a man of integrity and forethought not? I have fought hard to speak the truth and truth is never popular.'

'Or it could be Morna,' said Phoebe. 'She peeled the potatoes for the soup.'

'Morna!' said Sherwyn, surprised. 'Is she still around?'

'With the girls in Lausanne and Adela in Fontainebleau,' said Sir Jeremy, 'and me all alone in that great house, Morna was better than nothing. But white food, always white food! Now Phoebe's with me, I've been trying to get Morna to go home to Ireland where she belongs. But she's quite hard to dislodge, I find. We should all be where we belong in wartime.'

'It might all die down,' said Sherwyn. 'It might be just a storm that blows itself out.'

'I doubt it,' said Sir Jeremy. 'We are heading straight for an imperialist and unjust war for which the bourgeoisie of all the belligerent states bear equal responsibility. It is inevitable: the phoenix of equality will rise from the ashes. Are you taking this down, Phoebe?'

'Oh I am, Jeremy.' Another loving smile. Sherwyn was startled. It was the first time he had heard Sir Jeremy addressed as simply Jeremy, without his title. And lo! he was real flesh and blood: in Phoebe's eyes a moving, feeling, failing human being, not a publisher. He realised who Phoebe reminded him of. It was his stepmother with the face like a horse.

His stepmother had worn white shirts which were always damp under the armpits. And his mother, who his father always referred to as 'The Vamp', was like Adela, if not in looks in temperament; fun, dainty, murderous, an absconder. Never there. Sherwyn's father was like Sir Jeremy, untidy, bookish, ponderous, inept. So yes, probably, way back then Sherwyn had indeed pressed his drunken, charming Oedipal suit on both his stepmother, in Phoebe's shape, and his mother, in Adela's shape, thus aiming a blow at his father, in Sir Jeremy's shape. And it was sheer guilt, not necessarily hang-overs, which had rendered him amnesiac. Or so Mungo, Freud-mad, would have had it.

He was friends with Mungo again. It was Mungo who had brought Sherwyn to Sir Jeremy's bedside. Mungo had phoned Sherwyn weeks back, before even the advent of the death cap episode. He hadn't had a card from the girls for some time. Could Sherwyn check with the old man that the twins were safely back from Lausanne and in London, or preferably at Dilberne Court where bombs were less likely to fall?

Sherwyn said he knew Adela was back from Fontainebleau. He too had no word from the girls, but he assumed they too had returned. He asked Mungo why he didn't just ask Sir Jeremy himself. Mungo said that last time he'd seen the old man they'd all but come to blows. Sir Jeremy had said there was no way the working class or Communist Parties worldwide would support the war. Mungo had said all classes would unite against fascism. Sir Jeremy had said Mungo was a war profiteer gloating because the Ministry of War had decided all army uniforms would have zipped flies.

'You know how it works.'

'Oh I do, I do,' Sherwyn said. '*Unbuttoning's such a bore.*' He explained that these days he too tried to avoid Sir Jeremy's company. War talk was bound to end up in disagreements. Communists against fascists, appeasers and patriots and all stages in between – everyone took sides, claimed the moral high ground. Families split, peaceful dinner parties became rancorous. People walked out of rooms when others walked into them, as discord amongst the rulers found its echo in social and domestic life.

The twins were forgotten. Sherwyn and Mungo agreed to have lunch at Rules. 'Like old times,' said Mungo, 'but this time round you can pay the bill. Bet you're bloody richer than me.'

They argued about who had done better in life, who had bedded more women. Mungo acknowledged that his ambition was to write a novel one day, 'when he had the time'. They talked about Adela, They talked about Adela, who after she'd accused Sir Jeremy of having an affair with his secretary had packed the girls off to a finishing school in Switzerland, become a Seeker after Truth, refused to divorce Sir Jeremy in case he married the girl (which would be a humiliation worse than death) and gone to live in a Gurdjieffian commune in Fontainebleau which devoted itself to the Harmonious Development of Man.

'She was always that way inclined,' said Sherwyn, over smoked trout. He had decided to watch his weight since he'd been approached at his club by a certain Major Lawrence Grand from a hush-hush outfit he'd set up in a back room of the War Office, and known only as Section D. Espionage had turned out to be his fictional forte. Now, with a war in the offing, perhaps he and his alter ego Delgano could blend properly and become one. But he'd need to be fit.

Mungo had the roast beef. Still with the build and the geniality of the rugger Blue, he had, however, run to fat and was losing his hair. Sherwyn's remained luxuriant. He felt quite kindly and generously towards Mungo.

'Poor Adela,' said Mungo. 'Superstition. What daddy Freud would call faulty actions rooted in anxiety.'

Sherwyn said perhaps Adela did not deserve too much pity. She had indeed been distressed to find Sir Jeremy had a single lover to her dozens, but had quickly enough recovered sufficiently to run off with Igor, himself a Seeker after Truth and a long-term follower of Gurdjieff, as were several White Russians.

'Igor Kubanov, the equestrian? The gold medallist? Adela knows him? I'd no idea.'

'Together again,' said Sherwyn, enjoying himself. 'Turns out he's the twins' father.'

'Impossible,' said Mungo, after a second or two, sneezing into his roast beef, spluttering into his gravy. A waiter came running. The restaurant was being fitted with blackout blinds. Light and shade kept changing.

'I thought you knew. Igor has all this blonde hair. That's why he's such a favourite with the ladies. They lose interest when we go thin on top. But obviously. Think about it. Stella's blonde hair, Mallory's Cossack legs.'

Mungo took time to recover from the shock.

'Truly? I really assumed I was the father. Lord, what a mess!'

'Ah yes,' said Sherwyn, 'all those presents. Remorse. What Freud saw as the result of a struggle between ego and superego – parental imprinting.'

Mungo looked piteously and reproachfully at his friend and ordered apple pie and cream, and Cheddar cheese. Sherwyn took only black coffee. What was it that the mysterious Major Grand of Section D had said? '*Of course, the kind of people we'll need will have to be in fairly good physical shape.*' Sherwyn was an excellent French speaker but with no German. Grand, who seemed to be already planning for covert excursions into enemy territory, had intimated that he assumed France would fall. Now was not the time for apple pie and cream, thought Sherwyn, let alone a slab of Cheddar.

'It's something of a relief,' Mungo was saying. 'Not my responsibility after all. But you won't forget, will you, my friend? Just check the twins are back. They're nice girls at heart, though it's a pity about Mallory. Adela never deserved a daughter with those looks, any more than she deserved Vivvie, the monster you married.' And then, hastily, 'No, no, not that she wasn't a nice girl. I was so sorry about what happened. Dear boy, indeed, a loss.'

'Thank you,' said Sherwyn.

They left the table as friends. Sherwyn did not bring up the possibility that non-identical twins could be fathered by two different men. It seemed unkind. Enough was enough. And in so thinking Sherwyn quite forgot to ask about the twins' safe return, until he heard about the mushroom poisoning and hastened round to the London Clinic as soon as the great publisher was fit to receive visitors.

The streets on his way had been noticeably noisier than usual: the clattering and banging, shouts and whistles of a London preparing for war reminded him of being in Galveston in 1933 when the coastal town was expecting a hurricane and was being boarded up for something that might or might not happen. That was for *Delgano Goes Deep South*.

And here was Sir Jeremy the appeaser of appeasers, the likes of whom had led to the despoiling of the Czechs, and after the Czechs Poland, who next? Thank God there was Churchill, who'd never changed his tune about the need to stand up to the aggressor. Churchill was a fan of Delgano and had told Sherwyn so.
Whereas Sir Jeremy was still appeasing Adela.

'It could have been an accident; it could have been Morna the maid who meant it for Phoebe. Phoebe is my secretary, you know. Nothing more. Why blame Adela?'

'Of course not, sir.'

Sir Jeremy seized Phoebe's hand and put it to his chest. She let it stay.

'A single bad mushroom! What a fuss! It could have been any number of disgruntled employees. As I say, I am not a man without enemies. It could have been you, young man. Perfectly possible. I never trusted Old Paulines. Nest of fascists!'

'Unlike you, sir, an Old Etonian,' said Sherwyn, driven to sarcasm. 'Nest of bourgeois bohemians! Only the rich know how the poor should live, it seems.'

Sir Jeremy did not rise to the bait. He was staring at Sherwyn through rheumy, unnaturally bright eyes. Phoebe removed her hand and stroked his temples. Thus, Sherwyn thought, his stepmother had stroked his father's brow when the batty old man had a particularly bad headache. She had loved him. Sir Jeremy seemed not to be focusing properly, as if the mind behind his eyes was flickering in and out, an electric bulb struggling to maintain its proper connection.

'Don't you write thrillers?'

'I do, sir.' Had the old man forgotten even this? His screws were rapidly coming loose.

'I thought so. Never understood their popularity. Banal trash. Why can't people learn to think?'

'I believe "people" quite enjoy reading thrillers. Sales thereof rather suggest so.'

'Phooey! Sales! Weren't you the one who married my daughter Vivien?'

'I was, sir. I loved her very much.' His saying that surprised Sherwyn, but he could see it was probably true. No-one else had proved satisfactory – other than Rita, he supposed, and that was always on-and-off.

'If my grandson had lived he could have taken over the company. Little Arthur!'

'Yes, Sir Jeremy, but little Arthur didn't exist. He was all in someone's head. Vivvie had twins and died and Adela said they were hers and that you were their father. Remember?'

Phoebe shook her head at Sherwyn and frowned. She needn't have bothered.

'Ah yes, so she did,' said Sir Jeremy. 'Old men forget. Life gets confusing. One minute the Nazis have to be outcasts, moral degenerates, misfits; the next there's a non-aggression pact with Germany. I try to keep up. Readers think the Nazis and the Germans are the same. It's a linguistic confusion, not a political one. That's what that ass Mungo Bolt says. I may give him the Ripple account. He's done quite well with his zippers.'

'No doubt a mere semantic problem, sir. I was going to ask about the twins. I know you can't be considered their real father but I imagine you have a legal responsibility and certainly a moral one. You've sent for them? They're already home?'

'Oh yes, the twins. Palm them off on me, would you? Adela did mention them. I'm afraid she's very upset. Have you sent those train tickets off, Phoebe?'

'Tickets, Jeremy? No. I know nothing about train tickets.'

'But I could have sworn – oh dear, mea culpa! What a forgetful old person I am. But didn't Adela say they were in Lausanne? Switzerland's a neutral country. Why should the twins be sent for? They'll be perfectly safe where they are.

Our Swiss socialist friends are very active, though very torn by this sudden Ribbentrop–Molotov business. Who knows which way the Swiss will jump? Who knows anything, these days?

'Who indeed, sir.' Best to placate, not challenge. It was how Delgano managed the unexpected.

'I must say I too find myself, like the Swiss, rather torn. I really believe it's not so much the mushrooms as the pact that has brought me to this state. I am feeling rather faded even as I speak. Seven non-aggression pacts in one day, and every one a hidden declaration of war!'

'A portrait of domestic life, perhaps,' said Sherwyn.

'Married life,' said Sir Jeremy. 'You've no idea! But tell me, how can good communists ally themselves with fascists? I haven't felt so bad since Mayfair Lights fell at the sixth in the Grand National. It was damned Becher's Brook and the fool of a jockey didn't take it wide enough. Perhaps, dear boy, I need to be alone with Phoebe? She understands me.'

Sherwyn went straight round to Belgrave Square. Morna opened the door to him. Her hair was untidy and her apron none too clean. She seemed to be barring his way rather than letting him in. She was quite formidable, brawny bare arms and stains down her front but she had a nice face; she really was not the sort to put death cap mushrooms in the soup.

'Lady Adela's taken to drink,' Morna said. Perhaps she wasn't the only one, thought Sherwyn.

Morna seemed to feel the need to talk and the step was as good as anywhere.

'She doesn't know what she's doing, sir. Sir Jeremy has finally lost his marbles, and thinks he's been poisoned by a death cap.

Black shirts, brown shirts, green berets, death caps, what's the difference? How can he have been? His life's not in one of your whodunits though he seems to think it is. It was that horse of his having to be shot was the last straw, not herself walking out on him the way she did. Best thing that could have happened to him. But now she's moved back in and Phoebe's been sent off to stay in a suite at the Savoy, though she was only ever his secretary. I'm not saying she doesn't love him, though that's another matter. But I wouldn't suppose he can rise to the occasion any more, would you, sir, if you see what I mean? Would you like a cup of tea?'

Sherwyn thought he should accept in the circumstances, and he did. It would at least get him into the house. Morna led him down to the kitchen, her large rump swaying. The room was in a slovenly state: his servant at the Albany would have been shocked.

'And where are the twins, Mr Sexton? I have to ask. If we're going to have a war they ought to be back here where they belong.'

'I'm doing what I can,' said Sherwyn. 'That's why I'm here.'

'She can be a right bitch, but it's the way she says it herself – that children belong to those who look after them, not those who gave birth to them, and who's that except me, not her. Who's brought up the twins? Me. None of her strong spices and flavours. She got those from your books, Mr Sexton, if you ask me. Nice bland food, as white as white can be, that's what children need – and if they're with me that's what they'll get.'

'I am sure you are right,' said Sherwyn, horrified.

'And who did give birth to them, come to that? Was it the big sister nobody talks about?'

'It was,' said Sherwyn, giving up. A great burden seemed to fall from his shoulders. 'It was the big sister. Vivvie. My wife.'

'Stands to reason,' said Morna. 'It was the same back home. Everyone's mother turned out to be their sister, to save the disgrace. But I wouldn't have thought it coming from this lot, especially her. She's a walking disgrace. You mean to tell me the father's not Sir Jeremy either?'

'No.'

'Well, that's all to the good then. Poor wee things.' It was not how Sherwyn would have described the twins. 'In that case you being the father –'

Sherwyn opened his mouth to object but gave up.

'– you'll be doing the right thing. They need to be with you. I'd be prepared to carry on, for a consideration. What with the war and everything wages are going to be good in munitions; it's a temptation. But I'm fond of the girls, I'm not saying I'm not. I should miss them and they'd miss me.'

He could see that was true enough.

'I'll think about it, Morna.'

It was impossible, of course it was. The father Joseph analogy had long ago worn out. He lived in comfort in the Albany and they didn't take families there. It had been rewarding enough to take them gifts even though they never seemed quite the right choices. He didn't understand children and he didn't want to. They were grown now and he couldn't envisage a life full of shampoos and scent and strewn underwear and love letters and tears and hysterics and face powder spilt everywhere. He knew what female households could be like. Marjorie had left him with no illusions about that.

'Yes, you just think about it, sir. Just you remember those twins belong to me now.'

She went back to her room and wrote a letter to her sister in Galway telling her all about it.

Sherwyn found Adela in floods of tears, huddled up under a blanket on the sofa. There was a strong smell of alcohol in the air. The zebra-skin rug which Vivvie had so hated had long since been moved to the Square, but was in a pretty bad state. A decanter of Sir Jeremy's best whisky seemed to have broken over it and there were slivers of glass everywhere. Adela had not even had the will or energy to clear it up.

She was distraught and clutched at Sherwyn's arm. She buried her head on his chest and he let her. He pitied her. She was a little old lady in distress. It seemed she had found Phoebe's underwear in Sir Jeremy's bed. He had promised never to see the slut again and had not only broken that promise but had actually moved the whore into the house in her absence. What a stupid excuse – the coming war! Everyone was using it. The underground might get bombed on the slut's way to work. What did it matter if it was? Typists were two-a-penny. She had forgiven Sir Jeremy once before for upsetting her so and they had made their peace. But he had broken the terms of the pact. She would never divorce him, never. She did not approve of divorce, it was immoral. She had gone to join Igor in a religious retreat just to punish him a little, to show Sir Jeremy what it felt like to be jealous.

More tears, and more.

'Oh come off it, Adela, as if he didn't know. Give the poor man a divorce.'

'He'd only marry the slut.'

'She seems a nice girl, Adela.'

'You're just a man, what would you know?'

'Adela, you are a bit drunk.'

She sat up and dabbed at her eyes.

'I am not drunk, I am upset. If the place smells of alcohol it's because Morna tripped and broke the decanter. She's the one who was drunk. If she thinks I'm going to clear up after her she has another think coming.'

'Adela, stop making excuses. You are drunk.'

'Don't accuse me. Why does everyone always accuse me?'

'Because it's usually your fault.'

'You'd be upset if you were me. Igor's left me. That's why I'm here.'

'I thought it was because of the war. Aren't all foreign nationals advised to return to their country of origin?'

'Sod the war,' said Adela. 'What about me? Igor fell in love with a man and left me.'

Igor Kubanov a queer? That took some getting used to. Igor the consummate actor, Sherwyn considered, who just went wherever advantage led him?

'He saw all my powders and paints and said I was too old for him. He said it was disgusting, finding himself with an old baboushka. He said that Stefan was all young flesh and firmness. But Sherwyn, there was nowhere to keep anything secret at the Gurdjieff place. You were lucky to have a decent mattress or a cupboard with a door, let alone a proper meal. Bloody esoterics, them and their higher thoughts! They just hate comfort.'

Igor, of the greenery-yallery persuasion? Sherwyn remembered the hand on his sleeve in Upper Belgrave Street and could see it might be true. In which case, poor Adela. He had to remind himself she was a monster, responsible for Vivvie's death and all troubles in between.

'Adela, I have no time for these frivolities. Where are the twins?'

'In Lausanne, darling. Where they usually are. Switzerland is perfectly safe. It's always safe where the bankers are. Anyway, you keep denying the twins are anything to do with you, so why should you care?'

'Adela, that's mad. Two sixteen-year-old girls alone in a foreign land in wartime?'

'They're nearly seventeen. Their birthday is any day now. They were premature, of course. I could push it to September the third. I kept my head about me. I always did.'

'I shall go myself to fetch them if I have to.'

'I wish you wouldn't, darling. Always interfering.'

But he felt a surge of Delgano's spirit. It stirred his blood, flexed his muscles. He, Sherwyn, was ready for war. The war would bring out the best in him. It would be his salvation. He said so.

'Oh, do what you like. What does any of it matter?' said Adela. 'I'm too old to care. Igor and Stefan have joined the Waffen SS. He's always been such a snake. That's why my husband sacked him from the stables in the first place. He'd said he was a Russian Jew in order to get the job. Sir Jeremy discovered he was actually a White Russian *émigré* and threw him out. Fired him. All Igor's nonsense about Vivvie! He was just getting his revenge.'

'You mean he actually raped her?'

'I suppose you could put it like that if you like, isn't that what Cossacks do?'

'And you knew? And did nothing?' Poor twins, the children of rape! And Vivvie too stoical to even complain!

'Once something's been done, there's not much you can do.'

'As you said when you let poor Vivvie die.' He was furious.

'Oh, blame, blame, blame! There is no point in blaming me now. I am old. It is over. D'you know what Gurdjieff said?'

'No, thank God,' said Sherwyn.

'"*A man may be born, but in order to be born he must first die, and in order to die he must first awake.*" I died when I saw Igor walking off to join the enemy. He and Stefan, half his age, leaving practically hand in hand. They both had good calves and such excellent, well-polished riding boots. But now I have woken up. I am awake.'

She sat up straight on the sofa and seemed indeed to come to life. She rang the bell for Morna, but Morna didn't come.

'In that terrible place in Fontainebleau they made me stop taking my emminin pills. They did not think it was right to drink the urine of pregnant women. They were right. But the withdrawal can be difficult. One can become tearful.'

The blanket had gone. She seemed now like a dignified old matriarch. Some transition had been made. Still Morna didn't come. Adela just sighed.

'That girl will have to go,' she said. 'Nothing ever changes. Once it was Vivvie's mud, now it's Morna's whisky. My poor rug.' But she stirred herself to pick up the fragments of glass and place them delicately in one of Sir Jeremy's solid glass ashtrays, careful not to cut herself. Sherwyn found himself helping.

'The smell of drink will soon wear off,' she said. She looked better without make-up, but her eyes were almost as rheumy as Sir Jeremy's. She was right. She was old and over.

'"*A man will renounce any pleasures you like but he will not give up his suffering,*'" she said, 'That's Gurdjieff too. I have suffered so much from love, because all my pleasures have come from sex. One leads to the other and I have found it very difficult to give up either. I attribute that to the pills.'

'A bad woman blames her pills,' said Sherwyn, 'as a bad workman blames his tools.'

'Laugh at me if you must,' said Adela. 'It is better than hating me. Nature is all rewards and punishments. It rewards you with sex and punishes you with children. It does what it can to lure you into procreation, then makes you suffer if you succumb. It bribes women into loving their children when they're born. But I never felt that flood of love for Vivvie. It was a difficult birth and really hurt and I was so small and she was so big and Sir Jeremy looking on. I hated her.'

'Well, I loved her,' said Sherwyn.

'How admirable of you. It's Nature makes us mourn when people die so we take care not to die ourselves. If we were guided by reason we would rejoice. They are out of pain and we are the more prosperous. I rejoiced when Vivvie died because she no longer had to put up with the pain of being her. I wanted a child like Stella, I admit, and made sure I got one, but like all children, she turned into nothing special, just another person. It has not yet happened to Mallory, but it will.'

'This is very interesting,' said Sherwyn, 'but I really have to be off. Travel is going to be a nightmare. Half the world is getting up and changing places.'

'Do what you must,' she said. 'Nature makes some of us cleverer than others. The clever ones lead, the silly ones follow. I think you are being very silly. You are so very male, Sherwyn. Women are smaller, weaker, more talkative, more emotional little things than men. Fuelled by emminin I was the most female woman you ever met. Just as you, fuelled by the power of that great shiny Bentley, were the male-est man I ever met. Perhaps we could just both blame our fuels?'

Sherwyn left, in some haste.

September 1st 1939. Académie St. Augustine, Lausanne

Travel was indeed a nightmare, though at least he journeyed against the flow of human traffic, not with it. Passengers were desperate, frightened, suspicious of spies, intimidated by the policemen and soldiers who stalked the train corridors, overloaded with luggage they didn't dare put down, on their way to homes that for all they knew might turn out to be more dangerous than the ones they had just left. Between Paris and Geneva Sherwyn saw at least a dozen young men dragged away to an uncertain fate. What had they done? What happened next? Delgano would have to work it out. It took Sherwyn three days to reach Lausanne, and three times he was asked why he was travelling in the wrong direction. At least when he had the girls he would be going in the right direction. But he had left it absurdly late. Delgano would have moved faster.

The Académie St. Augustine occupied a handsome château set in well-kept grounds. Here there was no sign of panic or haste. Well-dressed, well-fed, beautiful girls looking healthy and happy wandered around in the sun with books and music cases in their hands and straw hats on their heads. After days of travelling chaos it seemed like paradise.

The twins seemed to think it was, too. Stella looked taller, somehow smoother and even lovelier than ever in an ingénue kind of way. Mallory's jaw still seemed to reach for her forehead and she was wider than ever, but seemed more comfortable in herself. They were graciousness itself. Sherwyn wished he had brought better clothes, and had had time to shower and shave. They served him a refined herb tea with lemon, and delicate cucumber sandwiches.

'Ah, Mr Sexton, we hear you are our father.' Mallory spoke.

'We know everything.' That was Stella. 'Morna rings us once a week. It is really nice to hear from home, but really nice to be here not there. It sounds really dreadful. And it seems our big sister is our mother.'

'That made us very angry for a time,' said Mallory. 'We have been brought up under false pretences. But we also hear our alleged mother, who turns out to be our grandmother, is in a pitiful state. Drunk all the time.'

Sherwyn opened his mouth to protest. He closed it again. Perhaps his breath smelt? Did he need a mouthwash? Delgano would never have suffered from such awkwardnesses as this.

'But it is hard to be angry for long,' said Mallory. 'My studies tell me that the need for sex can be very powerful in some women, and Grandma may still be a victim.'

'Sufficient punishment to be Adela and called Grandma for ever after,' said Stella giggling. Sherwyn allowed himself to relax a little. They were still the nice, funny girls he had always known. If his breath smelled a bit they would surely overlook it. He had come to save them, after all.

'We want to stay here, Uncle Sherwyn,' said Mallory. 'Or Papa, as I suppose we should call you. We know you're here to bring us back and it will all have been terrible getting here, and we're grateful but really we want to stay, not go. We are big girls and can look after ourselves.'

'We know how to look down our noses at other people,' said Stella, 'which we have found to be a great help.'

'I noticed that,' said Sherwyn.

'But we can stop when we want,' said Stella, 'and we're behaving now. Daddy, I've fallen in love with such a nice boy.'

'He is not nearly as nice as you suppose,' said Mallory. 'No boy is. But it is such heaven here, Papa. The food is divine. They all read your books. At first we were very angry, being sent away the way we were. At least Stella was. I am more sanguine. I have few excitements in life and that was one of them. And now I have got into the Geneva Institute for Psychiatric Genetics, the youngest person to be admitted and the first woman to study there. And the mountain air is so wonderful after London. We would have to go back to boring Belgrave Square and Morna, for who else is to look after us?'

'We know on which side our bread is buttered, Papa,' said Stella. 'And we were glad our paternity was you, not Uncle Mungo. Even though he did give the best presents. And so we mean to stay here. More tea?'

'Thank you,' said Sherwyn. They decided he needed more lemon, and possibly some soup, cheese and bread and rang the bell for it.

He enquired about their finances. They said they had explained the new circumstances to old Mr Baum only yesterday and he had assured them if they now inherited from Vivvie not Adela there would be fewer problems. Courtney and Baum still had their agent in Barscherau (a nice Swiss man with, to the German authorities, the reassuringly 'Aryan' name of Becht) and the girls could be supplied through his office.

'As we say,' said Mallory, 'we try not be angry, but just get on with things without rancour.'

'I had the best of Grandma,' said Stella. 'I loved all that shopping when I was small.'

'Alas, poor Stella,' said Mallory. '*A damsel of infinite jest, of excellent fancy.*'

They had even learned their *Hamlet* in the finishing school, along with fine cookery, manners, how to greet royalty and look down their noses. They would survive without him.

'We could have stopped you coming, Papa, but we needed you. We want you to take us to visit our mother's grave on our birthday. We believe it is at an abbey in what was Austria but is now Germany. We understand crossing borders may be difficult if we are unaccompanied.'

'The understatement of 1939,' said Sherwyn. He almost felt like crying, it had all turned out so well. And he was so relieved. If they'd gone home with him he'd have stood no chance with Elvira. He did not want that. Elvira was everything a man could want. And then suddenly he became Delgano again, restored and confident. He did not look forward to going back to London. But one way or another he would move the plot of his life to a satisfactory ending.

Sherwyn hired an odd little car, one of Herr Hitler's new populist Volkswagens, and they crossed without trouble into Germany, down to Munich and from thence to the Bavarian Alps. They were charged double what they should have been for petrol. Rationing was expected. Such deals were done cheerfully. The locals were buoyant. War was coming but who needed to be scared? The Nazis were at hand. The war would be sharp and short, restore the nation's territories and pride and show the rest of Europe who was master.

Barscherau was no longer the little village Sherwyn remembered. It was now a tourist destination: in the winter a cable car took skiers to the higher mountain slopes. Now, in the summer bird watchers and hikers thronged the streets, uniforms and KdF groups were everywhere; the swastika was everywhere; geraniums bloomed in the window boxes: no-one seemed cheerless or gloomy. The old Town Hall was now spectacular with traditional Bavarian Lüftlmalerei. There was a shop doing good business selling cuckoo clocks. The Gasthaus Post had been extended and refurbished. Sherwyn looked through the window and saw the Bielers sitting by the fire, old people, nodding and smiling.

It seemed prudent not to linger. The twins spoke perfect German but Sherwyn could be too easily recognised as an Englishman. They found the office of Herr Becht, Rechtsanwalt, on the high street, but it was closed for lunch.

As they took the new road up to the abbey, Sherwyn began to feel more at home. The mountain above was snow capped. Eagles soared, the long grass below was alive with Alpine flowers. It had been a glorious summer, indifferent to human affairs. Sherwyn marvelled at how nature seemed to apologise for the terrors other forces were about to unleash, by creating such spells of benign weather. One could become very suspicious, sometimes, of clear blue skies. The old abbey had been partially restored, which was a pity. He preferred it as a ruin. But at least the Painted Madonna stood where she always had, calm, smooth and perfect, now beneath an elaborate frescoed baroque ceiling that did not leak. Vivvie would be pleased.

Mallory found the grave under the long grass. Someone had cleared it lately and left some flowers in a jam jar. There was a simple cross and a small brass plaque on which was engraved *Vivien Ripple* and *Requiescat in Pace*. There was no date. Sherwyn was embarrassed to admit he had not been to the funeral.

'I was upset at the time,' he said.

'Because you loved her so much,' the twins said.

'She gave her life for us,' said the twins. 'Thank you, Mama.'

Sherwyn could see it behoved him not to elaborate.

Next to it they found a smaller cross and an even smaller plaque:

ARTHUR RIPPLE
Infant, one day old
R.I.P.

The cow, thought Sherwyn, enraged, the cow! Adela thought of everything.

'You mean we were triplets? We had a brother who died?'

All of it, all of it, Adela's fault. It was intolerable.

Fortunately Sherwyn found the person who had left the flowers. Actually there were two of them. One introduced herself as Maria Walker, the English doctor's wife. The other as her friend Berthe.

'We come here quite a lot,' Maria said. 'Such a blessed place. And she was so good. Almost a saint. She gives me hope still.'

'She had twins, you know,' said the other one. 'Not a son. I should know. It was two little girls I breast fed for their first day of life. One doesn't forget a thing like that.'

'I took them after that,' said the doctor's wife. 'For a whole month. My husband insisted. My own little girl had to go hungry. One was a little angel, the other one scratched and fought. So why the son? We've always wondered.'

'A genuine mistake,' said Sherwyn. But oh, beware, he thought, one's sins will find one out. He had not played fair with Vivvie. Some things may be confessed to, others never. But, as it occurred to him later, some benign influence he did not deserve came to his rescue. Delgano would have it that it was the Painted Madonna, with his reward for being Joseph.

The twins came back into the church at that moment looking for their Papa, and were met by cries of joy and delight from the two people who'd nourished them and known them when they were babies. For all concerned it made the day complete. The twins heard from Berthe that she had known their mother well before she died, and from Maria Walker that her husband had been present when Vivvie died, and there was nothing anyone could have done to save her. In the noise and tumult of reunion the matter of Arthur, infant, was forgotten; this poor baby that Adela never had.

Sherwyn conveyed the twins safely back to the Académie St. Augustine in Lausanne, content to get on with their lives. He was able to use his best Delgano skills in getting himself back to London and the Albany. It was the day after the declaration of war, and all borders were closed and closely guarded; a dis-gruntled fisherman managed to get him back to Dover for a price. The journey had been dangerous, but he had survived. Major Grand of Section D would be pleased. At last the real war could begin.